Praise
and her novels

"Valerie Wolzien is a consummate crime writer. Her heroines sparkle as they sift through clues and stir up evidence in the darker, deadly side of suburbia."

— MARY DAHEIM

"Wit is Wolzien's strong suit. . . . Her portrayal of small-town life will prompt those of us in similar situations to agree that we too have been there and done that."

— *The Mystery Review*

$2.25
2

By Valerie Wolzien
Published by Fawcett Books:

Susan Henshaw mysteries:
MURDER AT THE PTA LUNCHEON
THE FORTIETH BIRTHDAY BODY
WE WISH YOU A MERRY MURDER
AN OLD FAITHFUL MURDER
ALL HALLOWS' EVIL
A STAR-SPANGLED MURDER
A GOOD YEAR FOR A CORPSE
'TIS THE SEASON TO BE MURDERED
REMODELED TO DEATH
ELECTED FOR DEATH
WEDDINGS ARE MURDER
THE STUDENT BODY

Josie Pigeon mysteries:
SHORE TO DIE
PERMIT FOR MURDER
DECK THE HALLS WITH MURDER
THIS OLD MURDER

Books published by The Ballantine Publishing Group
are available at quantity discounts on bulk purchases
for premium, educational, fund-raising, and special
sales use. For details, please call 1-800-733-3000.

THIS OLD MURDER

Valerie Wolzien

FAWCETT BOOKS • NEW YORK

Sale of this book without a front cover may be unauthorized. If this book is coverless, it may have been reported to the publisher as "unsold or destroyed" and neither the author nor the publisher may have received payment for it.

A Fawcett Book
Published by The Ballantine Publishing Group
Copyright © 2000 by Valerie Wolzien

All rights reserved under International and Pan-American Copyright Conventions. Published in the United States by The Ballantine Publishing Group, a division of Random House, Inc., New York, and simultaneously in Canada by Random House of Canada Limited, Toronto.

Fawcett is a registered trademark and the Fawcett colophon is a trademark of Random House, Inc.

www.randomhouse.com/BB/

A Library of Congress card number is available from the publisher upon request.

ISBN 0-449-00629-8

Manufactured in the United States of America

First Edition: July 2000

10 9 8 7 6 5 4 3 2 1

ONE

JOSIE PIGEON EXAMINED her reflection in the dressing room's mirrors, a frown creasing her freckled face.

"It looks . . . You look . . . uh, lovely . . . dear." The slim, young saleswoman seemed to be having a difficult time finding the right words.

Josie didn't bother responding. She knew she didn't look lovely. She never looked lovely. Slightly overweight, with frizzy red hair that she had given up trying to control, she was usually satisfied with perky and thrilled if anyone thought she was cute. "Maybe I should try a smaller size?"

"It's not fashionable to wear them tight."

"I'm not trying to be fashionable! I'm buying them to work in," Josie explained. "They're carpenter's pants. I'm a carpenter."

"A carpenter?"

"Yes, in fact, I own my own contracting company." She was bragging, but after three years it still pleased her to say those words.

The saleswoman was not impressed. "I did think you were a bit old to be a student."

"I'm going to be on TV," Josie stated, trying to gain prestige. "On *Courtney Castle's Castles*."

"Courtney Castle! She's wonderful. So pretty and chic. You would never know she's a carpenter from just looking at

1

her. . . ." Realizing that she was possibly treading on less than popular ground, the saleswoman changed the topic. "And she builds the most wonderful houses! Did you see that log cabin in Minnesota? My husband was watching with me and he said it looked more like a log palace. Of course, that's why they call them Courtney Castle's castles, isn't it?"

Happily, the woman chatted on and on and Josie wasn't forced to admit that she had never seen the Courtney Castle show. To tell the truth, watching builders on television wasn't her idea of a relaxing way to spend an evening. And every time she happened on a show while channel-surfing, there seemed to be a man explaining just how easily the home-owner could do something Josie and her crew were well paid to do. "I'll take these and another pair, if you've got them in my size," she finally interrupted.

"Of course, and maybe you could tell that lovely Courtney to come in here if she needs any clothing. I'd be happy to put aside some things for her."

"Yes, I'll do that," Josie lied, fumbling around in her purse for the one credit card she possessed that wasn't maxed out and then handing it to her.

"Josie Pigeon." The saleswoman, reading the name on the card, was now gushing. "I'll be watching for you on television. Wait until I tell my husband I met someone who actually knows Courtney Castle. He'll be so excited!"

Josie just took her card back.

The level of excitement in the office of Island Contracting made the saleswoman seem blasé by comparison.

"I can't believe we're going to meet Courtney Castle. She's been my idol since I was a little girl!" At nineteen, the speaker was the youngest member of Josie's crew. To most of her coworkers, Annette Long still was a little girl. Sitting on the floor, legs crossed in a yoga position, blond hair tied in a skinny ponytail snaking between bony shoulder blades, she barely looked old enough to smoke the cigarette she was holding.

"You know, TV people are real snots. You probably won't like her at all in person." Dottie Evans was the oldest member of the crew as well as the most recently hired. In the few weeks she'd been with Island Contracting, no one had heard her say anything positive about anyone. Her graying hair was badly cut, barely covering her ears. Her skin was pale, puffy around the eyes, and the frown that was usually found on her face did nothing to enhance her appearance.

The third member of the crew spoke up. "I just wish they were filming a different job. I mean, Island Contracting has remodeled some great houses—old Victorians downtown, big modern things on the water, that little chapel we turned into a family home over the winter . . . Now that job would have interested television viewers. But a 1964 A-frame on the bay—it's so dull." As she was speaking, Jill Pike looked around at the birdhouses decorating the shelf that circled the room near the ceiling. Each one represented a remodeling job completed by Island Contracting. Brightly colored cottages covered with gingerbread sat beside modern duplexes, that were next to little Cape Cod boxes, and so on. A frown caused her sunburned nose to crinkle. "It would be nice if we made a really good impression," she said wistfully.

"Why? You think someone watching the show will see you working, fall in love with you, and take you away from all this?" From the blush on Jill's face, it was apparent that Dottie Evans's comment had hit at least one nerve.

"I don't think we should get our hopes up about becoming rich and famous. After all, how many people even watch those building shows?" Josie asked, hoping to change the topic.

"How many people? Thousands . . . maybe millions! They're

some of the most popular shows on television! And Courtney Castle's show is the best! There was an article all about her in *Parade* magazine just a few months ago. She lives in this fabulous penthouse apartment on the water in Boston. She gutted the whole place—even replaced the windows with huge made-to-order Pellas. It's fabulous!" Annette waved her hands around to demonstrate the size of the glass as she spoke.

"Working as a contractor for a television show must pay really well," Dottie commented sarcastically.

"Better than working for a contracting company," Jill agreed somewhat wistfully.

"No one gets paid anything unless we get going," Josie reminded her crew. "We've got to get three walls down before they can start taping our work."

"Do they want us to wear anything special?" Jill asked.

Josie remembered her new carpenter's pants. Should she tell her crew about them? Wouldn't it look a bit odd if they all appeared at work wearing new clothing next Monday? "No one has mentioned anything about it to me" was all she said.

"Maybe we should all get our hair done," Dottie suggested, more than a hint of a sneer in her voice.

"Do you think I should?" Annette asked, taking the suggestion at face value as she grabbed the end of her long ponytail and examined it anxiously for split ends.

"You look wonderful," Josie said honestly.

"Will they bring their own makeup artists and hairdressers? There was an article about the show in *Cosmo*, and Courtney said she couldn't do it without her staff."

Josie was stunned. "There was an article about a carpenter in *Cosmopolitan* magazine?"

"She's not just any carpenter! She's a celebrity!" Jill said vehemently.

"I don't get it." Dottie's flat voice interrupted them. "If

this Courtney Castle wants to use our remodeling job on her television show, doesn't she want us to wait for her arrival to start work? Or, with that big apartment and her hairdressers and makeup artists, is she too prissy to do the down-and-dirty demolition?"

"They have to condense weeks of work into a half-dozen shows, so they want the demolition done before they arrive," Josie said.

"Guess they figure any idiot with a sledgehammer knows how to smash the hell out of a wall," Dottie said.

"The trick is to keep the ceiling standing at the same time," Josie said. "So we'd better get going. The shoring up is going to take some extra time."

"Someone has to stop at the hardware store and get those metal braces we ordered last week," Jill reminded them.

Josie smiled. Betty Patrick, an old friend and previously the right-hand woman at Island Contracting, had left in the spring to get married, but Jill Pike seemed to be filling her shoes (or work boots, as was the case) nicely. "Why don't you take the Jeep and pick up that stuff? The rest of us can go together in the truck," Josie suggested, grabbing her toolbox— the signal that the work day had begun.

The women got busy. It wasn't eight yet, but the sun was strong and the day promised to be warm. Along with toolboxes and rolls of blueprints, two large thermoses of iced tea were tossed in the back of the 1969 Chevy truck, the pride, joy, and money pit of Island Contracting.

The house that was being remodeled was on the bay side of the seven-mile barrier island where Island Contracting was located. Built nearly forty years earlier on speculation by a man who had gone bankrupt waiting for an economic surge that had occurred one year too late, the house was the only one of the dozen original homes that had not been extensively remodeled during the building booms of the early seventies and late eighties, when families had discovered the joys of owning a second home where a boat or two could be docked.

The women chatted as they traveled and Josie was left to wonder—for the millionth time—whether or not she should have accepted the opportunity to appear on television.

The offer had been made a few weeks earlier via a message left on Island Contracting's answering machine from the show's producer, Bobby Valentine. That was how he referred to himself. "Bobby Valentine here," he had answered his phone. Josie, working on the assumption that each and every call to Island Contracting's office might be a potential client, had, initially, called back immediately. Bobby Valentine had a proposition—that's how he put it after a few minutes of flattery.

"We've heard about Island Contracting. You hire only women. Right?" Before Josie could explain that while there were only women on her crew, it wasn't really a company hiring policy, Bobby Valentine continued. Josie later learned that although he asked many questions, he usually didn't wait for any answers. "Make a great bit on the show, it will. Courtney loves to do something different, you know?"

"I—" This was before Josie had learned not to bother trying to answer.

"Yeah, I can see it now. Women crawling around on beams with the sun shining off their muscular biceps—that image makes a statement. Women can do anything men can do, right?"

"Certainly, and—"

"Maybe a short segment on what you women eat for lunch. You know, whether it's best to bulk up on carbs or if natural foods give you the most energy. Maybe we could even include your favorite recipes. Sort of a combination cooking and remodeling show. What do you think?"

She didn't think much of the idea, but since he didn't give her the opportunity to answer, he was never to know this.

"Yeah, we could emphasize the healthy lifestyle that you women live. Working outdoors, getting lots of exercise. Maybe include a segment on stretching. How you all prepare to do the backbreaking labor you do without . . . ah, without breaking your backs. How about that?"

She had no idea how to respond this time.

"We can work out the details later. So what do you think? Have we a great idea or what?"

It took Josie a few minutes to realize that it was time for her to speak up. "You . . . you want to hire us to be in a movie?"

"No movie. No way! Think video, not film. Think cable, not theaters. We're asking you to be on *Courtney Castle's Castles*. Turn your home into your castle. You know. On television."

"Oh, well—"

"We don't pay you, you know. But the publicity is priceless. Courtney's name is a household word. You'd be really happy if that could be said about Josie Pigeon and Island Construction, wouldn't you?"

"Island Contracting," Josie corrected him faintly. She had no idea what to make of this unusual offer.

"We understand you ladies are going to be starting work on an old A-frame down on the bay. The job's unusual and would fit right into our shooting schedule. How about it? I need an answer ASAP. You know how it is. I promise you we won't get in your way. If anything, the job will go faster. You'll have our crew to help out. What do you think? Can we make a deal?"

That had been three weeks ago, and to this day Josie had absolutely no idea why she had said yes so quickly. In fact, every day since then she had wondered why she had said yes at all, every single day, right after Bobby Valentine's daily phone call.

It didn't take long for Josie to begin expecting those calls.

Generally they came around noon; always they contained a
bit of information and a lot of lunacy. Bobby Valentine, as
he had told her himself, was full of ideas. She just wished that
he would keep them to himself and that they wouldn't have
anything to do with her or with her company. About half of
his ideas were easy to turn down. After all, Courtney Castle
wasn't paying for the renovation. The owners of the house
were. And Josie was able to contact them through a New York
City law firm. A series of faxes had gotten all the legalities
out of the way. The owners agreed that the job could be taped
and shown on TV. All they asked was that they not be disturbed. They were considering selling the house. That it
would be on television for all the world to see was a big plus
as far as they were concerned. So that part had been easy.
Dealing with Bobby Valentine was proving not to be.

So far, she had agreed to be interviewed in her wonderful
little office, which overhung the water, on the Friday before
filming began, to pose walking up the beach as the sun was
rising, (actually, Bobby Valentine had wanted a shot as the
sun was setting, but when Josie explained it was difficult to
arrange on the East Coast, he had changed his shooting
schedule), and to sit with her entire staff and talk over the
plans. She had refused to be interviewed in her home. She
knew that anyone who saw the mess in her apartment would
be unlikely to hire her or her company. She had refused to allow her son to be interviewed—in fact, she had insisted that
Tyler not be asked about it, as she was pretty sure he would be
thrilled to get his sixteen-year-old face on the boob tube. She
had refused to answer questions about her relationship with a
man Bobby referred to as a hotshot lawyer from New York
City before she even asked how he knew about Sam Richardson. When she woke up in the middle of the night, worried
that she had made a terrible mistake agreeing to do it at all,

she wondered why a producer from what her crew claimed was a popular television show was so interested in her life.

And now, as she turned the last corner to the house, it was time to get some answers. And the first question she was going to ask was: What the hell is going on here?

TWO

"DON'T YOU REMEMBER? I'm absolutely positive I told you I was bringing some people by this week to start taping."

But that wasn't the answer to the first question Josie had asked. The first question out of her mouth had been "Where is Bobby Valentine?" She asked a half-dozen people and she got six different answers. Bobby Valentine was "out back." Bobby Valentine was "inside." Bobby Valentine was "in the van." Bobby Valentine was "in the truck." Bobby Valentine was "in the living room." Or, possibly, Bobby Valentine was "off site for the morning." He might have been in all those places at one time, but right now he was by her side.

"Josie Pigeon, right?"

She turned and looked at the man standing beside her. "You're Bobby Valentine?"

"In the flesh. Don't I look the way you imagined?"

Josie didn't answer. She hadn't, in fact, imagined Bobby Valentine at all. But if she had, she had dressed him in more urbane clothing—the type of sports jacket and slacks that Sam wore in his store or possibly an Armani pinstripe. But Bobby Valentine was wearing pressed jeans and a shirt made of smooth white Egyptian cotton. Pigskin loafers covered sockless feet and a gold Rolex hung on his tanned wrist. He resembled one of the Wall Street moguls who vacationed on the island.

"What do you think? I bought this shirt just for the shoot." He pointed to his breast pocket.

Josie looked more closely. There was a tiny gray hammer embroidered on the silky fabric.

"I thought about a whale, of course, to stay with the seashore motif, but when I saw this thing, I couldn't resist. Courtney will love it."

"It's very nice," Josie said, moving aside to avoid being run over by a young man carrying a huge round metal frame with shiny white fabric stretched across it.

"Hey, you! Watch out for that reflector! Hold it at your side."

With a quick word of apology for bumping Josie's arm, the worker moved quickly out of range of Bobby Valentine's voice. "These damn interns. They come to us for the summer. By the time they know how to do their job, they're back snug in their dorm rooms at Princeton or Amherst or wherever. Sometimes I think they're worth less than what we pay them."

"What do you pay them?" Josie asked, glad the subject was no longer Bobby Valentine's clothing.

"Nothing. Zip. Nada."

Josie glanced back over her shoulder at the young worker, who had put down his burden and was now edging a massive black box off the lift at the back of a large truck. The strain caused his muscles to tighten beneath the Cornell T-shirt he wore. "He isn't on salary?"

"Nope. He gets college credit for doing all this. Pretty neat system, huh?"

"It sure is," Josie answered, wondering if it could be implemented in the building industry.

"So what do you think?"

"About what?"

"All this." Bobby Valentine swept his arms in a circle that encompassed the area.

Josie could only think of it as mayhem. Two large vans with COURTNEY CASTLE'S CASTLES—MAKE YOUR DREAM HOME COME TRUE emblazoned on the side panels were nose to nose in the driveway. An even larger trailer was parked at the curb. It was hard to believe that these three vehicles, despite their size, had provided enough space to transport all the flotsam and jetsam that filled the front yard. There were tables and chairs, folded and piled high, enough for a small wedding reception. There were big black lights attached to various poles and stands. There were strange metal boxes prickly with buttons and levers. The sidewalk was covered with enough coils of wire to hook up the entire island.

"Impressive, huh?"

Josie was blunt. "I don't see how we're going to work around all this junk."

"Oh, don't worry. Remember, we do this all the time. Inland Contracting will be just fine."

"Island Contracting. The name of my company is Island Contracting."

"Oh?" He looked at her, a surprised expression on his face. "Well, I guess you should know. Don't worry. Courtney is good with names. You'll get your free publicity."

"If you'll be able to see us in the middle of all this stuff," Josie said, frowning.

"That's all that's taking the smile off your pretty face? Hey, don't worry! Once we're set up, you won't even know we're around."

"You're going to hide all this?"

"Behind the scenes."

Josie realized that they were talking about two different things. Bobby Valentine was concerned about the show that was going to air. Her concern was to get the remodeling done well and on time. Free advertising was fine and good, but she needed the final payment for this job to keep her company in business. But they would fight these battles as each day came up. Starting now.

"I've got a load of Sheetrock coming the day after tomorrow," she began.

"I know what you're thinking and you don't have to worry about a thing. I promise you, all of this will be out of sight before my guys go home tonight. Courtney's going to be here to check out everything tomorrow morning. And you know what Courtney always says—"

"A place for everything and everything in its place," Annette chimed in enthusiastically.

"Exactly! Well, I see we have a fan of the show here." Bobby Valentine beamed at the young carpenter.

"You bet! I love Courtney Castle! I can't wait to meet her!"

"Well, you'll have that privilege tomorrow."

"You told me you weren't going to start filming until next week!" And they sure wouldn't be ready before then, Josie knew.

"No problem. No problem. We may tape a bit here and there, but Courtney's really just coming to get a feel for the place and the job. You don't have to worry about a thing. Go on with your work as though she wasn't even around. Believe me, that's what Courtney would tell you to do."

Dottie Evans stopped on her way to the small front deck, her habitual sneer on her face. "And she expects us to do things just because she tells us to. Right?"

"What time will she be here?" Josie asked quickly, frowning at Dottie. Annette's obvious hero worship might be a bit naive, but at least it wasn't hostile.

Apparently Bobby Valentine didn't mind—or notice. "You

don't have to worry about Courtney. She just wants what's best for the show. You're gonna love her."

Dottie hefted a huge box of nails up on her shoulder and stomped into the house. The expression on her face was plain: She doubted it. But Josie was thankful that she didn't seem to feel the need to say anything more.

Dottie let the old, ripped, aluminum screen door slam behind her, but Josie's attention was drawn to a heavyset man in filthy jeans and an even dirtier red T-shirt walking up the sidewalk. "You Josie Pigeon?" he asked, pulling a bandanna from his pocket and mopping his perspiring forehead.

"Yes," she answered, glancing over at Bobby Valentine for an introduction.

"I wanna see your blues," the stranger continued, referring to the blueprints, which, as far as Josie knew, were still stashed in her truck.

"I . . . I faxed a copy to your office," Josie answered, still expecting Bobby Valentine to join in the conversation.

"I ain't got an office. I run my business from my home, an apartment over on One Twenty-third. And I ain't seen no blues. And I gotta get any special orders in today." The bandanna went back into his pocket and a toothpick came out—and went straight into his mouth.

"You're the plumber!" Josie exclaimed.

"Yup. Wayne Wagner, at your service."

"It's nice to meet you," Josie said enthusiastically, starting forward with her hand outstretched.

"Whoa. Just wait one second here. You're who?" Bobby Valentine got between Josie and her subcontractor.

"Wayne Wagner. The plumber Ms. Josie Pigeon hired to add two bathrooms to this here project. And you are?" The toothpick went back in the pocket and a pair of glasses came out. Wayne used them to examine Bobby Valentine.

Bobby Valentine didn't waste any time responding to the

other man. "I need to speak with you in private, Ms. Pigeon. We've got ourselves a problem. A big problem." His elegant shoe dug into the lawn as he spun around and stalked off. Josie followed him across the grass, off the curb, and up the steps into the trailer.

"We have a problem," he repeated when they were alone.

Josie didn't reply; she was too busy staring. Unlike its utilitarian exterior, the interior of the trailer resembled a luxury spa. One entire side was mirrored. A beauty-parlor chair sat before a large buffet littered with pots and tubes of ointments and creams. A small refrigerator was built into a wall; a microwave hung above it. An exercise bicycle stood in the middle of the hallway. At the far end of the space a brocade-covered couch was piled high with lace pillows. The walls were frosted with framed awards and photographs of large estates. Josie peered at the large color photograph by her left shoulder. It was of a stone mansion larger than anything she had ever seen.

"Who was that man?" he asked, flopping down in a chair, not bothering to offer a seat to Josie.

"You heard him say his name. Wayne Wagner."

"And who is he?"

"The plumber."

"The plumber or a plumber?"

"Both, I guess." She paused. "I don't know what you're asking."

"Is he just a friend of yours who happens to be a plumber? Or is he Island Building's plumber?"

"We don't have a plumber on staff right now," Josie answered, understanding him despite the incorrect name. "But he is the plumber we hired for this project, if that's what you're asking."

He just frowned.

"That is what you want to know, isn't it? I've never met

him before," she added when there was no answer to her question. "My crew changes and sometimes we have a plumber on the staff, but right now we don't. And the plumber I usually use was busy and recommended Wayne." After a pause, she asked, "Is something wrong?"

"Is something wrong? Is something wrong, she asks," he said loudly, although Josie had no idea who he imagined he was speaking to. "Yes, something is wrong. I will tell you what is wrong."

"What?"

"Well, unless Wayne Wagner is going to have some very serious surgery before next week, he's not going to fit in with the image we have of this project."

Josie suddenly realized what he was talking about. "You mean the problem is that Wayne isn't a woman?"

"Got it in one! And we've sold this show to the stations as an all-female show. They were chomping at the bit to get it for a spring or summer fund-raiser. Now what the hell am I going to do?"

"I don't understand."

"Look, television shows don't make themselves. It takes lots of equipment, lots of people, and lots and lots of money to make a halfway decent show."

Josie remembered the piles of equipment and the large staff outside and nodded her head.

"And there's only so much money to go around."

"Of course." Was there anyplace where that wasn't true?

"So we sell our shows to the stations before we make them. And, frankly, finding your company was a godsend."

"Why?"

"Because the biggest pots of cash go to the shows that make money."

"I don't understand." Josie put up a hand to stop him. "I

thought this show was for public television. I thought only commercial television worried about making money."

"Yeah, you and everyone else. Why do you think they're always having those long fund-raisers?"

"Well, I don't watch PBS all that much," Josie admitted. "I did when my son was young. *Sesame Street* and *Zoom* and stuff like that."

"Ever wonder what it costs to make one of those cute little Muppets?"

"Not really," Josie admitted.

"Lots."

"But what does all this have to do with my plumbing sub?"

"That's right. You may have a point. He's a *sub*contractor, not a contractor. We might just manage to work this out. Depends on how we sell it." Bobby Valentine seemed to be speaking almost to himself.

"I still don't understand," Josie reminded him.

"Well, we sold this show to public broadcasting as a fund-raiser. I mean, we know contracting shows are a dime a dozen, but one that featured women workers . . . Well, it's different, if you know what I mean. And it sure would have more appeal as a fund-raiser and . . . and stuff like that. It's well known that women control where the contributions go in most families."

"Really?" Josie knew nothing about it. When her son, Tyler, was four years old, she had sent twenty-five dollars to Channel 13 because he longed for a bright blue stuffed Cookie Monster. That was her entire experience with fund-raising. But Bobby Valentine had bigger things on his mind.

"You know, there's nothing to get excited about here. That Wayne isn't really on the staff of your company. We'll just keep him in the background." Bobby Valentine got up and opened the trailer's door for Josie.

Once again she was struck by the amount of equipment

standing around. There was an awful lot of stuff that was supposed to be hidden in the background with Wayne Wagner. Josie just hoped that someone knew how to go about doing it.

THREE

JOSIE HAD MET Sam Richardson when he retired from his job as a prosecuting attorney in New York City and moved to the island to begin his new life as owner-manager of an upscale liquor store. That had been three years earlier. Most of the time she was wildly in love with him. And other times she wondered why they even bothered to speak to each other. This was one of those times.

Sam had just admitted to being a fan of the Courtney Castle show.

"If I was still living in my New York apartment, I wouldn't even have glanced at those building shows, but we've done so much work on my house, and I've even gotten an idea or two from watching them. In fact, those indents in the shower walls, the ones we're going to redo when Island Contracting has some free time, were an idea I got from watching Courtney."

"The idea isn't original with her. Half the decorating magazines have been featuring them for years," Josie said sullenly. Sam was almost twenty years older than she was and certainly more educated and experienced. Building and remodeling was the one—and only—area where she was the expert. It wasn't as though she was competitive, but still . . .

They were sitting in a booth at one of Basil Tilby's restaurants that had opened near the end of last year's season. A good friend, Basil had hired Island Contracting to remodel the place. Josie had come there expecting Sam to spend at least some of the meal admiring her work—and not spend any time talking about another woman.

"I've never seen the show," she admitted.

"Josie, you should. You're going to be working with this woman for the next few weeks. It's on tonight at nine-thirty. We'll skip dessert and go over to my house to watch it. I have a few pints of Ben and Jerry's in the freezer," he added when she didn't answer.

"I wasn't worried about missing dessert," she protested, somewhat dishonestly. "I was just thinking about Tyler. I told him he had to be home by ten-thirty, so I'd better be home to make sure he remembers."

"Josie, Tyler is a responsible kid—"

"Sam, he's sixteen years old."

"He does just fine away at school."

"Where there is a huge staff to keep an eye on the kids. And it's not just that. There's a lot to keep him busy at school. Tyler belongs to all sorts of clubs, he has to participate in a team sport each season, and he has piles of homework."

"Are you saying idle hands are the devil's playground?"

"Something like that. Tyler spent yesterday in his room in front of that damn computer."

"So?"

"I don't know. You hear so much about bad things on the computer. Sex and all . . ."

"Josie, he probably checked out the sex available in cyber-space years and years ago."

"I know. I just worry." She took a deep breath. "The truth is, I'm afraid I'm boring him. That he's happier at school than he is at home."

"He sure looked happy at my house Sunday afternoon."

"He was stuffing his face with junk food. Of course he was

happy. But unless you're going to spend the entire summer on your deck grilling hot dogs for him, he's going to need a bit more to stay busy."

"Well, once he starts working . . ."

Josie leaned forward so quickly that she almost tipped over her glass of wine. "You know something, don't you? You two were in the kitchen for a long time. Where has he applied for work? What does he want to do this summer?"

"He hasn't just applied for a job. He's got one. But I think you should wait for him to tell you about it."

"I . . . Why . . ." Josie was rarely speechless and then it didn't last for long. "My son has a job and he hasn't even mentioned it to me! What's going on, Sam?"

"Josie, he just wants you to see his point . . . to get to know . . . to understand . . ." Sam stopped and took an uncharacteristically loud gulp of the wine he had carefully chosen. "I'm blowing this for Tyler, Josie, and I hate to do that. I promised him I would help prepare you."

"For what? Why would I have to be prepared for any job Tyler would take?"

"Now don't start imagining all sorts of horrors."

"I won't have to imagine anything if you tell me what's going on."

"Look, it's a great job for Tyler. He knows a lot about . . . well, about the subject. He'll get to be around people. The pay is good—"

"It's off island, isn't it? My son isn't even going to spend the summer with me! That's it, isn't it, Sam?"

"No, it isn't. Now, see, you're doing exactly what I thought you would. You're imagining problems that just are not going to happen."

"Sam . . ."

"Josie, I'll tell you, but you must listen to everything I have to say before going nuts."

"Just as long as I can go nuts when you're done."

"I really think you won't want to when you hear what I have to say. Tyler got a job at Family Video."

"But, Sam, that's wonderful! He'll be able to ride his bike to work and he'll be just a few blocks away from you, so when it rains maybe you'll be able to drive him home. Why did either of you think I'd object to him working there? I'll even be able to see him in the evening when we drop in to pick out a video— Oh, no!" she cried, realization dawning. "It's a night job, isn't it? He wants to work the night shift."

"Josie, we're not talking about overnight in a ghetto convenience store. Tyler has been asked to work three full days and three evenings a week. The evening shift runs from three to midnight with an hour off for dinner."

"Midnight! Why midnight? The store's only open until eleven."

"I asked the same question. Apparently there's a lot to do after the customers leave. Tapes to check in. Shelves to clean up."

"He can't do it. He can work days, but not the evening shift."

"I suggested that, too, but the store's policy is that no one gets preference. If you work there days, you work there evenings. But, Josie, it's not as though he's going to be miles away from home. And he's not going to be hanging out on street corners, for heaven's sake. He's going to be working."

"But it's at night, Sam!"

"Look, I didn't say anything to Tyler, but I have to admit I think he's right about this. What difference does it make if he's home by ten-thirty or twelve-thirty as long as you know where he is, what he's doing, and that he's safe? If he were home, he'd probably be sitting in front of his computer or watching TV. In any case, you'll be in bed. So what difference could it possibly make to you if he's at the video store instead of in your living room or his bedroom?"

"I just like him to be home before I go to bed. I know it doesn't make any sense, but it makes me feel better knowing he's around."

"Then why did you send him to boarding school?"

"Because he's so smart he was ahead of most of the teachers on the island. When Noel's will was read and I found that he had not only left me Island Contracting but had put aside enough money for Tyler to go to boarding school, I was incredibly relieved. It's important that he get a good education. But I miss him! And that's part of the reason I like him to be home in the summer. He only gets short vacations the rest of the year. And if he's working nights, he'll end up sleeping all morning. We'll hardly see each other. Besides, I don't like him riding his bike late at night. The bars will be closing and there will be drunks on the road."

Sam refilled their glasses thoughtfully. "Look, I didn't mean to get involved in this, but since I am, let me suggest a compromise."

"Go ahead."

"What if you let Tyler take this job—with two conditions," he added quickly. "First that he'll get up in the morning and see you before he goes to work if at all possible whether he worked late the night before or not."

"Not a chance! Do you have any idea how long it takes a teenage boy to get out of bed in the morning? I won't make it to work on time."

"He has to agree to set his alarm and get himself up. Okay?"

"Well, maybe. What's the second condition?"

"He agrees to allow me to drive him home on the nights he works. That will mean he has to either get a ride to the store earlier or walk, but for a kid who's been on a track team all spring, that won't be a hardship."

"You'll drive him home? Really?"

"I just said I would."

"Oh, Sam, that's so sweet of you!"

"So you agree?"

"If he agrees to everything you suggested, how can I complain?"

Their waitress placed a huge platter of antipasti on the table between them.

"Perfect timing," Sam said, spearing a long strip of roasted pepper and popping it in his mouth.

"Can I bring you anything else?"

"Maybe some Pellegrino," Sam suggested.

"Fine. And I'll tell the chef to start your risotto in about ten minutes, shall I?"

"Excellent."

Josie was too busy digging into the pickled eggplant to reply.

"So what's this Courtney Castle like in person?" Sam asked.

Josie realized he was changing the topic and hoping for a comparable change in her mood. But he'd sure asked the wrong question.

"Why is everyone so interested in Courtney Castle? It's almost as if she's a sex symbol rather than a carpenter." The truth suddenly dawned on her. "She is, isn't she?"

"Sexy? Yes, in a wholesome all-American-girl sort of way," Sam admitted. "She has gorgeous hair."

"So she's young?"

"To me she is. I'd guess she's around your age actually."

"Do you think she ended up having a show of her own because of her looks?"

"I have no idea. But there aren't a lot of unattractive people on television," Sam said. "After all, if you're designing a show, you want people to watch, and most people would prefer to watch good-looking personalities.

"Josie, why did you agree to do the show? You keep saying that it will be good publicity for Island Contracting, but you have lots of work. And unless you're planning to work off island, most of the people watching will never hire you no matter how good you all look."

"I know that. But I was flattered to be asked and, frankly, it had a lot to do with Tyler."

"Did you think they might hire him?" Sam asked, obviously mystified.

"I never even considered it." Josie sighed and turned her attention to the platter of food they were sharing. "I thought it would bring status to Island Contracting. Well, to me, actually. I thought all those rich people who send their kids to Tyler's school would watch and they wouldn't think of me as just a carpenter anymore." She looked up at him, a blush spreading over her cheeks. "Stupid, huh?"

"Not really." Sam spoke slowly. "Have you gotten the impression that some of his classmate's parents look down on you? Has Tyler said something?"

"To tell the truth, no. I worried a lot about that happening when he started there, but it hasn't been a serious problem. I'm sure there are some snotty kids, but the school has a huge scholarship fund, so there are some kids who have all their expenses paid. Besides, it's a place that values intelligence and creativity. And, of course, Tyler excels in those areas."

"But you said—"

"I know. The problem is me, Sam. I go to things at school and I feel like . . . an employee of his friends' parents. Everyone is very nice," she continued before he could say anything, "but they ask questions about remodeling their homes as though I couldn't possibly have anything else to talk about. Not that I could contribute to conversations about vacations in St. Bart's or flying to Paris for the spring shows. I just thought that this would improve my image, if you understand what I mean."

"You're looking for status conferral," Sam said. He didn't remind her that if she had accepted one of his many offers of marriage, she could afford to see a bit more of the world.

"I guess. I sort of figured that these people watched public television and they would think more of me for being on it."

"And it might work. But you just might find out that these people are watching *The Simpsons* instead of *Masterpiece Theatre*."

Josie grinned. "I suppose." She hesitated, then continued. "Do you think I'm being stupid?"

"No, you see a problem and when an opportunity comes up to do something about it, you act. I think you're being smart. But . . ."

Josie didn't even have time to enjoy his compliment. "What? What but?"

"You've never watched Courtney."

"That's what I was telling you . . . Why?"

"I don't want to prejudice you. Let's finish up here and go home and watch. Then you can tell me what you think."

Their risotto had arrived, but Josie discovered that she'd lost her appetite.

Josie's bowl of ice cream was melting on the coffee table. She hadn't said a word while the show was on. She hadn't said a word in the nine minutes since it ended. Sam had been waiting patiently—until now.

"I'm going to get another bowl of ice cream. Would you like another one? Or maybe a glass of brandy or something?"

"No, I'm fine." She was silent for a few minutes longer. "She really is pretty, isn't she?"

"Yes."

"You know, she reminds me of someone. I can't figure out who—"

"You've probably seen her photograph in a magazine or a newspaper. So she seems familiar."

"I suppose that's it. She has awfully long—and clean—fingernails for a carpenter."

"Perhaps they're fake. Or maybe she just had a manicure."

Josie remembered the equipment she had seen in the van that afternoon and decided he could be right.

"What did you think?" Sam finally asked.

"I think I may have made a mistake. Courtney is the star of that show and the house is the costar. I don't see how being on it is going to help Island Contracting." Or me.

But she didn't say the last two words aloud.

FOUR

JOSIE WOKE UP with the uncomfortable feeling that the night had been filled with bad dreams. But she didn't have time to worry about vague phantoms; she had to talk to her son before she left for work.

Apparently their meeting was high on Tyler's agenda also. She walked into the large room that, in addition to their two bedrooms and two baths, completed their apartment. Her son was standing at the stove. No, she corrected herself before opening her mouth, he was *cooking* at the stove.

"Tyler?" Maybe she was still dreaming?

"Hi, Mom! What do you want with your blueberry pancakes? Bacon or sausage?"

"You made blueberry pancakes?"

"Yup. The batter's waiting to go on the griddle. So?"

Josie stared at her tall, good-looking son with disbelief. "So?" she repeated, confused.

"So which do you want? Bacon or sausage? There's only room for one on the side of the griddle."

"We have a griddle?" It didn't seem likely. The most professional equipment in her kitchen was the KitchenAid mixer Sam's mother had given her last Christmas. The half-inch of white stuff in the bottom of its bowl was dust, not flour.

"I borrowed it from Risa yesterday. Want some coffee? I filled your thermos and made extra."

Josie sat down at the small counter that served as their daily eating place. "Before you start looking up recipes for Chateaubriand and pressing your own grapes, I should tell you that you can take the job at Family Video—with two conditions," she added quickly, raising her hand to silence his enthusiasm.

Tyler stood quietly while she explained the ideas Sam had come up with and then a large grin spread across his face. "Thanks, Mom. I knew you'd be reasonable. You know what I'm going to do with my salary?"

"Put half of it in your college fund," she reminded him.

"Sure, but after that I'm going to start saving for my car."

"Your what? Tyler, you won't be driving for another year. And cars are expensive." Josie shut up. A year was a long way away and Tyler's enthusiasms could be as brief as they were intense. Besides, the smell of hickory-smoked bacon filled the air and there were more immediate things to worry about. "Did you check to see if we had any syrup?"

"The real stuff," he replied, pointing to the plastic jug she hadn't noticed at the end of the counter.

"You really planned this well."

"I figured we could celebrate my new job if you agreed to it. And if not, I'd try bribing you with a good home-cooked meal. You know what they say: The way to a woman's heart is through her stomach. Right?"

"That's not quite how I heard it," Josie admitted, reaching for the plate Tyler passed her. The plate, bought at a garage sale, was extra large. And it was in danger of overflowing. She picked up her fork and reached for the syrup, suddenly famished.

Josie was a good and enlightened mother. She had read her share of articles about the importance of self-confidence, so she forced herself to stop eating after the first pancake and compliment her son's cooking.

"So when do you start work?" Josie asked, putting down her fork and reaching for her coffee.

"Today. At nine o'clock. So I'd better get," Tyler said, standing up. He seemed to notice the pile of dishes in the sink for the first time. "I'll clean these up tonight, okay?"

Josie smiled. She doubted it. "Great. I'll have a hard time matching this meal for dinner tonight."

"Uh. Mom."

Josie knew what was coming. "You're not going to be home for dinner. I thought if you worked early, you'd be off by five."

"Oh, it's not work. It's just that I promised some of the guys that I'd meet them for pizza and we could watch a video or two." He grinned, for a moment resembling his mother. "I get free videos, you know. This could make me the most popular person on the island this summer."

"As far as I'm concerned, you already are." Josie glanced at the large grandfather clock Tyler had made for her in his shop class at school. "Damn. I'm going to be late if I don't get a move on. When will you be home?" she called over her shoulder as she hurried to the bathroom.

"I'm not sure. I'll call and tell you where I'm going to be and what time I'll be home. I can leave a message on the machine if you're out."

"Okay, but be here by ten—"

"Thirty. I know, Mom. I know."

Bobby Valentine hadn't lied. *Courtney Castle's Castles* had folded its equipment into its vans and vanished into the sunset (or wherever). Happily, everyone from Island Contracting seemed to be present, accounted for, and working busily. The windows of number 23 were open and dust was flying out of them. As well as noise. Lots of noise, as the heavyset man standing on the side deck of number 25 seemed anxious to point out.

"You Josie Pigeon?"

Josie forced a polite smile onto her face and admitted the truth.

"Howard, is that the contractor?" The question came from the dark interior of the house behind the man.

"I'll take care of this, Cheryl. You just keep trying on everything in your wardrobe."

Josie knew what was going on. It wasn't the first time she'd had to deal with a neighbor who came to the shore for a nice quiet vacation only to discover the realities of early-morning remodeling going on nearby. "This isn't going to last forever," Josie said, waving toward the house. "And this is the noisy part. In a few days the demolition will be complete and things will get quieter."

The man in the doorway seemed to consider her words. "There were a lot of television vans here yesterday."

"Yes." Was he the type of person who would be thrilled to have a bird's-eye view so near a production, despite the noise level? She could only hope. She certainly wasn't going to be able to hide it from him. "Courtney Castle is going to be taping some of the work next door."

"Yeah, Cheryl and me, we saw her name on one of the vans. Was she here yesterday?"

Josie had watched the show the night before and knew the answer to this. "Well, uh . . ." She sure hoped these two weren't going to be a problem, hanging around the work site, hoping to meet the celebrity.

"Cheryl's been shopping her little heart out trying to find something to wear on television. Costs a fortune, but I say what the hell? She's happy. I'm happy. You know what I mean?" He winked lewdly. "What a vacation this is turning out to be. First it rains for a week, then we both get goddamn sunburns. But things are looking up. Courtney Castle is coming to town." A grin on his face, he vanished into the house; the metal screen door screeched shut behind him.

Josie shrugged and hurried back to work. Keeping the bystanders in order wasn't her problem. The blueprints were in her truck. She needed to make sure the correct walls were coming down.

A loud crash caused her to speed up. She needed to see what was happening and she didn't want to waste time trying to explain whatever it turned out to be to the man next door. She dashed up the steps, across the small deck, and through the sliding doors into the combination living room/dining room/kitchen area that fronted the house.

The noise had come from a mahogany room divider that had been torn from the rafters and now lay across a huge pile of debris in the middle of the floor. A handmade canoe, still attached to the ceiling, was swaying back and forth.

"Is that thing secure?" Josie asked, stepping back in case it wasn't.

"Yeah. I sat in it to rip out the nails holding that thing together," Dottie said, indicating the pile of mahogany.

"Good. The canoe's going to stay up there. But why isn't that stuff in the Dumpster?" Josie asked a second question before realizing that she knew the answer to that one. "Where the hell is the Dumpster?"

"Yeah, we were wondering that ourselves," Dottie said, standing up and stretching out her back.

"Damn, I've been using those guys for years. They're always reliable—"

The squeal of pneumatic brakes interrupted her statement. Jill, who was standing close to the window, glanced out. "They are reliable, if twenty-four hours late is how you define reliable."

Josie frowned. "Keep working. I'll be right back." She ran out to the huge tractor-trailer being maneuvered to the curb.

"What's going on?" she asked, grabbing on to the rearview mirror and swinging herself up on the cab's runningboard.

"Whada ya mean?"

But Josie was distracted by the driver's unusual attire. "Good heavens, you're wearing a suit. Are you going to a funeral or getting married?"

"It ain't a suit. It's a sports jacket and slacks. A double-breasted sports jacket," he pointed out, flicking his lapel with a filthy thumb.

"Someone change the dress code at Moffat Hauling?" Josie kidded.

"You know, Josie, sometimes a man just likes to look his best."

"Fine with me as long as you're going to unload that Dumpster in the driveway right now and as long as you're going to pick it up a week from today."

"Scheduled pickup is a week from yesterday."

"But it was supposed to be dropped off yesterday and we paid for it to be on-site for one week."

"Tried to drop it off yesterday. Couldn't. Too many of those television vans around. Not my fault. And it's the busy season. We're booked solid. Sorry, Josie, even for a good customer like you we can't make any changes. I know how you women like to take your time"—he saw the look in Josie's eyes and changed the end of his sentence—"but you'll just have to work a bit harder for the next six days."

Josie realized she wasn't going to win this fight. "So why don't you drop this thing off and let us get down to it? I need it to open toward the house, so leave enough space between it and the garage for the doors to swing."

"No problem. Think the TV people will be here when we come to pick it up? I'm only asking because you'll have to make sure their vans aren't in the way—or maybe they will want to tape a segment about hauling. You know. Size of Dumpsters. How to fill them efficiently. Where the garbage goes. That type of thing."

Josie didn't smile at his enthusiasm. After all, she had been equally enthusiastic about the prospect of a television appearance just a very short time ago. "I'll sure suggest it" was all she said.

"Great." He leaned forward, turned the key in the ignition; the truck roared to life, making further conversation impossible.

Josie knew she could depend on him to do the right thing. Time to get back to work.

Once there was a place to put the debris, the demolition went quickly. The house was getting three additions. One front, one back, and the biggest one up as high as the current building code would allow. All interior walls except for load-bearing beams were being removed. The appliances had already been taken to a resale shop, the furniture donated to a shelter off island. Built inexpensively in the sixties, there were no architectural details worth preserving—except for two. The canoe and a sculpture. Josie turned amid the dust and noise and stared at the sculpture. It sure looked ugly to her. But it was considered priceless by the home's owners.

For decades, critics have been arguing over the merits of modern sculpture. One of the most controversial artists to ever tie a tree up in monofilament and charge many thousands of dollars for the result of his deed had rented this place one summer in the midseventies. It had been, apparently, a summer with dreadful weather. The combination of being forced to remain inside and the wind and rain, which had smashed almost incessantly against the house, had inspired the man. The result of this creative flow was something Josie had, at first sight, thought was a misshapen piling that had somehow ended up sitting on the hearth of the fireplace. Apparently she'd been wrong; it was ART, and at all costs it was to be protected during the renovation.

Josie was happy with the progress so far and got to work building a reinforced frame around the sculpture. It took her almost an hour and she was less impressed with the aesthetic virtues of the piece when she was done than she'd been when she started. In fact, her cover looked better than the sculpture, she decided, standing up and stretching her tendons. But it was finished.

"Anyone know where there's a large piece of plywood we can write on?" she asked, looking around. "And a can of paint or something."

Annette came running with both. Josie painted FRAGILE!! on the wood and hammered the sign across the front of the frame.

"What do you think the Courtney Castle people will think about that?" Jill, her arms full of debris, stopped on her way out the door to ask.

"God knows. But I do know that we won't get anything accomplished if we worry about their opinion every step of the way. Let me help you all." She grabbed a slab of Sheetrock that was falling from the wheelbarrow Dottie was pushing and joined her crew in the dirty, exhausting work of demolition.

Two hours later they were sitting on the front deck, exhausted, huge hoagies dripping greasy strings of lettuce and tomato onto their filthy laps when a silver Porsche roared up to the curb and an Armani-clad young woman jumped out of the driver's seat. The polite smile slowly faded from her face as she surveyed the scene.

"That's her! That's Courtney!" Annette announced.

"How can you tell in that getup?" A lavish Hermès scarf

swaddled Courtney's head and massive black sunglasses covered much of her face. Josie stood, unaware that a slab of bologna was sticking to the front of her overalls. She smiled despite her aching back and mounting apprehension and started down the steps to the sidewalk.

"This isn't going to stay here for long, is it?" Courtney asked, not bothering to introduce herself and staring at the overflowing Dumpster as though she'd never seen one before.

"It's due to be taken away in six days," Josie answered. "I'm Josie Pigeon." She offered a dirty hand.

It was ignored. "Courtney Castle. This really won't do. Our show teaches people how to do things right. We don't accept sloppy work."

"Ms. Castle, I'm so happy you're finally here. I'm Cheryl. My husband and I live next door. We're the neighbors to this project. Anyway, I couldn't help but hear what you said and I couldn't agree with you more! My husband and I have never seen anything like this. Disgraceful and very unprofessional." A huge woman, showing off her dimpled thighs and arms in a bright pink playsuit, stomped across the lawn next door. "Certainly not up to the standards of *Courtney Castle's Castles*."

Josie didn't bother to introduce herself to the woman or defend her crew's work. Instead she examined Courtney Castle's profile with a shocked expression on her face. "You know—" she began, but Annette Long interrupted.

"Oh, Ms. Castle, I can't tell you how excited I am to meet you. We're all just thrilled that you're going to put Island Contracting on the air."

"Yes, we haven't been able to talk about anything else," Jill added.

"Well, some of us are more thrilled than others." Dottie had joined them.

"And we were going to clean up the front lawn right after lunch. Right, Josie?" Annette lied.

"Yes. I . . ." Josie was still staring.

"I think Josie and I should do a walk-through of the site," Courtney announced. "Right, Josie?"

"I . . . You . . . Yes, that would be a good idea. You all finish eating. This won't take long."

"Let's start out back. The blues are there and we can compare the finished product with what's here as we go."

"Great."

The two women, one chic and clean, one dirty and dowdy, entered through the open front door.

"Isn't this exciting?" Annette bubbled.

But Dottie and Jill had gone back to their lunches.

FIVE

IT WAS ALMOST six o'clock, well after the official start of the island's cocktail hour, so Josie wasn't too surprised to find a parking place right in front of Sam's store. Most of his customers would already be home, immersed in their first or second gin and tonic of the day. They were, after all, on vacation. But Josie wasn't. Furthermore, she was upset and in a hurry.

Which probably explained why she smashed right into a display of Beaujolais, knocking six bottles to the floor.

"Oh, damn!"

"They made it all the way here from France without a break, Josie. You could at least let me sell them to thirsty customers."

Josie was fumbling with her overalls. "It was my hammer. I thought I'd left this in the truck," she muttered, pulling it from her back pocket.

Sam had finished replacing the bottles on the shelves. "No harm done. So, are you here to see me, or am I a convenient stop on the way to the video store?"

"Have you seen Tyler today?"

"I just happened to return the tape we rented while he was at work, yes."

"And?"

"And he was having a ball. I was in the store less than five minutes, and during that time, he explained a new system of shelving foreign movies to the owner, told a woman he was sure her preschool son would get a lot out of *A Clockwork Orange*—his words, not mine—and flirted with one of the cutest girls I've seen on the island in a long while. He was having a ball," Sam repeated. "And don't worry. The little boy is going to be watching *One Hundred and One Dalmatians* tonight despite Tyler's helpful advice."

"Do you think he'll get fired?" Josie asked, suddenly discovering something new to worry about.

"No way. Everyone in the place was getting a huge kick out of his enthusiasm and energy. You know Tyler. Besides, the store doesn't carry anything X-rated. Anyone who wants to get something like that will have to go a few blocks away to Island Video."

"But won't the owner be upset if Tyler recommends tapes he doesn't carry?"

"Both stores are owned by the same person. Doesn't make a bit of difference to him which place people choose to rent from."

"Oh, so you think Tyler is doing a good job."

"Yes, I do."

"Do you think I could possibly just stop in and—"

"I think—and you know—you should leave him alone."

"You're right. I just needed something to do. It's been a strange day."

"*Courtney Castle's Castles* couldn't already be causing problems." Sam opened a bag of gourmet potato chips and passed them to her as he spoke.

"Sort of," she admitted through the crunching. "You know, last night when we were watching the show, I thought Courtney looked familiar. But today when she was at the house—"

"Courtney Castle is already on the island? She's getting to work early, isn't she?"

"I don't think . . . That's not the point. Sam, there's something strange about . . . Courtney. You see—"

"Did I hear Miss Josie Pigeon saying something about Courtney Castle? Did you hear anything about that, son?"

"Well, Chief, I guess I did."

Sam and Josie exchanged looks and turned to greet Chief Rodney and his son, the official (and during the winter months the only) police presence on the island.

"I was just telling Sam that I met Courtney Castle this afternoon," Josie explained.

"Yeah, so we heard." Mike Rodney managed to make the simple statement sound menacing.

"Can I help you?" Sam asked politely.

Chief Rodney got right to the point. "Sure hope so. We're looking for donations for the Annual Police Association Auction, Sam. We thought a bottle of one of your imported bubblies could fetch a pretty price."

"Always ready to help out the local organizations, you know that," Sam said agreeably.

"What Annual Police Association Auction?" Josie asked. "I've never heard of an annual police association auction. I didn't even know there was a police association on the island. What is it?"

"Most municipalities have a police association. Among other things, they raise money to help the officers in times of crisis, to do things like help the widows of officers killed in action," Mike Rodney explained.

"You mean this money is to go to your mother if the chief dies on the job," Sam said.

"Not just Mom—"

"I have no intention of dying either on or off the job, and

that's just one of the uses for any funds we may raise. There's also equipment available that would help us do our jobs more efficiently that cannot, for one reason or another, come out of the town budget."

"Is the donation tax deductible?" Sam asked.

"It will be. The papers were filed as soon as we heard that Courtney Castle was coming to the island."

"What does Courtney Castle have to do with . . . this police association auction?" Josie asked quickly.

"She's going to be our auctioneer," Mike bragged. "It was Dad's idea."

"We thought it would be wise to take advantage of having a famous celebrity in our midst."

"You asked her to do this already?" Sam asked.

"You called her?" Josie asked at the same time.

"In point of fact, she called us. Or, to be more specific, her producer called. She needs police protection, you see."

"Police protection?" Sam repeated the words.

"She's a famous person. Sometimes famous people attract oddballs," Mike said.

"I don't think this is anyone's business, Mike," his father warned.

Josie realized that Mike was explaining more than his father wanted him to. "You mean Bobby Valentine called you?" she asked.

"Sure did."

"To ask for police protection for Courtney Castle."

"To watch out for things while the show is in town," his father explained. "Crowd control."

"Crowd control? What crowds?"

"According to this Bobby Valentine, there's always a crowd around wherever the show is taped."

"You're kidding."

"I gather you didn't know anything about this," Sam said.

"No one mentioned it to me," Josie admitted. "But I don't see why it should be much of a problem."

"Well, I wouldn't be so sure of that," Sam said. "A bunch of spectators could disrupt deliveries if they're kept in the street, to say nothing of what might happen if they're allowed to wander around on the property. It sounds to me like a police line of some sort is an excellent idea."

"Does this mean you're planning on hanging that yellow police tape around my work site?"

"No, that's just the point," Mike said proudly. "Courtney Castle doesn't want anyone to see a police line. We're going to prevent curious people from getting anywhere near your work. The entire block will be cordoned off."

Josie could just imagine what Cheryl's husband would have to say about that. "What about the neighbors? The other people who live on the street?"

"Right now we're working on having passes printed up," Mike explained.

"But . . ." Josie began.

"How large an area is going to be cordoned off?" Sam asked. "Surely the whole block is a bit excessive."

"We will do whatever Miss Courtney Castle asks," the chief of police answered.

Josie took another step backward. A fatal one for the Beaujolais, as it turned out. Glass and wine flew in all directions, drenching Josie's overalls as well as Sam's chinos and loafers. The ensuing cleanup didn't interest the Rodneys, and claiming urgent police business, they stepped over the mess and left. Sam called to an employee to bring a mop and he led Josie to his small office in the rear of the store. He seated her in his desk chair and grabbed a wineglass from a nearby shelf. "Red or white?"

"I'll stick with red," she answered, glancing down at her stained clothing.

Sam waited until she'd had time to taste the wine before he asked his first question. "Why do you object to this police line? Even if it's a bit excessive, it probably won't be a problem for you."

"Ha! Everything about Courtney and her show will be a problem for me!"

"How can you possibly know that? You've just met!"

"She doesn't make a good first impression," Josie answered after a short pause.

"Meaning?"

"Sam, you should have been there. She drove up in this hot car—a silver Porsche, for heaven's sake."

"Wow. I wonder if PBS pays for that."

Josie couldn't believe it; he sounded envious. "You know, Sam—"

"It doesn't matter. Go on. What did she do when she drove up?"

"She . . . she started to complain about everything immediately. She didn't like where the Dumpster was located or how we filled it. Ask Jill or Annette or Dottie. They all heard her complaining."

"I don't doubt you, Josie, but so what?"

"I don't know. It's just that she bugs me. I'm really beginning to regret agreeing to be on television."

Sam picked up his full glass, then put it down without drinking. "I think I'll keep my head clear."

Josie didn't have any such compunction. She drained her glass and stared at the desk before her.

"We could go out to dinner," Sam suggested. "Sounds like you need a break. And tomorrow's going to be a big day."

Josie frowned.

Sam knew what she was thinking. "How about if we just get a beer and a pizza at that new restaurant down on the boardwalk. You'll be home long before Tyler arrives."

"I hear that place is usually crowded."

Sam shrugged. "Let's give it a try anyway. We can take your truck."

"It's filthy," Josie warned him.

"So are we," Sam said, glancing at their wine-stained clothing. "So are we."

But the popularity of the new pizza place had apparently been exaggerated. They were almost the only customers in the gleaming white-tiled room. Sam looked around as he pulled Josie's chair out for her. "Guess we won't have to wait long for our food."

Josie looked over his shoulder, recognizing a member of Tyler's old Cub Scout troop. "Luke! Look at you! You look so grown up!" She knew she sounded stupid.

Apparently the teenager was used to the clichés of adults. "Hi, Ms. Pigeon. I saw Tyler at the video store this morning. Cool job."

"This looks like a pretty good place to work, too."

Another couple walked in the door.

"Hey, we make the best pizza on the island. We've been jammed every day since we opened. Course it looks like everything's changed now. Maybe you could do something about that," he added, handing Josie a menu.

"Me? What do I have to do with it?"

"You're what brought that carpenter lady to the island, aren't you?"

"What carpenter?"

"You're talking about Courtney Castle, aren't you?" Sam asked.

"Yeah. She's over at Basil's new place tonight."

"So?"

"So that's where all our customers have gone."

"They followed Courtney Castle to dinner?" Josie asked, amazed. She herself was thrilled to be away from Courtney for the evening.

"Damn right. There's a line around the block over there. The line that should be going out that door," Luke added, nodding to the pizza parlor's entrance.

"I don't think you have to worry about this being permanent. Courtney is new to the island. After a few weeks, people will become accustomed to seeing her around and maybe they won't be quite so starstruck," Sam said.

"I sure hope so, Mr. Richardson. This is a great job. I get all the leftover pizza I want at the end of each day. And the tips are good, too. If they go out of business, I'm dead meat."

Josie had been looking around the large room. "Did you mention any of this to the couple sitting at that table by the window?"

Luke followed her glance. "No. What do they have to do with it?"

"Well, the pretty young woman is one of my carpenters. But the young guy is a summer intern on Courtney's show. Maybe if he likes the food, he could mention it to Courtney and she might start coming here."

"Hey, cool. Do you think maybe I should give him a menu and he could take it to her, and then she'd try the pizza and like it and start coming here?" Luke asked.

"It's possible."

"Hey, I'd better make sure they get good service. And they could order out. I'll tell them we deliver."

"You have takeout service?" Sam asked as Luke turned to rush off.

"Well, not for just anybody, Mr. Richardson. But for Courtney Castle . . . well, that's different."

"Things are different for Courtney Castle?" Josie mused, a frown creasing her face.

"I think, Josie, you'd better get used to it."

SIX

IT WAS SUMMER. People who had struggled to earn enough money to buy summer houses at the beach were enjoying those homes. Rental agencies had NOTHING AVAILABLE THIS SEASON signs posted in their windows. Daytrippers from inland lugged tons of paraphernalia to and from the sandy beach, many of them with children in tow. The island had only two main roads that carried most of the vehicles traveling north or south. But a traffic jam at seven-thirty in the morning? Josie was glad she had a mug of coffee propped between her toolbox and a new sweatshirt on the seat by her side. She had gotten up early and left her apartment quickly, pausing only to greet her very sleepy son. She thought there wasn't a chance she'd be late the first day of taping. But now . . . The car behind her was honking and she threw an angry glance over her shoulder. Probably some damn tourist rushing to his rented house with a bag of warm doughnuts from the bakery.

"Damn idiot. How the hell does he expect me to move? Maybe I'm supposed to run right over the cars in front of me?" Annoyed, she reached out for her coffee and succeeded in spilling it over the sweatshirt. "Damn!" At least it hadn't splashed on her new carpenter's pants. As she raised the mug to her lips, a hand jogging her arm through the window did just that. "What the—?"

"Hey, I'm trying to help you, Miss Pigeon. Thought you might want to get to work."

Josie looked up from her wet clothing into the eyes of the police chief. "How can I . . ." she started her question and then realized she was being ungrateful, stupid and ungrateful. The way had been cleared for her truck to move around the block and out of what seemed to be a continuous line of stopped cars.

"You can go right around there and then Mike will lead you through the traffic up to your work site. We don't want Courtney Castle to think you're going to make a habit of being late for work."

"Courtney—"

"Hey, lady, we cleared people out of the way. Are you going to sit there and sulk about your dirty clothes or get going?"

She got going. With any luck, she'd still beat Courtney and Courtney's crew. But when she drove up to the house, she realized she was wrong. There were, if possible, even more trucks and vans in front of the house than before. Courtney, wearing worn overalls that were tight in places most overalls didn't even skim, a bright red T-shirt bearing its allegiance to Yale across the chest, immaculate Donna Karan sneakers, a red bandanna around her neck, and a bright red barrette in her thick, shimmering hair, was leaning against the Dumpster she had been so upset about the day before, munching on a rice cracker.

Josie got out of her truck and forced a smile onto her face. "Hi."

"You're late." Courtney didn't bother to raise her eyes higher than the stains on Josie's carpenter's pants.

"There was a traffic jam." Josie looked around. "I guess you know that. You are the traffic jam."

"We've been here since five. Been taping since six A.M. It doesn't take very long for word to get out and for crowds to appear. Bobby told the cops that we would need all-day protection, but I guess they assumed we worked a nine-to-five schedule or something." The stains were still fascinating Courtney.

Josie was acutely aware of the crowd milling around. Of the many things she wanted to say to this woman, none of them were for public consumption. She swallowed. "I don't understand. I thought the show was about this house, about the job we're doing on it. How could you get started without us?"

Courtney's eyes raised to Josie's face and then drifted off to a space just above her left shoulder.

Bobby Valentine filled the silence. "We have lots of standups to get on tape. Cutaway shots, things like that."

"You're not needed for any of that," Courtney stated, popping the last of her cracker in her mouth and wiping imaginary crumbs off her hands.

"And I've had our intern interviewing members of your crew. We need background information. Something for Courtney to say as she introduces everyone. You know, a little snippet about their pasts, how they became carpenters, how they ended up working for Island Contracting."

"You put that information on television?" Josie asked, looking around.

"Yes. Our audience loves that sort of stuff."

"But I thought this show was about the remodeling job. What does the background of my workers have to do with anything?"

"Hey, you're gonna be amazed! Some of these women will get fan letters. Hell, Courtney gets at least a half-dozen marriage proposals a year."

"Doesn't surprise me," Dottie said, joining them. "She's

what every man wants—blond, sexy, and capable of fixing anything that goes wrong around the house."

"I'll bet that young woman with the great body—Jill, I think she said her name was—will be getting fan mail," Bobby Valentine continued. "She sure fills out a T-shirt nicely."

Josie saw a frown forming on Courtney's face. If she had to make a prediction, she'd guess that Jill was going to be receiving limited airtime. "She's a good carpenter. That's all I care about. Speaking of which, we'd better get to work."

"We're ready for you at the back of the house." Courtney started in that direction as she spoke.

"What? I was . . . We were . . ."

"Our cameraman is set up at the end of the dock."

Josie was confused. "The show starts out there? I thought—"

"No. We just want to get a few cover shots while the sun is shining on the bay."

Josie looked down at her pants. "I don't suppose I have time to go home and change?"

Courtney laughed. "Not only don't you have time to change, you need to keep those clothes around in case we want shots on either side of this one to match."

"You mean everyone has to spend the entire series in the clothing they're wearing today?"

"Nope. But you do need to be wearing one thing in each show. We don't want to be cutting back and forth between shots and discover some sort of fashion show going on. And if you're going to be changing your clothing, you'll have to help us out and remember what you're wearing when. We don't have a continuity person on the show. This is public television, remember, not Warner Brothers."

"But I haven't even started working and I'm filthy," Josie protested, looking down at the coffee stains.

"You're a carpenter. You're not supposed to be immaculate. I'm going to check my face and I'll be back in a few minutes," Courtney announced, then turned and headed toward the large trailer Josie had visited yesterday.

"Remember, Courtney wears work clothes, too," Bobby Valentine said aloud. But Courtney's work clothes had been translated into a fashion statement by the likes of Ralph Lauren. She also wore tons of makeup and had recently had her blond hair done. "So let's get started."

"Shouldn't we wait for Courtney?"

"Nope. We don't need her for this."

Josie hurried after him. "I don't understand. I thought this was an interview. You know, that she was going to ask me questions and I'd answer them, and so on."

"We already taped her questions. Now we'll tape your answers."

"But how will I know what to say?"

Bobby Valentine chuckled. "I'll ask you questions, the same questions we taped Courtney asking. And we'll tape your answers. It's the only way we can do this type of thing without multiple cameras. This is public broadcasting, you know, not Turner Broadcasting."

"What if I make a mistake? You know, stutter or say something stupid?"

"We're not live. Everything will be edited. And no one wants you to look anything but your best."

Josie wasn't so sure of that, but she figured she had to trust someone.

"And this isn't a quiz, remember. I'm just going to ask you a bit about your background. The same type of things we're asking the rest of the crew."

"Shouldn't I have on makeup?"

"Not unless you're planning on wearing it while working during the rest of the project. You might want to run a comb through your hair though."

She started to search her pockets.

"Use mine," he offered, handing her an elegant tortoise-shell model.

"Thanks." She scraped it across her unruly curls. "What do you think?"

He looked at her doubtfully. "Better, I guess. But don't worry. Our viewers will probably assume it's windy on the dock."

They circled the house, walking around planks of wood. Josie noticed everyone on her crew hard at work, except for Annette, who was talking with the show's intern as she rather lackadaisically sorted through a delivery from the lumber-yard. They made a cute couple, Josie thought, jumping up onto the dock. The cameraman was waiting for them. He pointed to where he wanted her to sit, and after a bit of rearranging her clothing and another ineffectual combing of her hair, the interview began.

Bobby Valentine read from a sheet of paper.

"Tell us a little about your background, Josie. Where were you brought up?"

The question took Josie by surprise. "Ah, not on the island. I was raised in . . . in the suburbs."

There was a moment or two of silence. Then Bobby Valentine spoke up. "Cut. You can tell us a bit more about yourself. You know, not just the suburbs but the suburbs of what city, in what state. You know the type of thing. Give our viewers something to relate to. Now let's start again.

"Take two. Tell us a little about your background, Josie. Where were you brought up?"

"I grew up in the suburbs, Bobby—"

"Cut!"

"Why? Do I have to name a place? I . . . Oh, sorry."

"Take three. Tell us a little about your background, Josie. Where were you brought up?"

"I was raised in the suburbs, Courtney. Like a lot of women, I had no idea how to use tools. And I didn't expect to need to. I took home economics in high school, not shop."

Bobby Valentine's eyes narrowed, but he asked the next question on his list. "How did you come to live here on this island?"

"I was lucky. I was looking for a place to live, a community where I could raise my son and earn a living, and I remembered this place. I had . . ." Here she stumbled at bit. "I had been on the island when I was a kid. I came back here just to look around. And I stayed." She smiled, realizing what a sanitized version she was presenting of her life. No mention of dropping out of college pregnant, no mention of the irreparable rift with her parents. But also no mention of someone who needed recognition, who needed mentioning. "I was very lucky to meet up with Noel Roberts when I got here," she added quickly.

Bobby Valentine looked startled, but he picked up on her cue. "Noel Roberts?" he repeated the name as a question.

"Noel was the owner, the creator actually, of Island Contracting. He trained me as a carpenter, and when he died, I inherited the company from him—"

"Cut!"

Josie was startled. "What's wrong?"

"Did you just tell all our viewers that this man, this Noel Roberts, was your lover?"

"No, I told you. He was my friend."

"He left you a company out of friendship?" Bobby Valentine asked.

"Some friend," the cameraman muttered, fussing with his lens.

"Yes. He did. And he deserves credit for creating the company. Why did you stop the camera?"

"Thought we needed to chat for a minute. Let's get going."

Josie nodded. The cameraman looked through his view-finder. Bobby Valentine asked another question. "How long have you owned Island Contracting?"

That one was easy. "Over three years."

"Do you happen to know how many remodeling projects you've been involved in during that time?"

Josie frowned before remembering that making faces on camera wasn't particularly appealing. "Heavens, I don't know. At least five houses, maybe more. And we've done other projects as well. Small carpentry jobs like building shelves over at the island's hardware store and putting in skylights for one of the realtors on Ocean Avenue. We built the Christmas display that is set up on the island every year. And we do some nautical things—we've worked on docks just like this one." She smacked the rail for emphasis and was startled when the wood cracked and a piece fell into the water. "Not this one, of course. The docks we've rebuilt don't fall apart."

"Island Contracting's location is unique, but there's something even more interesting about your company. I understand you hire only women workers. Why is that?"

"That's not exactly true. I mean, it's not a company policy. It just happens to work out like that." She stopped. The questions were getting closer to things she didn't want to discuss. "Island Contracting, in Noel's time, did try to hire people who needed a second chance in life." She paused again. "A lot of them happened to be women. And," she added, becoming enthusiastic as she realized they had segued to a safe topic, "you have to remember how much things have changed since Island Contracting was created. Women began training in the trades in the late sixties and early seventies, but even now there are companies that go out of their way to only hire men. For some women, a place like Island Contracting is a miracle as well as the only opportunity they've been offered to use their skills professionally.

"You know, Bobby, there are government-sponsored programs to get women off welfare and into the workforce. And some of those programs have only recently discovered that people in the trades—electricians, plumbers, carpenters, rockers, and others—are in an ideal position to change their lives. We pay living wages and sometimes can adjust the work hours to accommodate women who are raising small children and— Oh!" She broke off. "I'm sorry. I called you Bobby. I forgot."

"Don't worry. Your answer was too long. And Courtney has included information about those programs in two of her show introductions. We'll just edit that out.

"Now, let's see." He looked down at his list. "Where did you learn your trade? Did you go to school?"

Josie remembered Courtney's Ivy League T-shirt and sighed. "Actually, I . . . ah, didn't finish college. And I learned my job right here. At Island Contracting." At least she didn't have to admit to only completing one semester of college. But between the coffee stain and some judicious editing on the part of Courtney's staff, she was fairly sure she'd come off looking stupid as well as sloppy. Why, she wondered as Bobby Valentine asked the next question calling for a revealing answer, had she agreed to be a part of *Courtney Castle's Castles*?

SEVEN

A S THE FIRST day of shooting *Courtney Castle's Castles*
continued, the crowds, discouraged by police efforts
to keep anyone from seeing anything interesting, dispersed
and returned to the sand and surf. Josie and her crew weren't
lucky enough to have that option.

After the interview was over, Josie hurried back to work.
They were going to frame in the extension at the back of the
house before opening that wall to the outside. The same thing
would be done in the front, and then, when the interior walls
had been removed and if the good weather held, the upward
expansion would begin. The entire project was scheduled to
take six weeks. Each week Courtney and/or her crew would
be on hand for at least two days of taping. The end result was
to be a completely remodeled house and one fund-raising
television series.

Her crew had begun marking out the new foundation. Here
on the bay, the only foundation possible was of pilings pounded
into the ground by the same company that did underwater
work for docks and bridges. It was a unique process, and the
show was interested in taping this part of the construction.

And Josie was interested in moving beyond the interview
stage.

Apparently, she wasn't the only one who felt this way. As

soon as the television crew was out of hearing range, the complaints began.

"God, why do they want to know so many personal things about us?" Jill said, pulling her T-shirt away from her body. The sun was bright and the women were sweating as they worked.

"Nosy parkers," Dottie muttered.

Josie raised her eyebrows. That seemed like an awfully subdued reaction from the person she had expected to find the most upset. "They did ask some awfully personal questions," she commented.

"At least the producer interviewed you. We got stuck with that kid intern. He asked me where I grew up, when I decided to be a carpenter, how I learned my trade, what led me to Island Contracting. I wanted to tell that young punk that he could just mind his own business!" Jill said angrily.

"I think he's cute." Annette spoke up. "We ran into each other last night at that pizza place on the boardwalk and had dinner together."

"That kid wearing the Cornell T-shirt? Are you nuts? He's the product of some prep school in a wealthy suburb. His parents have so much money, he doesn't even have to get one of those easy summer jobs that most kids have. He's an intern. An intern!" Dottie made the term sound like something awful. "And just in case you're getting any ideas, I can tell you that he's not going to be interested in a carpenter. Those Ivy League types are only slumming when they're being nice to the likes of us."

Annette put down the plumb line she was using and looked straight at Dottie. "What about Josie and Sam? He's a lawyer and she's just a carpenter. . . ." She glanced over at Josie.

"I don't think of myself as 'just a carpenter.' And Sam doesn't either," Josie said. "And if you like this guy, go for it."

Annette's face broke into a large smile. "He asked me to go

out with him tonight. I said I didn't know what time we'd be finished work—"

"We'll be done in time for you to see him. Why don't you go tell him it's a date? And if you need an excuse to be out front, get the thermos of coffee and the bakery box from the front seat of my truck. We may as well take a coffee break now."

Annette bounced off happily.

"You and Sam are an exception," Dottie stated flatly. "And you probably know it. How many college-educated men have you dated since you entered the trades?"

"Not many—not that I've dated all that much. But Annette is young and it's nice to be young and think all things are possible."

"You're right," Jill agreed, nodding. "Let Annette keep that feeling for as long as she can— Why are you back so soon?" she asked as Annette reappeared. "And where's the food Josie told you to bring?"

"I ran into Chad—that's his name, Chad Henshaw—and he told me there's food set up on a table in the driveway."

"Yeah, I saw the truck delivering it," Dottie said. "They hauled out all sorts of goodies. But it's for the TV people, not for the likes of us."

"No! That's not true. Chad was on his way here to tell us that Bobby Valentine invited everyone to eat there, for breaks as well as for lunch. The food is provided by merchants on the island for a credit—I think he called it a credit—at the end of the show. I saw it—it's a feast!"

They didn't have to be invited twice.

Josie's first thought, upon spying the lavish spread laid out on two large tables and shaded by multicolored beach umbrellas, was to wonder why anyone would ever eat a rice cake when such delicious bounty was available. She was piling sugary Bismarcks on a large paper plate when she noticed

Courtney walking by, a can of Diet Coke in one hand and a sheaf of papers in the other.

"I see you still have that sweet tooth," Courtney said, speeding up so that Josie didn't have time to respond.

Josie opened her mouth and then, realizing what she was looking at, closed it again. Son of a gun, she thought. "I see you're still a sourpuss" was what she called out, picking up a doughnut and taking a large bite. Too large, it turned out. A chunk of sugary coating stuck in her throat and she began to choke. Embarrassingly enough, everyone came to her aid. By the time her back had been slapped and offers to try out newly acquired Heimlich skills refused, Courtney was standing in the middle of the sidewalk, smiling at the camera set up before her.

"If you're feeling better, they're going to need you in a few minutes," Bobby Valentine said.

"Why?"

"Courtney wants to tape the show's opening introducing you and the project."

"But I thought that wasn't going to happen today!"

"Courtney thought this would be a good day. I guess she's had time to glance at the background notes on you and Island Contracting and she's ready to go."

"And when Courtney is ready to go, you go?"

He shrugged. "She's the star of the whole shebang."

"Do I have time to put on makeup?"

"Well, we were aiming more for the natural look." He glanced over at Courtney.

Josie looked, too. Courtney's cheeks were pink, her eyelashes black, and her lips bright red. She looked wonderful, but not . . . "That's natural?" Josie asked.

"That's what Courtney looks like on the air. Always. Period."

Josie took a second look at Courtney. "Oh, well, I suppose

she would look better than I do even if I had makeup on and a fresh haircut."

"Let's face it. If you were better-looking than Courtney, you probably wouldn't have been chosen to be on the show. Besides, you look very alive, very perky."

"Thanks." Faint praise was better than none at all. "I think you're being waved at."

"Time to get this baby on tape. Want to borrow my comb again?"

"I think I'll settle for the windblown look." She tried to tuck in her T-shirt as they walked over to join Courtney and the cameraman. "I've heard the camera adds five pounds."

"Ten actually. Ready to tape, Courtney?"

"Just waiting for you." She scowled at Josie.

"I'm here now." Josie scowled back. Just like old times. "Where do you want me to stand?"

"We were just thinking that you both could be perched on the deck railing—on either side of the corner." The cameraman pointed. "Light's good. House is in the background and if I pan to the right, there's a nice view of the bay."

Courtney smiled. "Sounds good to me. What about you, Josie?"

"Fine." She tried to emulate the energetic little jump that put Courtney up onto the railing and heard the wood creak ominously. "Shouldn't I be prepared? What are you going to ask me?"

"You know, we used to give guests lists of questions and what we discovered was that they prepared answers and the show lost some spontaneity."

"Besides, you're only going to be asked about your life and work. You know the answers," Bobby Valentine added, probably seeing the worried expression on Josie's face.

"We're going to lose the light behind us in an hour or so," the cameraman warned them.

"I'm just going to introduce you and then off we go," Courtney explained, and then, without a pause, did just that. "Welcome to *Courtney Castle's Castles*. Would you like to own a summer home? Someplace to kick back and relax? Maybe someplace with a dock for your boat? Well, we've found a place just like that. But it needs a lot of work and that's where Josie Pigeon and Island Contracting come in."

And suddenly Courtney turned to face her and Josie realized she was on. "Hi, Josie."

Well, that was easy. "Hi, Courtney." She tried to match Courtney's enthusiasm.

But Courtney was talking to the camera. "Josie is a carpenter who owns her own contracting company here on the island. The company employs only women." Courtney smiled. "I always like to think that my feminist sisters are getting a break, but tell me, is this type of discrimination legal, Josie?"

It came at her out of left field. "Ah . . ." She thought furiously. "We don't hire workers just because they are women. But there are still many companies that do discriminate against female workers, so these women need jobs. And, you know, we would hire men . . ." She realized she was talking to the side of Courtney's face.

"Do you find the women are as well trained as men doing the same jobs?"

"As well or better. And some of the women we've hired have unique skills. Jill Pike, who is working on this project with Island Contracting, has spent some time in the Northwest, where she participated in building cob homes."

"She made a home from corncobs?"

Josie felt as if she had the upper hand for a moment and decided to make the most of it. "No, Courtney, cob construction is an ancient building technique. Cob is a mixture of sand, straw, and clay. Jill and the group she was working with built six homes from that material over the course of two summers."

"In the Northwest?"

"Yes, and I know what you're thinking. The material is completely impervious to rain once it dries."

Courtney seemed speechless for a few minutes. "How interesting. Ah . . ."

"It's really fascinating," Josie continued. "Families can actually build their own homes without much professional help and save considerable amounts of money—"

"Speaking of women, work, and families, Josie. How does your family feel about the life you've chosen?"

Josie smiled. "My son, Tyler, is sixteen years old and I think he's proud of what I do. When he was small, he and I used to bicycle around the island in good weather and he would point out what he called Mommy's houses."

"I was referring to the rest of your family. Your mother and father. How do they feel about you being a carpenter? Are they also proud of your handiwork?"

"I haven't . . . that is, they haven't . . ." She took a deep breath and tried to figure out what to say. "My parents don't live on the island" was all she came up with. She was busy trying to keep a scowl off her face. That damn camera was still going.

"That's too bad. They might be proud to see how successful their little girl is." Courtney turned back to the camera, smiled, and changed the subject. "So we'll be meeting more women than we usually do on our shows during this project. Tell us a bit about the island, Josie. I gather you're not a native? How long have you lived here?"

Josie tried to keep her voice modulated. "No, I'm not. I came here right after . . . over a dozen years ago."

"So you were here during the boom years of the late eighties, when real estate values increased dramatically."

"Yes." Josie decided it was time to get the attention away from her personal life. "But this house was built before that time. This house was built in the midsixties by a developer who put up at least a couple of dozen of these homes, usually doing exactly what he did here—buying up an entire block and filling it with a line of identical little A-frames.

"There aren't many left in their original state," Josie continued, wondering why the questions had stopped. "This job is interesting because instead of tearing down the entire structure and building something new, the owners have chosen to retain parts of the original house. We're even extending the chimney from the first floor up through the roof of the new addition."

Josie didn't know what else to say, so she stopped talking and waited for Courtney to pick up the ball.

But Courtney was sitting quietly, looking a bit like she'd adopted some Buddhist practice. There was a slight smile on her lips and her eyes seemed to be focused on something far away in the distance.

"Cut!" Bobby Valentine ended the moment. "Do you want to do the walk-through of the house now or wait until after lunch?" he asked Courtney.

"I suppose we may as well block it out now."

Josie was amazed by the transformation. When the camera was on, Courtney was bright and alert. But without an imaginary audience, she almost seemed deflated. "Block it out? Do you need me?"

"What do you think, Court? Do you want to do the walk-through alone or with Josie?"

Bobby Valentine's question pulled Courtney back from the vast beyond. Her eyes focused on her producer and she seemed to consider the question.

"Maybe it would be best if Josie came along and she could

suggest where we run into her crew members," Bobby Valentine suggested. "We probably won't introduce everyone during one show, but we try to give the audience an opportunity early in the series to recognize the people who will be on the set. It serves two purposes. First, it's less distracting. Viewers don't need to be wondering about the man—or woman—in a background shot while Courtney is talking or doing an interview. And it helps the viewer relate to the project."

"Why does that matter?" Josie asked, thankful for the arm he offered to help her get off the railing more gracefully than she had gotten on, and then followed him through the door into the house.

"Our show is supposed to be educational, at least that's how it's billed. And we do show almost every new product on the market as well as the ways to use them. And certainly anyone planning to work on a house can get lots of great ideas by watching. But most of our viewers will never do anything as extensive or expensive as the jobs we show. They tune in because it's fun to imagine being involved in a large-scale remodeling project without the grief or the expense involved in real life."

"You're saying *Courtney Castle's Castles* is entertainment."

He grinned. "Yup. But don't tell anyone involved in public broadcasting. We used to get government funding to do this stuff, remember."

Josie noticed he was looking over her shoulder through the still open doorway. "Isn't Courtney coming?"

"It's difficult to know just what she's doing these days." The words seemed to be said more to himself than in answer to her question. "But," he continued firmly, "why don't you and I go through the house and we can discuss how your work is going to connect with ours. Courtney can catch up later."

"Great."

"Courtney will introduce you on the deck in the first shot

of the first show. And since she'll mention your unique crew at that time, we think another introduction should take place within that half hour. Maybe someone could be finishing up a last bit of demolition in here?"

"Well, we're protecting the chimney and hearth down here. Maybe—"

Josie was interrupted by a loud screech. It was so loud and frightening that at first she feared someone had been murdered. But it turned out to be the beginning of a Courtney Castle temper tantrum.

EIGHT

ANNETTE LONG WAS pink with excitement. "You should have seen her! She was completely off the wall!"

"You're right. I couldn't imagine what was going on," Jill agreed, nodding furiously.

"Hysterical bitch." Dottie was typically succinct.

Josie looked down at the plate in front of her. Caesar salad with grilled shrimp. Marinated roasted red peppers. Fresh rolls and butter. And there were three cheesecakes being cut up for dessert. Plain, chocolate, and raspberry. "But there are fringe benefits for putting up with her," she reminded them.

"She's so thin. I don't know how she eats all this stuff without gaining weight. Do you think she has a personal trainer?" Annette asked.

"Ha!" Jill was sarcastic. "She doesn't eat real food. Every time I see her, she's taking tiny little bites from one of those disgusting rice cakes. I'd rather eat sawdust!"

"Anorexic bitch." Dottie patted her protruding stomach fondly.

"I suspect we won't be seeing all that much of her. I'm beginning to get the impression that Island Contracting is just scenery for *Courtney Castle's Castles*," Josie said, a frown on her face.

"Oh, good, can I be a tree?" Jill asked. The women were

sitting together on the dock behind the house, and Jill reached out, plucked a branch from an evergreen bush overhanging the water, and stuck it jauntily behind her left ear.

"Me, too," Annette said, giggling and running off the dock to collect more branches. "Here." She handed one to Dottie, who jammed it into her hair so that it stuck up like a feather in a child's Native American headdress. "You, too," she said impulsively, and, forgetting that Josie was the boss, began tucking leaves and tiny branches into her mop of red hair.

Josie laughed and stuck a curl of red pepper in her mouth like a lizard's proboscis. "You guys be the flora and I'll be the fauna," she said, giggling. These women hadn't been working for her for long and she was usually reluctant to "let down her hair" with new employees, but the taping was creating a lot of tension and she couldn't resist the temptation to let off a bit of steam. Apparently the others felt the same way—except for Dottie, who was still scowling. Or maybe scowling was something Dottie enjoyed; she certainly did it enough.

Josie picked up a long roll, held it like a microphone in front of her face, and stood. "Allow me to introduce myself. I am Josephine Pigeon, host of *Pigeon's . . . Pigeon's Palaces*."

The women shrieked with laughter.

"And I would like to introduce you to my crew." She held the roll out to Annette. "This is Annette Long, star of *Annette's Adobes*, a build-it-yourself-with-the-stuff-in-your-backyard show. And this woman is Dottie Evans, star of *Dottie's Duplexes*, building for two—"

"How about *Dottie's Dives*?" Annette suggested through giggles.

"I was hoping for *Dottie's Dumps*. Build your own trashy place to crash," Dottie admitted, almost smiling.

"And me! What about me?" Jill demanded.

"*Jill's . . .*" Josie drew a blank. "*Jill's* what?"

"I have it," Dottie said, really getting into the swing of things. "How about Jill Pike, builder of the *House of Jill Repute*."

"I love it!" Annette jumped up and down, causing the whole dock to shake. "*House of Jill Repute!* That's a good one!" She seemed to notice a lack of enthusiasm in Jill's response. "Don't you get it? Jill Repute. Like Ill Repute. Like a whorehouse."

"I get it. I get it." Jill sounded weary, and Josie jumped in to rescue the moment.

"How about *Jill's Joints*? It can go on the air right after *Dottie's Dumps*. We'll create a new Saturday-night lineup for PBS. *Dottie's Dumps, Jill's Joints, Annette's Adobes,* and then . . . ta da . . ." Josie took a deep bow before continuing. "*Pigeon's Palaces*. Who needs Courtney Castle and her dumb show?"

"Yeah, you're better than that snob any day of the week," Annette said enthusiastically. "They should give you a show. And we could all be on it! We'd knock Courtney Castle dead!"

"I'm afraid someone's beaten you to it."

The women turned to see who was speaking.

Two men, their regulation police uniforms covered with international orange vests, stood together, arms crossed, serious expressions on their closely shaven faces. Josie recognized one of them. "Mike, did you say something?" she asked Mike Rodney, police officer, son of the island's police chief, and all-around pain in the ass as far as she was concerned.

"Well, I guess I did, didn't I, Mark?" he asked the man standing by his side.

"You sure did, Mike. You said—"

But Mike Rodney apparently wanted to offer the information himself.

"I said I was afraid someone had beaten her to it and that's what I meant."

"Beaten who to what? What are you talking about?" Josie was pulling the leaves from her hair as she spoke. She was becoming nervous. Mike was an idiot, but she had seen that expression on his face before. "What's going on? Has something happened?"

"I'll say something's happened. Tell them, Mikey."

That distracted Josie. She had never heard anyone call Mike Rodney "Mikey" and she had known him ever since she came to the island. "Who are you?"

"I'm Mikey's cousin. My name's Mark."

"Mark Rodney?" Josie asked, slightly incredulous.

"Mark Stern. He doesn't have to have the same last name to be my cousin. Mark's father is my mother's brother," Mike explained. "And don't call me Mikey," he told Mark.

"So why are you two here? Why aren't you out doing crowd control? What's going on?" Dottie asked.

"We have a bigger problem than crowds," Mike said.

Mark looked as though he might burst if he didn't speak up. "Yeah, somebody may have killed Courtney Castle!" he blurted out.

"Killed?"

"Don't talk to these guys. They're idiots," Dottie ordered the women under her breath.

Josie ignored the good advice. "Where? When? Who says?"

"He doesn't know anything. And he should learn to keep his mouth shut," Mike answered, scowling at his cousin.

Despite the seriousness of Mark's statement, Josie found that she wanted to smile. Mike sounded just like his father. "Where is your father?" she asked. "Is he with the body?"

"There is no body," Mike answered.

"I thought you said Courtney had been murdered." Jill joined the conversation.

"It's all those rice cakes," Dottie said. "She just wasted away. Poor thing."

"Mike, what the hell is going on?" Josie asked. This was turning into a very long lunch hour. Little had been accomplished this morning. They needed to make up for it this afternoon. "We have to get back to work. Has there been a murder or not?"

"That Bobby Valentine . . . he's the show's director, right?"

"He's the producer," Josie said. "What about him?"

"He found a note in Courtney Castle's dressing room."

"And it said she was killed!" Mark sounded excited.

"What is this? Some sort of game?" Dottie asked.

"We really don't have time for this!" Josie insisted. "Do you think you could start at the beginning? What exactly did the note say?"

"And did anyone think to ask Courtney who killed her?" Dottie's question was sarcastic.

"The note said 'Kill Courtney Castle,' " Mike answered. "And Courtney Castle has disappeared."

"Disappeared? You mean she's just vanished?" Annette asked.

"How could she have disappeared?" Josie added.

"She's not in her trailer, which is where her producer says she should be. And she's not anywhere on the property," Mike answered seriously.

"So maybe she went for a drive," Josie suggested.

"Her truck is still parked out front," Mark explained.

That diverted Josie. "Since when does she drive a truck? What happened to the silver Porsche?"

"Apparently she drives a truck for the show—" Mike began.

"You mean that truck is just a prop?"

"I don't know what you'd call it. I just know what that Valentine guy told us. She came in the truck, and if the truck is still here, she is, too."

"You just said she isn't here," Dottie reminded him.

"Or maybe she hasn't left of her own accord," Jill suggested, lowering her voice and opening her eyes wide. "Maybe someone killed her and took the body away."

"Nope. Not a chance. We've had a police line around the block since early this morning. No way anyone got through with Courtney Castle—or with her body. Dad is double-checking with all the guys, but I can tell you that our line was—and is—impenetrable."

"And Mikey . . . Mike . . . and I have searched every square inch of this property as well as all the vans and trucks out front. She's not here," Mark asserted.

"Then she's not dead," Josie suggested.

"Yeah, it's a hot day. Maybe she went for a swim," Dottie said.

"Or maybe she got into a boat and rowed off for a bit," Annette said.

"Yeah, there have been lots of kayakers around all morning. Maybe that's what she did," Jill added.

Josie knew they were trying to be helpful, but she was aware of the logistics of what the women were suggesting. "You're sure she didn't drive away or go for a jog on the street? She loves attention. That's just the type of thing she would do."

"Nope. If she left the property, she did it back here." Mike Rodney had a grin on his face.

"You mean she had to pass us if she left," Dottie said slowly, folding her arms across her ample chest.

"When did this happen?" Josie asked loudly. "How can we possibly know where Courtney might or might not have been?"

"We . . ." Bobby Valentine appeared in the open doorway at the back of the house, his appearance in uncharacteristic disarray. His hair was standing on end, his shirttail half in and half out of his slacks. But he was, as usual, clutching his cell phone.

"Let this guy tell you," Mike continued, waving the producer over.

"Have you found her?" Bobby Valentine asked immediately, putting his hand over the mouthpiece, his face brightening at the possibility.

"No—"

"Nope, not yet." Bobby Valentine relayed the message to his unseen caller. "Gotta go. I'll keep you informed." He flipped off his phone. "So did they see her?" he asked the police officers.

"Why should we have seen her?" Josie asked.

"You see a helicopter around here?" Mike asked. "Because she either left by air or walked by you girls."

"Maybe she walked by and swam off during a time when no one was here," Dottie suggested.

Josie thought she knew what was coming.

"You girls were working back here taking down the deck and marking out the . . . whatever it is that you're all marking out, right?" Mark asked.

"We're not girls," Josie stated flatly.

"Ms. Pigeon is one of those women's libbers," Mike said sarcastically. "She doesn't like the term *girls*. Call them women."

"Courtney is the same way," Bobby Valentine said, ending that part of the conversation.

"So tell us, *women*. Was there ever a time when you were all out of the backyard?"

"This morning—" Dottie began.

"Let's pin it down a bit more," Mike said. "Was there ever a time when fewer than two of you were back here after Courtney ended her opening interview with Josie?"

The women looked at one another.

"I don't know about my crew, but I would have to think about that for a minute or two," Josie said very slowly.

"Damn right," Dottie agreed.

Annette looked up. "I don't know about everyone else, but I was back here the entire time. I . . . I watched Courtney interview Josie and then came right back here. Dottie and Jill were almost finished marking the new foundation out. And I've been back here since then."

"The three of you have been here since then. Is that what you're saying?"

"I—" Jill began.

"No, that's not it at all. I was here all the time. Everyone else came and went and did . . . well, they did whatever they had to do," Annette explained haltingly.

"Did Courtney come back here?" Bobby Valentine asked.

"No." Annette answered slowly. "I don't think so." She glanced at the others. "I really don't think so."

Josie frowned. "You would remember if she'd been here though, don't you think?" After all, Annette seemed to be so fascinated by Courtney. Surely she would remember the last time she'd seen her.

"Yes. Of course."

"And I came back to get something from my toolbox and I don't remember seeing you," Josie continued.

"I saw you," Annette said quickly. "I was working over there." She waved to the left. "You just didn't see me."

"Oh, I guess you're right."

"You didn't look around or anything. I figured you were just thinking and didn't want to bother you," Annette explained.

"What about the rest of you?" Bobby Valentine asked. "Did anyone else see Courtney?"

"No." Jill was brief.

"Definitely not," Dottie said with emphasis.

"And you're saying no one was alone back here. And you're sure of that?" Mike asked Annette.

"Yes."

"So where did she go?" Mark asked.

"And who wrote the note about killing her?" Mike added.

Josie took a deep breath and glanced at her crew. Was one of these women the answer to those questions?

NINE

JOSIE WAS SITTING at the kitchen table in her landlady's
apartment. There was a glass of wine in her hand, an
untouched bowl of pasta on the table in front of her. She had
finished telling Risa of her day and now found herself, uncharacteristically, not hungry.

"You like this Courtney Castle?" Risa asked. She stopped
stirring a large pot on the stove, unrolled the voluminous silk
sleeves of the shirt she was wearing, and poured herself a
glass of Chianti.

"I didn't really know her," Josie said, staring down at her
food. It was true. That poised, perfect television personality
was an unknown quantity—no matter what had happened in
the past.

"I have watched her show," Risa said flatly. "I did not like it."

Josie smiled for the first time since she'd heard of Courtney's supposed disappearing act. "Really? Everyone keeps
telling me how much they love her."

"Her? Sì! Her, I like. Beautiful blond hair. But that show.
No, I do not like that show."

Josie was momentarily diverted. "Why not?"

"It's not what it says it is."

"What do you mean? You don't think you could learn a lot
about remodeling from watching?"

"I think you would learn a lie from watching."

"What sort of lie?" Josie reached for her wineglass.

"I would not have known this if I had not known you," Risa answered obliquely, sipping from her glass.

Josie followed suit; she was beginning to relax. "What do I have to do with it?"

"I see you after you work. When you come home, you are tired, you are filthy, some days you are disgusting and you actually smell."

"I work hard!" Josie protested.

"But she . . . that Castle person. She doesn't. She's like a . . . a tourist on the work site."

Josie took another sip of her wine and didn't speak for a few minutes. "A tourist on the work site," she repeated quietly. It was an interesting image. "Yeah, that makes sense. The makeup. The hairdo. Those long fingernails."

"No, not the nails. They are acrid . . . or something like plastic. They are very hard. They break after everything else."

Was this true? Josie looked down at her split and cracked nails. Could she go to one of those manicure salons that seemed to have popped up all over the place in the last few years and come out with beautiful hands? And would they last throughout her workday?

"They are also ugly." Risa, never one to keep an opinion to herself, continued. "And unnatural. Plastic attached to the end of the digits . . . the fingers . . . No, not good."

"You're saying that you don't like the show because you know what hard work it is to remodel a house."

"Sì." Risa nodded. "She makes it look easy. It's not easy. People do not know this. They start work. They make mess. They unhappy. That's not good. Not fair."

"No, you're right." Josie took another sip of wine. "And that's the right word. It's not fair to the people in the audience." She frowned. "What about Courtney Castle?"

"I like her better on her other show. She made polenta almost like she was Italian. . . ."

Josie put down her glass. "What other show?"

"I do not remember the name . . . Not *Viva Italia*. It was not just Italian food. Also French and, I think, maybe Spanish . . . *Mediterranean Cooking*. No, *Mediterranean Cuisine*. They show not just recipes but also travel to places where food is made. Fascinating. The show on the fishing for scungilli. Fascinating," she repeated.

"You're telling me that Courtney was the hostess—or host or whatever they call it—of a cooking show on public television?"

"Sì. It was not recent though. A while ago. She was younger. Hair not so blond."

"She's really a brunette," Josie muttered bitchily, and then sighed. What Risa was saying was interesting. Josie picked up her fork and speared a piece of pasta. She asked another question before putting it in her mouth. "Do you remember when it was on? How long ago?"

"Oh, years. You eat. I think." She pushed a bowl of freshly ground Parmesan cheese across the table. "It was the year little Tyler played on that bad team for Little League. I learned to make those little orange rolls that he loved to eat when they lost from Courtney on TV."

Josie was accustomed to understanding her landlady's convoluted syntax and didn't question her statement. "That was the spring before he started boarding school. Three years ago."

"Sì. Who is that at the door?" Risa asked, standing.

"Risa! Josie! Tyler!"

Josie, a smile on her face, got up for one of the few things as interesting to her as food or her son. "It's Sam!"

Risa, ever the good hostess, headed to her stove. "I get him some dinner. He must be hungry."

"We're back here, Sam!"

"Josie, I heard about what happened today. I can't believe it!" he said, not bothering to greet her properly.

"I know, Sam, I—"

"You sit right down and eat this pasta," Risa interrupted. "You think better on a full stomach."

Momentarily startled, Sam stood still. "What in particular should I be thinking about?" he asked.

"About how to make sure Josie and Island Contracting are on TV. To make sure they still get good covers."

"She means coverage, Sam. And I'm not so sure I want to be on Courtney's show if she is going to pull stunts like this."

"Stunts? You think this is a stunt?"

"Yes. No one has talked about the handwriting of that note. I'll bet she wrote it herself."

"Why would anyone pretend to be murdered?" Sam asked.

Josie had thought about it for a while and come up with what she thought was a logical answer. "For publicity. Everyone knows how television people are always after publicity."

"Sì. She just hiding." Risa nodded vigorously.

"That's not what the police think. They seem to be taking this very, very seriously."

"Really?"

"I was told they were talking of bringing dredging equipment to the island."

"What? Dredge the ocean? They are mad!" Risa exclaimed.

"No, the bay," Josie said. "That's what they're talking about doing, isn't it, Sam? They're planning to dredge the bay."

"That's what I've been told." Owning the largest and most exclusive of the two liquor stores on the island, Sam was in a position to hear most of the gossip going around.

"Is there any evidence at all that she was killed?" Josie asked slowly. "More than the note, I mean."

"Well, what I heard was that she hadn't been seen since doing the interview with you."

"Really? *Cara,* what are they saying about you?"

"Were you two alone together for the interview?" Sam asked.

"Alone? Are you kidding? I've only been exposed to this stuff for a few days, but, believe me, it takes more than one person to do anything for television. It almost takes a crowd!"

"Was the interview done in the house? Or on some sort of set?"

"It was done in a corner of the deck in front of the house. They wanted to see me, the house, and the bay in the background. That, apparently, was the best place to see all three."

"And how big was the crowd it took to do this?" Sam asked. There was a smile on his face, but whether it was from Josie's answer or Risa's pasta, she didn't know.

"Well, there were only the cameraman, the producer, Bobby Valentine, Courtney, and me. But there were lots of people milling around. And it wasn't the first time I'd been interviewed. Bobby Valentine had asked me a bunch of questions earlier in the day. He told me that Courtney would use the information he got to figure out what to ask me."

"Perhaps this Bobby Valentine made up the questions and gave them to Courtney. It's not unheard of for on-air personalities to work from scripts provided by other people."

"No. She made up these questions herself." Josie stopped and glanced at Risa. "I'm sure they were her work."

"How do you know?" Sam asked.

"I just know," she answered.

"Woman's intuition," Risa suggested.

"Oh?" Sam looked at Josie for confirmation.

"I guess." She shrugged and changed the subject. "When is the dredging supposed to begin?"

"As soon as possible, is what I heard. Of course, knowing the police on this island, that could mean anytime in the next decade. There were two guys talking about it in the store when I left. I got the impression that they were summer cops."

"I don't suppose one of them was named Mark."

"I don't know either of their names. But they were buying soda and complaining about having to work late and, more significantly, go without beer for the evening while they figured out how to get the dredge into the bay without calling the Coast Guard for help. Although I don't understand why they wouldn't want to call the Coast Guard in. I don't understand the delineation of duties here, but it seems to me that a missing person, presumed to be in the water, is exactly the type of thing the Coast Guard does get involved in."

"On any other island, yes. But the local police and the Coast Guard have a history of . . . um, of not getting along."

"Isn't that a bit foolish?" Sam asked.

"Sure is, but you've been around long enough to not be surprised by it."

"What happened?"

"You didn't hear about it? It's a great story."

"So tell it."

"It happened one Fourth of July. You know what a big deal we all make of that day. It's pretty much the height of the summer season. All the tourists are here. When I moved here, there were fireworks shot off the old drawbridge at the south end of the island. Then someone suggested that an even bigger and better display could be created from the new causeway up north. But the smaller display at the other end of the island was a tradition and, well, you know how things go around here. We ended up with what we have now."

Sam nodded. "Fireworks at both ends of the island."

"Exactly. And you know how people head out to sea in their boats so that they can see both displays at the same time?"

"Yes."

"Well, a year or two before you arrived, one of the party boats that had been hired for the evening lost its engine and couldn't get back in after the shows ended. Unfortunately, the people in the boat were so drunk, they didn't notice they had a problem until they had drifted almost twenty miles out to sea. And then there was a storm that night and the boat drifted back toward land and ended up stuck on a sandbar about a mile off the coast. Well, to make a long story short, the Coast Guard rescue the next morning was very dramatic and could be seen by everyone sunning on the beach."

"So what does this have to do with the police?" Sam asked.

"They were the police," Risa explained. "In the boat. They were our police."

Sam grinned. "The island police were in the rescued boat? Surely not all of them. What about crowd control and traffic and all the other things they're supposed to do before, during, and after the fireworks?"

"Exactly the question everyone else was asking. And you can imagine how Chief Rodney reacted."

"Badly."

"And publicly. He accused the Coast Guard of incompetence for no reason at all. And he was quoted in the island newspaper. And the next week a reporter interviewed the captain of the rescue ship and that was the first mention of the empty beer kegs found in the hold of the boat."

"At least they didn't toss them overboard and pollute the ocean," Sam suggested.

"Sam, you own a liquor store. You know they didn't want to forfeit their deposit on the kegs!"

"Good point. So the police were embarrassed by the interview with the Coast Guard."

"Yes, but it didn't stop there. Some enterprising reporter went back to Chief Rodney the next week. Well, you can guess what happened. That man never has the sense to shut up. And since the Coast Guard had right on their side, they continued to respond to whatever idiocy he uttered. This went on week after week until the reporter went back to college for the fall semester. Everyone on the island was amused. Until there was a real crisis during one of the big fall storms and Rodney refused to call the Coast Guard for help."

"That man can be extraordinarily stupid," Sam said. No one in the room was inclined to argue.

"Definitely. Well, obviously that couldn't continue. The Coast Guard is equipped to deal with lots of problems that the police can't help. So they call them in an emergency. But not until they've tried to do everything themselves."

"Well, that's what's going on now," Sam said. He had finished his pasta during Josie's explanation and he passed the plate over to Risa for a refill.

"Hey, I hope there's some of that left for me!" Tyler appeared in the doorway.

Risa loved Sam. She hoped, prayed, and tried to arrange for Josie to marry him. But Tyler was her baby. She dropped what she was doing and reached for the large pottery bowl reserved for the young man's meals.

Knowing what was coming, Tyler plopped himself down at the table. "Hi, Sam. Hi, Mom. Thanks, Risa."

"How was work?" Josie asked, resisting the urge to reach across the table and push the hair out of his eyes. Her son had inherited her flyaway hair. The older he got, the longer he wore it.

"Great. We get to watch videos when there's no one in the store. And with that television crew on the island, no one has much time to watch TV, so we're not all that busy. Thanks, Risa," he repeated before digging into the food she'd given him.

"I saw three John Waters films," he said, chewing and talking at the same time. "Great stuff. I really loved *Polyester—*"

"They're pretty weird," Sam said. "What did you think about . . ."

Josie had no idea what they were saying. But she was happy to just sit and watch her son eat. She started to listen more carefully when Courtney Castle was mentioned.

"They're saying some strange things," Tyler was explaining to Sam. "About"—he glanced at his mother from under his long bangs before continuing—"about Mom, too."

"What about me?" Josie asked.

"Well, I heard that Courtney told someone that you would like to kill her."

"That's ridiculous!" Sam protested. "Your mother doesn't get that mad at people she doesn't even know!"

Josie glanced up at Sam, over at her son, and then down at her empty bowl. She wouldn't, she decided, say anything. It was safer that way.

TEN

IT HAD BEEN a long time—a very long time—since Josie had felt so completely alone. Awake in the middle of the night and too worried to remain in bed, she had gotten up, planning to walk on the beach for a bit. Instead, almost without thinking, she had found herself driving to Island Contracting's office.

Now she sat in her truck, engine and lights off, staring at the tiny building, remembering the first time she'd seen it.

Back then her life had been a mess.

Brought up with the expectation that she would continue her education after high school, she had dutifully headed off to the ivyless college her mother had attended. But that was as far as the dutiful daughter role had taken her. No one had expected her to fall in love with practically the first young man she met there. Or to get pregnant by him. And as far as her family was concerned, her decision to keep her baby had been the last straw. They broke off their connection with her, possibly to try to force her to come around to their way of thinking and if not to get an abortion, at least to give up her child for adoption.

Confused and more than a bit frightened, Josie had come to the island where she had spent many happy summers as a child, allowed to run free from parental control on the wide beaches and in the two small towns that made up the community. She had come back for comfort. What she had found was a life.

It's always easy to get a low-paying menial job in a resort community during the high season. Workers can be difficult to find, and her employer had been willing to ignore her slightly bulging waist when he put her on the payroll. Josie had been a waitress at a local restaurant when she met Noel Roberts. Other than surviving, she'd made no plans either for herself or her child. She had walked from her rooming house to this very spot early in the morning the day after Noel had offered her a future.

And standing near where now she sat, she had decided to take Noel up on his offer. She would work for Island Contracting. He would train her as a carpenter and she would have her baby and raise him or her on the island. At the time, it had sounded like a miracle. And it turned out to be true. Then, after Noel's death, when she discovered that he had left her his business as well as a trust fund just big enough to send Tyler to boarding school and college, she had been more grateful than ever.

She thought she had left her past behind. Until Courtney Castle arrived on the island. Josie sighed and got out of her truck. If she couldn't sleep, maybe she could get some paperwork done, she decided, walking down the familiar path in the dark. She unlocked the door and flipped on the lights. The office cat, a regal tabby known as Elizabeth, looked up from the bed she had made for herself in the piles of paper on Josie's desk.

"You're going to have to move if I'm going to get anything done," Josie murmured, heading for the coffeemaker atop a file cabinet at the back of the room.

The cat ignored her, carefully positioning her head on her paws and closing her eyes. Josie frowned. Oh, well, she was too tired to concentrate on figures anyway. She proceeded to make a pot of coffee. She grabbed the mug with the words "Super Mom" on the side, poured out a cup, and walked out on the tiny deck that hung over the bay from the fishing shack Noel had converted into Island Contracting's office. The sky was turning pink, reflecting the sunrise beginning over the Atlantic behind her. Josie plopped down on a plastic folding chair, sipped her coffee, and wondered what she should do.

It all depended, she decided, on what had happened to Courtney. But what had happened? Josie didn't for a minute believe that Courtney had been killed or was even missing. She had thought it all out while tossing and turning and trying to sleep.

The police line that had kept the curious from intruding on the work site had, in a sense, created an island on the real island. Courtney couldn't have walked or driven away without being seen; that was something everyone seemed to agree upon. Unless . . . Josie balanced her mug on the deck railing and went back into the office for a pen and paper. There was just enough light for her to see, and she wrote three words each followed by a question mark. *Disguised? Hidden? Alone?* It was the third word that interested her the most.

She doodled as she thought it all through again. Someone—or Courtney herself—had written a note about killing Courtney. That was either true or false. But, she decided, it didn't make all that much difference. What mattered was that Courtney had vanished. She could have left alone. If dead, she must have been carried. But the third possibility, the one Josie hadn't thought of until the caffeine kicked in, was that Courtney had left, alive and kicking, and aided and abetted by someone. Someone who had either hidden or disguised Courtney in some way. Someone who knew why she had disappeared, where she had gone, and what, exactly, was going on.

"That woman hasn't changed a bit since we were kids,"

Josie muttered to herself, straightening her spine and propping her legs up on the rail, and accidentally kicking her mug into the water. "Oh no!" She leaped to her feet. A small whirlpool was the only sign of her mug's entrance into the water.

She was still staring at the spot when she heard the door open behind her.

"Josie, it's me."

She smiled. Sam was such a sweetie, identifying himself quickly so that he didn't scare her. Then a thought struck. "Why are you here? Is something wrong? Tyler . . ."

". . . is just fine."

"Then why are you here? Why are you awake?"

"I always wake up when the phone rings. Risa called. She saw you leave your apartment and was worried about you."

"How did she . . . How did you know I would be here?"

"I didn't. In fact, I assumed you were on your way to your current work site, but I didn't want to cross the police line to find out if you were there unless it was absolutely necessary. I've decided that the best thing to do to maintain any peace of mind around here is to stay as far away from the Rodneys as possible. So I drove around a bit looking for your truck." He brushed her hair off her forehead. "Did I smell fresh coffee inside?"

"Just made."

"Do you want some?"

"The mug Tyler gave me for Mother's Day is down there." Josie looked over the rail.

"That's what you were looking for just now? I thought you were checking your trap." Sam looked over at the water, shimmering in the first light of day. "It is down there, too, isn't it?"

Josie reached behind him to the rope tied to the rail. "It's a bit early for blue crabs, but I couldn't resist putting the trap out last week. The bait's probably gone. I sometimes think I spend the first month of the season feeding minnows." She was pulling on the rope as she spoke and a large commercial crab trap broke through the surface of the water. Her mug was sitting, eerily upright, on its top. "Hey, look at that!"

"Careful. Just pull it straight up and I'll try to grab it." He had done it before he said it.

"And look! Crabs!"

"Frankly, I'm more interested in coffee right now," Sam admitted as Josie lowered the large wire box back into the bay.

"And I got my mug back!"

"Maybe you should volunteer to help with the dredging if they ever decide to do it," Sam suggested, a broad smile on his face.

"I wouldn't hold my breath. You know, I've been thinking about Courtney all night. It's why I couldn't sleep. And I have some ideas about her disappearance."

"Let me get some of your dreadful coffee and you can tell me all about it."

Josie spent a few minutes organizing her thoughts. She'd present Sam with her theories in a manner he couldn't ignore.

"Okay. Start," he ordered, passing her some coffee and sitting down on the old ice chest that was a permanent fixture back there.

"Well, think a minute. The first thing we need to know is whether Courtney was working alone or with someone else—"

"Not whether she's dead or alive?"

"I'm assuming she's alive."

"Really? That's interesting. Go on."

"Well, as I was saying, the first thing we need to know is whether or not Courtney had someone helping her disappear. I think she probably did."

"Why?"

"Because you can't be in two places at once, right?"

"I wouldn't even consider arguing with you—or anyone else—about that."

"So I think the other person was necessary to leave the note in her dressing room."

"And when do you think that happened?"

"I should tell you this in order. I figure Courtney and this other person—"

"Call him—or her—X, why don't you?"

"Good idea. I think Courtney and X either wrote the note together or Courtney wrote it and gave it to this X. So while Courtney was with me on the front deck of the house—"

"What were you two doing on the deck?"

"I told you. She was interviewing me. And we weren't alone. Bobby Valentine was there as well as the cameraman. I guess that means neither of them could be X, right?"

"If your logic holds, yes."

Josie smiled. "So while Courtney was interviewing me, X put the note in her trailer. Then, probably . . . I'm a bit less sure about this," she admitted. "Then Courtney either disguised herself or . . . X somehow packed Courtney in . . . something and carried her away."

"Alive."

"Oh, yes, alive."

"Josie, it's early and perhaps I'm missing something here, but why are you so sure Courtney is alive?"

"Because she's the type of person who would do something like this!"

"Something like fake her own death?"

"Yes, she was always like that . . ." Josie shut up, appalled at what she had done.

Sam was quiet a moment, looking out over the bay. A few gulls had appeared, gliding on the air currents, apparently thrilled to have made it through the night. A slight breeze was blowing, spreading the unmistakable scent of the littoral plain. Josie raised her mug to her lips and waited for Sam to speak.

"When you say she was always like that, you are referring to what time?"

"I knew Courtney before," Josie admitted.

"I was beginning to get that impression. How long ago did you meet?"

Josie thought for a moment. "I guess it was in the Brownies."

"Excuse me?"

"I think we were in the same Brownie troop. That would be about second or third grade, right?"

"I honestly have no idea."

"I thought maybe no one would have to know about this," Josie admitted.

"About what? Your past relationship with Courtney?"

"We didn't actually have a relationship," Josie protested. "We just knew each other."

"You mean you haven't seen her since . . . you were in elementary school?"

"Oh, no, we went through junior high and high school together." She paused. "And we started off at the same college. I suppose she may have stayed around long enough to graduate."

"Let me get this straight. You were—are—lifelong friends with Courtney Castle."

"No, Sam! It's not like that at all! We weren't friends. We could hardly stand each other."

"I was hoping you weren't going to say something like that." Now it was Sam's turn to sigh. "Josie, I would really appreciate it if you would tell me all about your relationship—friendly or not—with Courtney Castle."

"It's sort of a long story."

"I really think it's worth taking the time to tell it."

"Well, I don't know where to begin." She took a deep breath. "Our mothers were best friends, you see. They were roommates in college. Which is why Courtney and I ended up at the same college years later."

"You're not telling me that you and Courtney were college roommates?"

"No way! We were hardly speaking to each other by the time we went to college."

"Josie, I've done my share of questioning of witnesses. Some tell you nothing. And some tell you so much that it takes a lot of work to figure out what's important. The second type is the most irritating. And you're beginning to remind me of them."

"I'm sorry. It was stupid to think I wouldn't have to tell you this.

"At first I didn't believe it," she continued. "I mean, I thought I must be imagining things. That maybe Courtney Castle just looked like the woman I used to know. It's been years, remember."

"It is a rather unusual name though."

"Oh, her name wasn't Courtney Castle when I was growing up. I knew her as Courtney Casell. The spelling is different," she explained when Sam gave her a strange look.

"But you did recognize her," Sam prodded her.

"Not at first. She was older, of course. And when I knew her she had straight, thin brown hair."

"It's amazing what money, time, and a good hairdresser can do," Sam commented.

"Yeah, I guess." She hoped that wasn't a hint.

"But you did recognize her eventually."

"Yes. I don't know why I didn't say anything. I just couldn't believe it! I mean, here we were in the same business, sort of. Of course, she's famous and on television and all, and I just have Island Contracting here, but we're both carpenters and all. At least, that's what I thought at the time. I was so stunned that I didn't really think about how little building she actually did. She's more of an interviewer than a carpenter."

"You met her when you were in second or third grade?" Sam's question headed her back to the point.

"Yes. Our mothers had known each other forever, but my family moved that year. Up."

"You moved up?"

"Exactly. My father got a promotion—I guess—and we moved to a bigger house in a nicer neighborhood. I changed schools and started in the Brownies. And met Courtney."

"And you were friends?"

"Never. I don't remember all that well, but I've been thinking about it for the past few days and I don't think we ever had a chance to become friends. You see, my mother wanted me to be like Courtney and she was very open about her feelings. Even a kid isn't going to like someone her mother holds up as a good example. Courtney was thin. Courtney was a straight-A student. Courtney was popular. Courtney could play the piano. Courtney was on the swim team and, despite my extra fat, I sank like a stone to the bottom of the country club pool." She noticed Sam's eyebrows rise at the mention of her family's club membership, but she didn't feel she had to explain her entire past right then. "You get the idea. I couldn't like someone I was always being compared to."

"I won't argue with that."

"And I was jealous as hell of her. Over little things. Like my mother's idea of an appropriate bedroom for a young girl included lots of ruffles and fake French-country furniture. I slept in a canopied bed until I went off to college. In fact, I may have gone off to college just to get away from that horrible room. I wasn't even allowed to put up posters on my own walls. And that wallpaper desperately needed to be covered! My mother," she explained, "loved cabbage roses."

"I don't think I know what they are."

"You're lucky. So was Courtney. She slept in a room furnished with teak Scandinavian furniture. I used to think she could stay in that room and imagine she was living in an apartment in Greenwich Village even though she lived a few blocks away from me in a conventional upper-middle-class suburb. And when she was in high school the rock posters were so thick on her walls that she probably didn't even have to turn on the heat in the winter." She paused. "I was jealous of her."

"Sounds reasonable."

"I don't mean to sound stupid. I guess a therapist would say that we have a lot of unresolved stuff between us."

Sam seemed to be thinking for a moment. "You didn't change your name, did you? I mean, you grew up as Josie Pigeon."

"My family called me Josephine, but everyone else always knew me as Josie. Why?"

"Just wondering. What did she say to you?"

"About what?"

"About the past. What did she say about you two meeting again after all these years?"

"Nothing. Nothing at all."

ELEVEN

"NOW WAIT A second. How was Island Contracting chosen to be on *Courtney Castle's Castles*?"

"I don't know."

"Who contacted you?"

"Bobby Valentine."

"How?"

"He called on the phone. Why?"

Sam ignored her question and asked another of his own. "When?"

"About a month ago."

"Did you take the call?"

She had to think to answer that question. "The answering machine actually picked up the call. I called him back."

"And what did he say?"

"He asked if Island Contracting would be on the show. What else?"

"Josie, try to remember exactly what he said and when he said it. On the tape and during your first conversation."

"I'm not sure I can," she admitted.

"Try. It might turn out to be important."

"Okay. I think he just introduced himself. You know, I'm Bobby Valentine and I'm a television producer and I need to speak with Josie Pigeon immediately. In fact, I'm sure that's what he said because I remember Dottie was listening and she said he would be a difficult client since he was so snotty that he thought I should know right away what he did for a living. Of course, that was before we knew what he wanted. We thought he was calling about a normal remodeling job at first."

"Of course. But you called him back, right?"

"Yes, immediately. And he explained that he didn't want to hire us. He wanted Island Contracting for a television show. I . . . I'm not sure if he said the name of the show then. But he did say that he wanted to feature the remodeling project we were going to start this month, the one we're doing now."

"How did he refer to it? I mean, you usually say things like the Richardson project or the Jones project, right?"

"Sure. We refer to it by the owner's name. This one we've been calling the PBS house though. Um . . . I think he may have called it the house on the bay."

"How did he know about it?"

"Oh, that's easy. He said that someone who worked on the show had told him about it and that they were always looking for interesting projects, which made a lot of sense at the time. Do you think he was lying?"

"I have no idea. But I sure would like to know which staff member knows the owners of that house. Who are the owners, by the way? Do they live on the island?"

"I doubt it. I've never met them."

"What? Doesn't that worry you?"

Josie laughed. "Are you kidding? You've been around long enough to know that homeowners frequently are big pains in the ass, always in a panic that the job won't get done on time while making extensive and time-consuming changes. This job would be the easiest ever if that television show wasn't involved."

"So how did you get the remodeling job?"

"It just dropped in our laps. Like the TV show, come to

think of it. The house is owned by a company called Island Homes. My contact has been through some lawyer. He called a few days before Bobby Valentine did and asked if I would look at an architect's plan and submit a bid for the job. I did, and it was accepted."

"That simple?" Sam, who had been around for more than one of Josie's projects, was surprised.

"It was. I couldn't believe it. The bid was accepted in a day. Amazing."

"Have you ever had that happen before?"

"Yeah, once or twice. But usually with repeat clients. What happens is we do a job and the clients are happy with our work, so when they need something else done, they think of us. But everyone wants a bargain and there are a lot of contracting companies, so they ask for a few bids. But once the bids come in, they discover that our bid, if not the lowest, is in the ballpark and since they know our work, they really don't have to think about it. They hire us right away."

"But this is the first time it has happened with a new client?"

"I guess. I didn't think anything of it at the time. But so what? What could it have to do with Courtney's disappearance?"

"Probably nothing. It's just interesting." He frowned. "Didn't you tell me that you had two big jobs this summer and the first was on one of those Cape Cods at the foot of the dunes? Did that job disappear?"

"Oh, no. It's still on. We're going to start that the third week of July. But you're right. We were going to do them in reverse order. But things changed suddenly . . ."

"And Bobby Valentine just happened to want to tape the bay job for the show at the beginning of the summer?"

"How did you know?"

"Just a good guess. Seems to me there are a few too many

coincidences here, Josie. Who made the change? The lawyer for Island Homes?"

"No. It was the other job. The family who owns that house had a change in plans. They were going to spend the second half of the summer in the house and I'd remodel the kitchen and add on a breakfast slash family room before then, but they decided to do it the other way and asked if Island Contracting could accommodate them."

"But you had the Island Homes job by that time, right?"

"Yes, but I called their lawyer—he has an office in New York City—and asked him if we could make a change in the schedule. I didn't think he'd go along with it, but he agreed and . . ."

"Why were you surprised that he agreed?"

"Well, usually the people who hire us have many things to consider when they schedule a job. Like getting the money to pay for the work. I mean, getting a bank loan can take quite a while. And then, of course, people have to adjust their lives—move out of the house, or the kitchen, or whatever. But apparently Island Homes doesn't have to worry about any of that. The lawyer was quite happy with the change when we spoke on the phone and he sent back an annotated contract right away."

"So apparently his client wasn't planning on spending the first part of the summer in the house."

"I haven't the foggiest. I don't get the impression that the owner is terribly attached to the house, to tell you the truth. I mean, when I've called about changes in the architect's plans or brands or anything, the lawyer leaves most of the decisions up to me."

"And that's unusual."

"Damn right. I sure wish we had more clients like him. The house will probably be put on the market at the end of summer, at least that's my guess."

"Why?"

"The lawyer wants the best—and recognizable brand names—which is what high-end developers usually insist on. And he hasn't conveyed a single personal preference from anyone except for taking care of that damn sculpture in the living room. Most people are very vocal about their likes and dislikes."

"But the sculpture is different?"

"It's ugly as hell, but apparently, to some people, it would be a selling point."

"But no one has specifically mentioned selling?"

"Why? Are you interested in buying a second home on the island?"

"No, just curious. Not that a second home wouldn't be an excellent investment."

Josie wasn't interested. She couldn't afford to buy a first home; a second home was just too far out of her frame of reference to discuss. "Well, Island Homes may be planning to use it as a rental property instead."

"So things just happened to work out for Courtney Castle's show. Did you ever ask Bobby Valentine for more specific information about how they found out about this project and why they thought it would be interesting enough to put on television?"

"Not really. But it wasn't just the house on the bay and the unique aspects of that sort of building that interested them. They were interested in Island Contracting. He said that they thought their audience would love an all-female contracting company. But how did they know about us?" she asked, suddenly realizing that there were questions she hadn't considered before.

"How was it explained to you?"

"It wasn't. I . . . I was so flattered that I never even thought about it. Stupid, huh?"

"Completely understandable. And it could have been a co-incidence. I mean, the show could have been told about this interesting house, and then when they investigated the story, they discovered that a unique contracting company was going to be doing the work and that just sold them on the entire thing."

"Do you think that's what happened?"

"I think it *could* have happened. But frankly, Josie, I doubt it."

"Me, too."

"What did Courtney say?"

"About what? This?"

"Yes."

"Nothing."

"You two hadn't seen each other in how many years?"

"Wow. Let me think. Tyler is sixteen and I left school when I was two months pregnant. . . . I guess it's been almost seventeen years." She grinned. "In fact, she was there when I discovered I was pregnant. Although she couldn't know that, of course."

"What do you mean?"

Josie frowned. "I was so young and stupid. I don't like to think about those times." And she sure didn't want to tell him about them.

"We all did stupid things when we were young," Sam said gently. "Tell me about it."

"Okay. See, I thought I couldn't get pregnant." She paused and, happy that he hadn't asked why, continued with her tale. "So when I didn't get my period, I went to the school infirmary to see a doctor. I wasn't just surprised and upset to find out I was pregnant; I was embarrassed to be so naive. The doctor I saw was less than kind. In fact, it was obvious that he thought I was too stupid to be in college. He told me I was pregnant and said he was busy and had to see students who were really sick. I walked back out into the waiting room in shock. And Courtney was there."

"She just happened to be there? You weren't meeting her there for any reason?"

"No. Heavens, no. I spent a lot of my first two months on campus avoiding her."

"Did you two speak? Did you tell her what you were doing there?"

"I wasn't thinking straight. I was in shock. My whole life had changed in just a few minutes. And . . . there was something else." It was becoming more and more difficult to talk about it.

Sam didn't say anything. He just waited for her to continue.

"See, she was dating the guy who . . . who got me pregnant." She didn't say "Tyler's father." She didn't think of him that way. She hadn't thought of him that way since his response to her announcement that she was pregnant.

"She was dating him while you were dating him?" Sam's voice was gentle.

"I think so. She was still dating him at that point. They could be seen necking all over campus."

"That must have been horrible for you."

"It was. But more before I discovered I was pregnant than after. Once I knew I was going to have a baby—or an abortion—nothing else mattered a lot."

"Josie, did you tell the guy you were pregnant? Or did Courtney find out in some way?"

"I told them both. I told you, I wasn't thinking. I actually blabbed it out to Courtney right there in the waiting room."

"You just told her you were pregnant?"

"I don't actually remember the words, but she knew I was pregnant and who . . . the father was."

"Do you remember what she said?"

That she remembered as if it was yesterday. Courtney had

looked up from the book she was studying, brushed her long hair back over her shoulder, and said, "It doesn't surprise me, Josie. I always said you were stupid."

Sam's response to her statement was gratifying. "What a bitch!"

"Yeah, but she was right. I was stupid to get involved with that guy, even stupider to get pregnant, and then I did something else stupid. I told him."

"Since you ended up here, I gather he didn't offer to do the right thing."

"To marry me? No way, but I don't think I would have married him." She frowned. "At least I hope not. But, anyway, you're right, he never offered. He didn't even offer to help pay for an abortion. But I guess I should be glad about that. I probably would have done it without thinking about whether or not it was what I wanted to do. When I think back on that time—and I don't much—I realize that most people, including my family, thought I should have gotten rid of the baby, changed schools, and gone on with my life, but then I wouldn't have Tyler."

"And everyone who knows him is glad of that," Sam assured her. "He's quite a kid. And you've done a remarkable job of raising him and creating a life for yourself."

"He really is wonderful, isn't he?" Josie smiled. "But I was lucky, too. I came to the island and Noel offered to help me. I don't like to think about where Tyler or I would be if that hadn't happened."

"But go back to Courtney," Sam urged. "What happened to your relationship?"

"Nothing. That day in the infirmary office was the last time I saw her until this week. The word on campus was that she and her boyfriend broke up. Of course I knew why, but I didn't tell anyone. That would have meant letting people know about my pregnancy." She decided to skip over the rest. "Christmas break started two days later and I was planning on going home. I think . . . I think Courtney and her family went to St. Bart's over vacation. I . . . My parents and I stopped speaking to each other and suddenly I found out that I was on my own in the world. I came here. And I've been here ever since."

"And you're not in contact with anyone who might have told you what Courtney was up to?"

"I hadn't even thought of her in years and years."

"What about her? Doesn't it strike you as odd that she came here to tape a show? Did you get the impression that she knew she would find you here?"

"I have no idea."

"And she honestly didn't say a word when the two of you met again? Certainly she expected you to know who she is."

"Why?"

"Don't you think she probably assumed you would have watched her show and recognized her on TV?"

"I guess. Probably."

"So what did she say when you two met?"

"Hello. I mean, she said hello, like she'd never met me before. Or maybe she didn't remember."

"Josie, I've got to tell you this. I think she remembered you. In fact, this may all be based on circumstantial evidence, but I'll bet they are taping here because you are here."

"But why, Sam?"

"I don't know. But I think we should get busy and find out."

TWELVE

JOSIE WAS NOT accustomed to anyone other than herself ordering her crew around. But she had to admit that Bobby Valentine was doing a good job of it.

"She is not here. She probably had important personal business to attend to. That's the key phrase for you all to remember. Courtney had important personal business to attend to. That's what you say if anyone asks. But nobody, and I mean nobody, is to say anything to the press! Understand? Now we're going to continue work on the show as though Courtney was still here."

"And how the hell are we going to do that? Do you have some sort of Courtney dummy that you're going to lean against the wall to watch us work?" Dottie sneered.

"We have already shot some of Courtney's cutaways, and we can do interviews without her. You don't have to worry about that part of it. We know what we're doing. We do this all the time."

That got Josie's attention. "She's disappeared like this before?"

"Not like this. No, not like this. But Courtney Castle is a very busy woman with many diverse demands on her time. She's frequently called on to be someplace else while we tape a show, and when that happens, we are required to work around her absence."

"Really? It's interesting to know how television works, isn't it?" Annette asked her colleagues enthusiastically.

Apparently the other women weren't so impressed. "So what do we do now?" Jill, ignoring Bobby Valentine's lecture, asked Josie the question.

"Let's get to work out back," Josie answered. "If that's all right with you?" she asked the producer rather sarcastically.

Apparently he didn't notice or care. "Whatever. I'm going to be in the trailer if anyone needs me. But, remember, no talking to the press!" With those parting words, he turned and left the house.

Jill leaped to her feet and, grabbing an imaginary microphone, said, "Please, no interviews! No interviews!"

Annette joined in, laughing and protesting to a crowd of imaginary paparazzi. "No pictures, please, no pictures!"

"Yeah, as though the press would be interested in the likes of us," Dottie said.

"Well, let's get to work," Josie said, standing and stretching. "Courtney can do her thing and we'll do ours."

The women picked up their assorted tool belts and boxes and headed out of the house and toward the bay.

"Am I the only person who thinks it's a little strange that Courtney has vanished?" Annette asked.

"Hey, she's not a carpenter. She's on-air talent. Probably thinks she can do anything she wants to do." Dottie slung her heavy belt across her shoulder and followed Josie.

"Sure, but still . . ." That was Annette's only comment. The intern was sitting on the dock, writing furiously in a spiral notebook. He jumped to his feet and brushed his too-long hair off his forehead. Annette unconsciously mimicked his movement, smiling nervously.

Josie grinned. "Why don't you see if he . . . what is his name? . . . needs anything from us before we start work?"

"I'll . . . Oh, you're asking me to do it?" Annette was flustered by the suggestion.

"Yup."

"Chad. His name is Chad Henshaw," Annette said, hurrying down the path to the dock.

"An adolescent crush. Why do you encourage them?" Dottie asked rhetorically.

"I think they're sweet," Jill said.

"I do, too. And as long as Annette keeps working, I don't see what harm it does," Josie commented.

"God, you're all romantic fools." Dottie sneered. "Wake up and smell the coffee, as my dad used to say."

"What I think is that they're both young and a summertime romance is appropriate."

Jill put down her toolbox and looked back at the house. No one could hear them. "Doesn't anyone else think it's strange that Courtney has disappeared? I mean, today that producer is acting like it's normal, but yesterday he was real panicked when she wasn't around. What happened to all that police interest? What happened to dredging the bay?"

"Heaven knows," Josie answered slowly. What *had* happened to dredging the bay? "Listen, you all know what to do and I'd appreciate it if you'd go on without me. I left my phone in the truck. I need to make a few calls."

"While you're at it, you might give the lumberyard a nudge about the gutter they should have delivered last week," Dottie reminded her.

"There's always something. If it's not a missing television personality, it's a missing piece of gutter." Josie sighed dramatically and started back to her truck. She was pleased to hear chuckling behind her. Courtney's disappearance was making her nervous. And she was afraid she wasn't the only one who felt like that. Dottie seemed to be affected and it didn't surprise her. But she was surprised by how jumpy Jill seemed to be. Of course, Annette was in the midst of summer love. Josie grinned at the memory of Annette's expression when Chad Henshaw appeared.

The police line was still protecting the work site, but Josie had been allowed to pass through this morning and her truck was parked behind the row of trailers queued at the curb. She grabbed her phone from under the seat and sat down on the runningboard to make her calls. The first one was not to the lumberyard. It was answered on the first ring.

"Sam! Thank heavens you're there. Do you have a moment?"

Happily enough, he claimed to have as many as she needed.

"Sam, there isn't any dredging going on! Do you know why? Well, could you find out? Well, I know, but . . . If you could just make a few calls. Maybe Basil knows something? No, she hasn't shown up yet. Bobby Valentine says it's normal. Apparently she's disappeared like this before. Well, that's what he claims. And he doesn't want anyone to talk to the press. What do you think?"

She was silent for more than a few moments while he shared those thoughts with her. "Well, what I think—" She tried to interrupt, but he wasn't finished.

The gist of Sam's thoughts was that Josie should go on with her work and ignore anything having to do with Courtney Castle or her disappearance. And that she should be quiet concerning their mutual past.

She frowned and listened to his suggestions. But he wasn't saying anything surprising and so her attention wandered . . . to a very interesting conversation that seemed to be taking place right behind her truck.

". . . look, you're not going to be able to keep it quiet forever," a deep male voice was insisting.

"I'm not talking about forever. I'm talking about now. Right now." The second speaker was also a man.

"What about her friends? Her family? Her masseuse? Her hairdresser? Her therapist? Won't they all wonder where she's gone?"

"Courtney is seeing a therapist?"

"I don't know. I just assumed—"

"Just because someone is crazy doesn't mean they're doing something about it. But that's not the point. We'll just tell anyone who calls that she's not available and that she'll get back to them."

"But what happens when she doesn't?"

"Hey, anyone who knows Courtney knows that she doesn't spend a whole lot of time worrying about other people. Her not returning a call is par for the course."

"Yeah, I won't argue with you about that. The promises she made us, you wouldn't believe."

"Oh, I'd believe it. I'd believe anything. She's talent, remember."

Josie was fairly sure the second speaker was Bobby Valentine. It sounded like the other was someone he trusted with his problems. She wished she knew who it was. But, more important, it was obvious that Bobby Valentine was more concerned with Courtney's disappearance than he had claimed to be. Josie bit her lip and thought for a moment.

Sam was apparently waiting for a response to something he had said. "Josie?" his voice called out of the receiver.

"Sam. Shh!" she hissed back at him. "I'm listening."

But the two men had either stopped talking or moved away. Josie got up cautiously and looked around. No one. Then she noticed an open window in the trailer. The voices could have come from inside; if so, the speakers might still be there.

"Hang on, Sam. I'm just going to go into the house and . . . get those specs you want." Resisting the urge to look over her shoulder, she hurried up the sidewalk, chatting into the receiver as she went. "I'm going to the house. There's no one around. Don't hang up. I need to talk to you some more. Sam? Are you there? Sam?"

"I'm here, Josie. What's going on? Are you in trouble? Is something wrong?"

"No. No. We're . . . I'm . . . Everything's fine. I'm in the house and . . . I don't want . . ." She looked around. She was alone. "Sam, you'll never guess what!" Without waiting for his response, she related the conversation she'd just overheard. "What do you think?"

"Nothing. It seems to me you don't really have any new information. We knew yesterday that the people who worked with Courtney were shocked by her disappearance. It was just today that they regrouped and decided to present it to the world as a normal event."

Josie was silent. "That's true. But . . ." She paused. "Yeah, that is true," she repeated slowly.

"Maybe it means nothing," Sam said. "Or maybe it's a problem, but it's not your problem."

"Yeah, I suppose you're right." Not that she believed it for a second. "I suppose I'd better get back to work."

"I'll see what I can find out about the dredging."

"Great." Josie leaned back against the wall and propped one foot up on the frame protecting the artwork. She knew what she wanted to do. She wanted to find out more about what Courtney had been doing during the past . . . what was it? Sixteen years. Sixteen years and seven months to be more exact.

Sixteen years and ten months since she had been in contact with her family. Well, to be more accurate, seventeen years and ten months since they had been in contact with her. Sixteen years and one month since she had gotten her courage together and sent them the short, perky letter announcing the birth of Tyler Clay. The short, perky letter that had not been answered. For a moment, she relived that pain.

Did she want to feel it again? Did she *need* to feel it again? Could she find out what Courtney had been doing during this time without evoking those feelings? Sam had once hired a private detective who could probably have done it all easily, but she couldn't afford to pay for a detective and she didn't want Sam involved. She had chosen to move beyond her past. If she was going to return to it, she sure wasn't going to drag the man she loved along for the ride.

There was one other person she didn't want following her into her past: Tyler. Her son had gone through periods when he was curious about his heritage. He'd asked more than a few questions about his father, who he was and where he was. But Josie had insisted on keeping her secret and Tyler had become interested in other things. His fifth-grade class project had been to make a family tree and so the question arose once again. With the insecurity of his teen years approaching rapidly, Josie had been about to panic when Risa had come to the rescue. "You are a lucky child. You choose your own family. You make a tree anyone would be proud of," she had told him.

Tyler had done just that. From baseball players to presidents, he had collected relatives and hung them on his tree. The end result was the envy of his peers—and it amazed the adults in his life. While Albert Einstein might look like a great-grandfather to many people, only Tyler would have claimed him for his own.

When Noel Roberts died, Tyler had lost the closest thing he had to a father, but Josie's relationship with Sam had provided him with a surprisingly good substitute at an age when he desperately needed a male role model. Josie really believed her son had come to terms with and accepted a life without a traditional family. She sure didn't want her slightly abnormal relatives to enter the picture and screw everything up.

Why had she ever agreed to do this damn television show?

THIRTEEN

JOSIE KNEW WHAT she had to do. And she hoped she could count Risa as an ally. She was going to need one. She headed for her landlady's apartment right after work. Risa was sitting on a lounge on her screened-in front porch, an exotic aperitif on the table by her side, and a pile of magazines sliding off her lap.

"This year I take a holiday," Risa announced as Josie stopped in the doorway.

"When?" She didn't ask where because she knew Risa would consider only Italy an appropriate destination.

"In the fall. After little Tyler goes back to that school you send him to."

"Is Tyler home?" Josie asked, suddenly realizing her son might be bounding down the stairs at any minute.

"He is at video store. He is always at video store." Risa begrudged every minute Tyler Clay spent in the company of others.

"He's only been working there a few days. I'm glad he enjoys his job. We wouldn't want him to be miserable, would we?"

"No, and he says he will get me some foreign movies I have been wanting to see, so that is good."

"Foreign movies? I thought Family Video only rented family tapes." Were there any family-oriented foreign movies? What did European children watch? she wondered.

"That is true. But my Tyler, he can order—special order—anything I want. Privately. Between friends. So I have my own private film festival this summer."

That was okay then. "I need to talk to you. Before Tyler comes home," Josie stated flatly.

"Sì. You have a problem? Not with little Tyler?"

"No, not with Tyler. With me. But I don't want anyone to know about it."

"Sit. Tell me."

Josie knew that the less she told Risa, the better. Not because she couldn't trust her to keep a secret but because Risa was a worrier. "I need to track down someone, someone I knew years and years ago. Before I came to the island."

"Ah." Risa nodded her head, a suitably serious expression on her face.

"I . . . I don't want Tyler to know about this."

The nodding became more vigorous and a hairpin fell onto the floor.

"I may have to leave messages and to have . . . uh, people . . . call me back. I wondered . . . I mean, I don't want messages left on the phone at home because of Tyler . . ."

"Sì. Sì." More nodding. More pins falling to the floor.

"And I don't want anyone else to overhear, so I think that leaving my office number would be a mistake."

"Definitivamente. Sì." Risa had long and luxurious hair, but just how many pins could she lose before it fell to her shoulders? "You need to use my number. Of course. What about address?"

"What?"

"Do you need also to give out my address to these people you need to get in touch with?"

"I . . ." She hadn't thought of that. "I may, in fact."

"Then you just give out my apartment number instead of yours. Easy, no?"

"Yes . . ."

"But maybe too easy." The nodding stopped and the frowning began. "Do you want this person to be able to find you just like that?" She snapped her fingers.

"I . . . You know, I never thought about it. Maybe not." Josie thought for a moment. "I suppose I could rent a box at the post office. But this is an awfully small island and there aren't a whole lot of people who live here all year long. If someone was to look for me, he or she would probably find me."

Risa seemed to hesitate, which was unusual for her. "Is Pigeon your real name? Your family name?"

"Yes. Of course. Yes." The question surprised her. "Why do you ask?"

"Well, we . . . I . . . There were people who thought maybe you had been married at one time when you first came to the island. I didn't like to ask too many questions back then and now . . . well, now you are you. I no longer have questions. If you know what I mean."

Josie thought she did. "Now no one questions who I am or where I came from. But I was born Josie Pigeon . . . well, Josephine Pigeon to be exact. Why?"

"Because I watch a show on television about computers searching out people. You can be found if you use your right name. So people not look for you. Or else they would have found you."

"But I'm not connected to the Internet," Josie protested.

"That does not matter. It searches phone books, address books, credit records." Risa shrugged dramatically. "I not know how it does it, but it does."

"Interesting. I guess that means no one has wanted to get in touch with me." She had a moment of feeling hurt by this fact, right before she decided to appreciate it.

"It means you can find who you look for," Risa reminded her.

"Oh, that won't be a problem. I'll just have to make a few phone calls. Maybe only one."

"And you leave my phone number to call back to." The nodding had started again.

Josie had another thought. "But how will you answer the phone? I mean, what excuse will you give that you're answering the phone instead of me?"

"I leave on answering machine."

"All the time? Even when you're home?"

"Sì. All the time. Even when I am here. Why not?"

"No reason. And I really will try not to use your phone number."

"You do what you have to do. I take care you get any messages. Sí?"

"Yes. Yes, and thank you, Risa. I don't know what I'd do without you." After a few more words, Josie headed up to her own apartment. She knew what she had to do. Although she had rarely given serious consideration to contacting anyone from her past, she thought of the one person she could go to: Naomi Van Ripper, reference librarian at the town library. Miss Van Ripper (she had insisted on Miss rather than Ms. even though she had certainly grown up during the consciousness-raising sixties) had acquired all of the official information about the town—newspapers, maps, public service flyers from various civic organizations—and she kept her ear to the ground about all else. And like a good librarian, Miss Van Ripper loved sharing her information. Josie grabbed the portable phone while the door to her apartment was swinging shut behind her.

Now what was the information number she was always seeing on TV? After five wrong tries, she got through and asked for the number of her hometown library. She wrote down what she was told and then punched in a new set of dig-

its. "Hello, I'm . . . calling to speak with Miss Van Ripper."
Josie held her breath, hoping no one would ask her name and
thinking furiously about a good alias if someone did. "Oh,
Dr. Van Ripper. I didn't know . . . Really? That's wonderful. I
knew her . . . well, I guess it was years and years ago. Oh, old
friends," Josie lied. Inspired, she continued. "I was supposed
to call her this week—not at the library but at home, and I
seem to have lost the number. Oh . . . yes, exactly, that's what
I mean . . . call her at the place she's staying . . . at the shore.
Yes. Right near here, in fact." Josie grabbed for a pen and a
magazine and wrote furiously on the cover. "That's perfect.
Yes. Thank you. I appreciate it." Resisting the urge to ask how
things were in her hometown, Josie hung up.

Just in time. Tyler walked in the door.

"Hi, Mom. When's dinner?"

"Whenever you get it on the table."

"I thought I was going to be cooking on Monday and
Wednesday nights." When Tyler turned thirteen, Josie had insisted that he share in the kitchen chores. He had turned out to
be a better cook than she was. Tyler leaned across the counter
that divided the kitchen space from the rest of the room and
peered at the Sierra Club calendar hanging on the wall.
"Yeah. You wrote it down. Right here. Tonight is your night!"

"Then how about pizza?" She was anxious to call the number she had just been given. If she could talk her son into
walking around the corner to the Italian takeout that had
popped up in the first floor of an old Victorian mansion that
summer, she would have the time.

"I had pizza for lunch. But . . ." He perked up. "How about
a large calzone?"

To Josie calzone was just rearranged pizza, but as long as
he was happy with that solution . . . "Sounds good to me.
Why don't you call and place the order?"

"Okay. Diet Coke?"

"Sure. And make sure you get a drink for yourself. I meant to go to the grocery store today, but . . ."

"I'll pick up a six-pack there—that way is the cheapest," Tyler offered.

"Great."

"And I can go down and place the order, then wait there until it's ready. That way it won't have to wait around on the counter and get cold or anything."

Josie suddenly remembered that the cutest girl on the island was working at the pizza place this summer. "My wallet is in—"

"I'll take care of it. I still have some money from my allowance. You can pay me back."

"Fantastic."

Tyler dashed out the door and bounded down the stairs. Josie waited until the front door slammed behind him before dialing the phone. She was making a local call. It turned out that Dr. Van Ripper was on vacation—less than ten miles north of where Josie was standing right now.

The phone was answered before Josie had decided what to say.

"Hello?"

"Is this Miss . . . I mean Dr. Van Ripper? This is Josie Pigeon." The words were out of her mouth before she had considered what announcing her presence might mean.

Happily, the name seemed to mean nothing to the librarian. "Yes?"

"I . . . You . . . I need to ask you some questions," Josie blurted out.

"Miss whatever, why are you calling me? I am no longer a reference librarian. And I am on vacation. Why do you imagine I would want to answer any questions you might ask—even if I could?"

"I . . . It's about Courtney Castle." It was the only answer Josie could come up with—and it seemed to work. At least the phone wasn't slammed down.

"Courtney Castle? What about her?"

"She's . . . Well, I need to ask some questions about her. I'm . . . doing research."

"Are you a reporter? Why didn't you say that up front? Why would you expect me to answer your questions unless you tell me why you're asking them?"

"Well, I—"

"Are you calling from nearby? From the shore?"

"Yes, I—"

"From the island where Courtney is taping her television show, right?"

"Yes, exactly." Josie was relieved to be telling the truth at last.

None of this seemed apparent to Dr. Van Ripper. "What do you need? Background information for an article you're doing?"

"Background information would be a good place to start," Josie admitted, glancing at the large grandfather clock that held the place of honor in the middle of the room. She sure hoped Tyler took his time getting dinner. She had just remembered how Naomi Van Ripper loved to talk.

"I've known Courtney since she was a small child. She was beautiful even then. I remember how her blond hair would glimmer in the light coming through the library windows as she studied at the table in the reference room on Saturday mornings."

Dr. Van Ripper must have been asked this many times before because Josie recognized a prepared speech when she heard one. And so far, while the image produced might be a publicist's dream, it was also a lie. Courtney had not been one to spend her weekends in the library. In fact, now that Josie thought about it, she remembered the rumors about how Courtney had bragged about getting the librarians to do her research so that she didn't have to spend long hours in the library. And her hair had been brown and stringy, not something that had shimmered ethereally in the sunlight. Not that there had been any sunlight. The Carnegie Foundation, which had generously donated the library to the town, had been fond of dark stained-glass windows through which natural light could not penetrate. And the fluorescent bulbs that hung from the reference room's ceiling turned everything beneath them a sallow hue. But the tale of Courtney Castle's early life was continuing.

"She was a unique child. Popular with adults as well as her peers. A wonderful student, of course. Although she didn't take shop or anything like that when she attended our excellent public schools." An artificial chuckle punctuated this statement. "I'm not surprised that she ended up on television. With her looks and brains, she is a natural. But I have to admit that her interests in the building trade must have developed after she left town."

"When was that?" Josie leapt in with a question.

"When was what?"

"When did Courtney leave town?"

"Why, just like most young people, she left when she went to college. Not that she just vanished from the scene, mind you. With all her interests, she was a busy young woman, of course. I seem to remember that she did a student service project somewhere in Africa after her freshman year of college. And she took classes at Harvard between her sophomore and junior years. But she is close to her family. She always visits her parents at Christmastime. And frequently joins them for their annual jaunt to the Caribbean in the spring."

Josie could just imagine her own mother drooling over this dutiful daughter and comparing Courtney with the unwed mother slash carpenter she herself had brought into the world. "And did you always see her during these visits home?"

"Naturally. That's Courtney for you! She stops in at the library to say hello whenever she is in town. Without fail. That's what I mean. She is just the most considerate person. She never forgets the people who helped her when she was young. That's the sign of an unusually fine person, I think. Courtney Castle is a success—well known, wealthy, famous. And she still appreciates her old friends. She's done quite a bit for our town, you know."

"No, I didn't. What?" Josie was relieved that the conversation had moved to more concrete ground. She had almost been expecting Dr. Van Ripper to refer to herself as one of the little people. From what she remembered of this woman, it would be extremely out of character.

"Why, she's been the speaker at more than one of the high school commencements over the years. She was given the key to the town by the mayor just a few years ago. And she was at the opening ceremony for the new gazebo in the town square—"

"The what?"

"We have a beautiful new Victorian gazebo in the town square. Bands play there on summer evenings. The elementary-school children hold their graduation ceremony there in the spring. Brides for miles around have their pictures taken there."

"Sounds nice." Josie was wondering where the town square was located.

"It seems to me that you people are always around when Courtney comes home," Dr. Van Ripper was continuing.

"My people?" Josie had a moment of wondering about her parents before she realized the librarian was speaking of her imaginary position as a member of the press.

"Yes. You sure love everything Courtney does, don't you?"

"She does appear to have a very interesting life," Josie admitted.

"And she's such fun to be around. I can't wait until tomorrow to see her." The librarian was now gushing.

"To see her? Where is she? I mean, where are you going to meet her?" Josie asked.

"Why, on the island. She invited me to the house her company is filming. I cannot wait! So fascinating, don't you think?"

Josie, in fact, didn't know what to think.

FOURTEEN

THERE ARE PEOPLE who feel that sleeping on a problem will help to solve it, that the subconscious will take over and answer questions. But it wasn't true for Josie. When she went to bed with a problem, she found neither solution nor sleep.

The next morning Josie was exhausted and she was asking herself the same questions she had asked the night before. Where was Courtney Castle? And what was she going to do when Naomi Van Ripper appeared at the work site today? How would she feel when she saw someone from what she thought of as her past life for the first time in seventeen years?

Well, houses don't get remodeled by lying in bed and worrying, Josie thought, stretching her arms over her head and swinging her legs to the floor. If she dressed quickly, there would be time for a bowl of cereal before she left. Grabbing clean but old overalls and a T-shirt from her closet shelf, she headed for the bathroom, running her fingers through her hair as she went.

But she had forgotten one of the realities of a home with a teenage boy living in it: cereal vanishes. Sighing, she considered the other possibilities. A dirty plate in the sink and an empty grease-stained box in the garbage indicated that her son had finished off the calzone as a midnight (or later) snack. A can of Slim-Fast on a shelf remained untouched, as did a package of Rye Krisp, but she was going to have a hard day. She deserved a good breakfast. Dumping a packet of cat food in her son's cat, Urchin's, empty bowl, she grabbed her key chain and wallet and headed out the door. Tyler knew where to find her if he needed her. And she knew where to find the best greasy breakfast on the island.

A few minutes later she walked through the door of an institution: Sullivan's (as the sign she had just strolled under informed anyone who cared to read the small print) had been established in 1927 right after the hurricane the year before had damaged or destroyed most of the buildings on the island. It was the only general store on the island and a lunch counter had been added the next summer. In the early fifties, an addition had been tacked on with room for a row of plastic upholstered booths and a dozen small tables. Not too much had changed since then. In fact, there were rumors that the grease in the deep-fat fryer qualified as original equipment. Few tourists ventured into this part of the store, satisfied to fill their needs for sunscreen on good days and playing cards and gizmos to keep the kids happy when it rained at the front. Glancing at a display of garish beach towels, Josie followed her nose to the source of one of her favorite meals.

"A number four. Over easy," she said to the young waitress in a turquoise uniform almost before her bottom touched the chair.

"Coffee?" The woman took Josie's abrupt order in stride.

Jose nodded. "Please. With cream and sugar."

"Gotcha."

Josie had barely finished her first mug of coffee when a massive oval plate was put on the paper placemat in front of her. Two fried eggs, yellow with butter, sat in the middle encircled by strips of crispy bacon, links of sausage, and rectangles of golden French toast. A large pitcher of sweet syrup whose antecedents had nothing to do with any tree was plunked down on the table, then the waitress left to satisfy the needs of another noncholesterol-fearing customer. Josie dug in.

She was halfway through the platter when she was joined by a friend.

"Mind if I sit with you?" Basil Tilby stood by her side. A fixture on the island, he was a notorious clotheshorse. Today his lanky frame was decked out as a sailor—not the type actually to travel over the water, more like someone from a Broadway production of a Gilbert and Sullivan operetta.

"Sure. Why are you here?"

"To eat. Of course."

Josie was surprised. Basil was a gourmet; this was about the last place she would have expected him to be eating. "You're kidding."

"Nope. Kristina makes one of my favorite breakfasts. I stop by every few weeks."

Josie couldn't wait to see what Basil ordered. "Really? How's the summer going for you?" As another businessperson dependent on the vagaries of seasonal profits, he would understand that her question translated as "How's business?"

"Great. But not as interesting as yours. What's going on with Courtney Castle?"

"She's disappeared."

"So I hear. Any idea why?"

"No. What have you heard?" While hosting in any of his restaurants, Basil chatted with the clientele and picked up a lot of information.

Basil leaned across the small table and whispered his answer. "That the police believe you killed her."

"What garbage! No one even knows if she's dead!" Josie was outraged enough to stop eating for a moment. "Her producer says she does this all the time." She was aware of the exaggeration, but she was upset and tired.

"All the time? Makes you wonder how they manage to film all those television shows, doesn't it?"

Josie recognized sarcasm when she heard it, but the arrival of Basil's meal distracted her. "What is that?"

He looked down at his own large platter with a smile and picked up his fork. "Fried scrapple. Kristina makes her own. Wonderful." A small pitcher with light amber liquid was placed by his plate. "Real maple syrup," he explained. "Wouldn't touch that stuff," he added, glancing over at Josie's pitcher.

She ignored his criticism of her taste buds. "What's scrapple?"

"One of those foods it's better not to ask about and just enjoy. Want to try some?" Knife raised, he offered a piece to her.

"No, thanks. What did you hear about Courtney?"

"That the Rodney clan believes you killed her and dumped her in the bay, but they're too cheap to have the water dredged for the body."

"So what does that mean? They're going to wait for it to float to the surface?"

"Well, there's a gruesome thought for this early in the morning." However, it didn't seem to stop him from enjoying his breakfast. "What do you think?" he asked, when he stopped to pick up his mug of tea.

Josie noticed that he had brought his own tea bag. Her bitchier self wondered if he had also insisted on using bottled water. "If you mean do I know what happened to Courtney, the answer is no."

"There's a rumor going around that you knew her before you came to the island."

"Sam told you that?" She felt betrayed.

"Sam? No, I haven't seen Sam since I placed a wine order with him late last week." Basil stopped eating for a moment and looked up at Josie. "So it's true, is it?"

"No . . ." She stopped. What was the point in lying? Basil,

like everyone else on the island, would find out sooner or later. Sam knew. Risa knew. The island's grapevine was working. Soon everyone would have heard the news. She looked at Basil and saw sympathy in his eyes.

"Yes, it's true, but I don't want anyone to know, Basil! My past is my past. It's private and it doesn't have anything to do with . . . whatever is going on here. We . . . we knew each other when we were kids. We weren't really friends. We didn't even like each other." She pushed her platter away even though there was a piece of French toast left on it. "What did you hear? And who told you?"

"Nothing really specific. There was a young man at Café Portofino last night trying to impress his date. I think he might be one of those horrible young police officers Chief Rodney hires—good-looking, of course, but with less brains than your average turnip. Anyway, throughout most of their meal he was bragging loudly about being on the crime scene. Discussing clues and evidence like some sort of Columbo wanna-be. Among the things he said was that the police thought Courtney had been a victim of foul play. And that you and the members of your crew were possible suspects—"

"Members of my crew? Why the hell would any of them kill Courtney? They didn't know her well enough to hate her!"

"From what this young kid was saying, the police think that you did," Basil said.

"Well, it's not true. I didn't. Kill her, that is."

"But you admit to knowing her before she came here?"

Basil had lowered his voice and was leaning across the table. Josie glanced around. It didn't look to her as though anyone was paying undue attention to their conversation. Three men at the closest table were arguing about a recent fishing trip. A young mother was correcting her small son's table manners. Another mother was criticizing her teenage daughter's choice of beach attire. An elderly couple was sharing the local newspaper as they ate breakfast. No one seemed particularly interested in anything the two of them were saying. "Yes. But that was a long time ago. Before Tyler was born. It can't have anything to do with her . . . disappearance the other day."

"I don't see how you can know that."

"I haven't seen her in years and years! I haven't seen anyone she knows. I didn't even know that she was doing that damn television show! How could I have anything to do with whatever has happened?"

"Josie, I'm just telling you what I overheard. And I would have even if you hadn't asked me. Josie, you know what idiots the Rodneys are. It's almost as though they are genetically programmed to arrest the wrong person. And, in this case, it sounds like the wrong person is you!"

Josie glanced down at her wrist and then up at the clock hanging on the wall.

"You know, doctors do all sorts of implants these days. Maybe you could have something done with a watch." Josie's inability to keep watches with her was well known among her friends.

"I'm going to be late for work."

"You'd better get going. Unless I miss my guess, the Rodneys and their minions are going to be hanging around with questions. And you know how they never believe the answers anyone gives them. Makes you wonder, doesn't it?"

"What?"

"If the reason they believe everyone is dishonest is that they're basing their judgments on themselves."

"Yeah." Josie tossed all the change from one of her overall pockets on the table and waved to the woman behind the counter. "Thanks. That was great—as usual."

"Bye, Josie. Don't get yourself arrested!" the woman called out cheerfully.

"Hard to keep a secret on this island," Basil said knowingly.

"So it seems," Josie answered, thinking about how, in this case, many secrets were being kept quite successfully—so far. She said good-bye to Basil and hurried out to her truck. Now that she had two visitors to worry about, it seemed even more urgent that she get to work. The drive took less than five minutes and she had not decided who she wanted to see less—the police or Naomi Van Ripper—when she turned onto the street by the bay. And realized she had been wasting time and mental effort. On the front lawn of her work site the chief of police stood talking to the librarian.

Josie parked the truck, took a deep breath, and got out with what she hoped was a welcoming smile on her face.

As she approached, toolbox in hand, the two people stopped talking and turned to look at her. Their expressions did not match her own.

"Is this the woman you knew as Josephine Pigeon?" the chief of police asked without preliminaries.

"I'd know that hair anywhere," Naomi Van Ripper said. "Josephine, you never returned *The Best Guide to Northeastern Colleges* to the library!"

"Uh . . . wouldn't it be a little out of date by now?"

"How many years has that book been out?" Mike Rodney Senior had a huge grin on his face.

"Since I last saw Josephine. It must have been the early 1980s. Let me think for a second. It was 1983! That book has been overdue for seventeen years, Josephine!"

"Everyone calls me Josie now," she told her. "And I think you'd better just make out a bill for that book."

"Saving it for Tyler to use in a few years, Josie?"

Naomi Van Ripper picked up on the name right away. "Tyler? Who's Tyler?"

"Why, Josie's son. Smartest kid on the island, I'll admit that. Guess the apple fell pretty far from the tree that time."

"You're married, Josephine?" Dr. Van Ripper sounded as though she didn't believe it could possibly be true.

Which, of course, it wasn't. "No. I'm not."

"Divorced?" She made it sound as though such a thing were unheard of.

"No." The two of them could tie her up and torture her, but she wasn't going to say more.

"How unfortunate. I guess the rumors I heard about you were true."

"Our Miss Pigeon is what you call a thoroughly modern young woman." Chief Rodney sneered. "An unwed mother."

The questions stopped while the librarian caught her breath. "Did you say an unwed mother? Josie . . . how . . . who . . . when . . ."

"I have a wonderful son. He's sixteen years old." And that was all she was going to say.

Apparently, it was enough. "I did hear that you had been involved with various men while you were in college. I hoped, of course, that you wouldn't be so foolish. And I gather you've been busy since you disappeared."

"Disappeared?"

"You left college and vanished. According to your mother, no one had any idea where you had ended up. There were even rumors that you had been killed or hurt in some way, but then your family got that message from you . . ."

So they had received her announcement of Tyler's birth!

". . . from some sort of hippie commune in California. At least that was what everyone in town was saying."

Josie opened her mouth, closed it, and opened it again. She had no idea what to say. She had imagined a lot of scenarios, but none of them had included gossip and lies being told about her. She realized Chief Rodney was enjoying her discomfort. "I guess we have a lot of catching up to do. But I should get to work."

"Yes, your crew seems anxious to see you." Chief Rodney was looking over her shoulder.

"You're a carpenter?"

"I own Island Contracting," Josie answered proudly. "And we'd better get down to work. When Courtney decides to show up, we want to be ready for her." She managed a slight smile, grabbed her toolbox, and headed into the house.

Her crew really did appear anxious to know what was going on. Jill was perched on a tall ladder. Dottie and Annette stood at the bottom. All three had concerned expressions on their faces. "Nothing to worry about," Josie assured them. "She's an old acquaintance. Someone I knew when I was a kid. She's here to see Courtney Castle."

"Then she has a problem," Dottie announced. "Courtney Castle is dead."

FIFTEEN

WHO? WHERE? HOW? Josie realized she was asking the same questions Naomi Van Ripper had asked just a few minutes ago.

"She's—"

"Shh! They're coming in. Don't say anything!" Dottie hissed the order.

"Chief Rodney—" Josie began as he and Dr. Van Ripper appeared in the open doorway. She didn't get a chance to finish. Jill Pike jumped down off the ladder—and onto Josie's right foot. "Ouch!"

"She's hidden. Don't say anything!" Jill whispered in Josie's ear, pretending to be checking on any damage she had done. "Sorry," she said more loudly. "Guess it's lucky you were wearing work boots."

"I just wish you hadn't been, too," Josie said, looking around. Where had they put the body? she wondered. There was a pile of furniture covered with a large blue tarp against the wall opposite the door. She realized she was staring at it. "No harm done. And we have to get started working."

"We're just passing through. College kid out front said that Bobby Valentine is on the dock. Thought he might know when Courtney Castle is going to be back," Mike Rodney said.

"She invited me for lunch. She will be here. Courtney is very well brought up. When she accepts a social commit-

130

ment, she lives up to it. And SHE always returned her books on time. That says a lot about a person in my experience." Naomi Van Ripper glanced at Josie to see if her barb had met its mark.

Josie didn't respond. She had more important things to worry about. Forced to be content with a parting harrumph, Dr. Van Ripper followed Chief Rodney from the house. The back door swung closed behind them, but it was a minute or two before anyone moved or spoke. Then Josie dashed across the room and ripped the blue tarp from the pile. Sawdust and dirt flew in all directions.

"What the hell?" Jill was stunned.

"Why did you do that? Do you think we should cover her?" Annette asked the question.

But Dottie understood why Josie had done what she had done. "She's not there. Up there," Dottie explained briefly, and pointed at the ceiling.

For one wild moment Josie considered the possibility that someone as bitchy as Courtney Castle had made it into heaven. Then she looked up and realized what Dottie was saying. "She's in the canoe?"

"Yup."

"She is!" Annette added, her eyes wide with shock. "We all saw her."

"I found her," Jill said. "I was so surprised, I almost fell off the ladder."

Josie took a deep breath and then walked toward the ladder. "I guess I'd better see for myself."

"Be careful. It's a little weird," Jill cautioned her.

"More than a little. It's horrible," Annette added.

"Go up. You'll see what we're talking about," Dottie said, holding the ladder still as Josie climbed.

She went up slowly, dreading what was awaiting her. Blood, gore, rot . . . She had imagined that and more when she reached the canoe. Taking a deep breath, she peered over the edge of the boat. "My God."

"Strange, isn't it?" Jill asked.

"Yeah." Strange was one word for it. Courtney Castle looked almost as good dead as she had alive. She was lying on her back, eyes closed, hair combed, hands crossed on her chest, no expression on her face. She even seemed to be wearing makeup. A heavy wool Hudson Bay blanket covered her from the waist down. She might have been napping. Except that she smelled—just a little.

Josie wrinkled her nose.

"Yeah, it's hot up there and that blanket isn't helping things either. We're going to have to get her down before the entire place stinks."

Josie looked down at Dottie. "We—"

"You ladies need some help or can you handle that thing yourself? Them wooden ones can be damn heavy. Give me a nice aluminum or fiberglass model any day." Chief Rodney was back.

"I—"

"We can handle it ourselves," Dottie told him. "Do we look weak?" She flexed an ample biceps as she spoke.

"Yeah, I guess you can manage. Gotta get going. Can't spend the day escorting people around. See you." He actually tipped his hat at Dottie Evans before leaving.

Annette giggled. "I think he's got the hots for you."

"Oh, yeah, me and a cop. That'll be the day." But, Josie was surprised to note, Dottie seemed to be blushing.

Josie was still standing on top of the ladder. "We should have said something. I . . . I should have told him that Courtney was up here. That she was dead."

"Are you nuts?"

Josie looked down at Dottie. "What do you mean? We can't just leave her here."

"Yeah, I know. In this heat and up there near the roof, she'll start smelling in no time at all. But I agree with Dottie, that doesn't mean we should tell the police about her," Jill said.

"Do you have anything to say about this?" Josie asked Annette.

"I . . . I don't think we should say anything either. I mean, I know you should. You know, that you're supposed to tell the police about stuff like this, but, well, considering what people are saying . . ." She stopped speaking and suddenly seemed to discover something of interest on the toe of her boot.

"About what?"

"Huh?"

"People are saying what about what?" Josie asked, becoming impatient.

"About you and Courtney Castle. You know, about your past." Annette seemed to find it impossible to look at her boss. "Your past together."

Josie climbed slowly down the ladder, not speaking until she was on the floor. "How do you know what people are saying?"

"I . . . You're mad at me!"

"Annette, I'm sorry. I'm not. It's just . . ."

"It's just that there's a dead body hanging over her head, you dummy," Dottie broke in.

"I . . . Yes. Let's all sit down and have some coffee. That way if anyone comes in it will just look like we're on a break," Josie suggested, suddenly realizing how likely that was.

"Good idea." Jill nodded.

"I could use some coffee," Annette admitted.

"I could use a shot of bourbon, but ya gotta make do with what ya got," Dottie said, kicking her tool chest open and pulling out a thermos.

"Maybe it wouldn't be a bad idea if we sort of kept a lookout—you know, just to know when someone is coming,"

Josie suggested. They were, after all, sitting in a large, cleared space with an open door on either side.

"Yeah, smart." Dottie obviously approved. "If I sit up here"—she lifted her hefty hips onto the blue tarp—"I can see straight out the back-door way, right down to the dock."

"And I can just plop myself down here." Jill leaned her shapely body against the covered work of art. "And I'll be able to tell you if anyone is coming from the front."

Josie, still at the base of the ladder, looked around. Her crew was spread out, but, unless anyone came in looking for something strange, no one would notice. Annette was still standing nervously by one of the windows. "Why don't you sit down and relax and you can tell me all about what you heard and how you heard it," she added.

"It's Chad."

"Who?"

"The college kid who works with the television people." Dottie identified him. "That kid is always snooping around."

"He's not a kid and he's not a snoop," Annette insisted. "He's just doing his job. And his job is to do whatever he is told to do. He's what they call a gofer."

"He's what we used to call a rat."

"He's not!"

"What do you call someone who creeps around listening and then reporting what's said . . ." Seeming to realize she'd gone too far, Dottie suddenly became quiet.

"Look, we've got a problem and we're all better off if we don't waste time and energy fighting with one another," Josie said loudly.

"She's right," Jill said.

"Yeah, I guess."

"Do you still want me to tell you what Chad heard?" Annette asked quietly.

"I sure do. And when he told you about it."

"Well, we sort of had a date last night. I mean, he took me to dinner and then we went for a walk on the beach."

"Sounds like a date to me," Dottie said.

"Yeah, well, he's really nice, like I said, and he told me about himself and school and how he got this job. You know, he thinks he might be interested in going into television as a career and his parents thought this would be a good experience, so they're paying for him to live here and everything."

"Lucky kid."

"Go on," Josie urged.

"Well, he does whatever anyone tells him to do. You know, he goes out and picks up coffee, unloads equipment from the trucks, helps set up stuff, goes to Kinko's to Xerox things, and lots, lots more. So he's all over and he hears things and . . . well, this is going to sound a little odd."

"What?"

"His mother solves murders."

Dottie stood up. "She's a police detective or something?"

"No. She's a mother . . . you know, a housewife. She just does it in her spare time—or something."

"You mean—"

"What does that have to do with this?" Josie interrupted Dottie.

"Well, he's been around murder investigations before. You know? And he's also in a position to hear things. That's what I'm trying to explain."

"Go on. We can't be on this coffee break forever."

"Oh, sorry. Well, he said that Bobby Valentine said that you and Courtney Castle knew each other years and years ago. That you were old enemies."

"He used that word? He said we were enemies?"

"That's the word Chad used. I don't really know if it's exactly the word Bobby Valentine used."

"Good distinction," Josie commented. "Go on, you're doing just fine."

"He . . . didn't explain. You know, he didn't say what had happened to make you two hate each other or anything like that. Chad thinks it's all rather odd, in fact. He says why did Courtney choose to do a show with Island Contracting if she didn't get along with the owner?"

"Good question," Dottie said.

"I don't think she knew I was the owner," Josie began.

"How could she not know that?" Dottie asked. "Your name is on the letterhead, right? And on any contract they signed with you, right?"

"Yeah. Well, not really. It's on the letterhead, all right, but I'm not sure I ever sent them a letter. Most—maybe all—of our contact was on the phone." She paused for a minute and thought about it. "In fact, all of it was," she concluded. She hated writing letters and had pretty much created a form for most of her contacts, so she would remember if she had had to write something special. And now that she thought about it, everything had been done on the phone. The only papers pertaining to *Courtney Castle's Castles* was one letter from the owners of the house giving permission for their home to be taped and waiving Island Contracting from responsibility for any damage that might occur during the taping. Josie had thought that perhaps Sam, as a lawyer, should look at it, but she was reluctant to ask him for professional favors, and somehow they had been busy with other things and she had never gotten around to showing it to him. But her problem now had nothing to do with liability. "Anyway, she probably didn't know I was here. I think Island Contracting was chosen because we're different, working down here on the island and being made up of women and all."

"I don't remember being around," Jill said. "What did Courtney say when she saw you? 'Ah, my old enemy from . . .' what was it, college?"

"High school actually, and we weren't enemies, damn it. We were . . . well, we weren't friends. You know how kids are at that age. There are cliques. An in group and an out group and dumb stuff like that. That's how things were with us."

"I gather Courtney Castle was a member in good standing of the innest of the in groups?"

"Yeah," Josie admitted ruefully. "That's not much of a surprise, is it?"

"Nope."

"Not really," Annette agreed with Jill.

"I hate people like that," Dottie growled. "I'll bet she was a cheerleader."

"And vice president of the student council, editor of the yearbook, president of the French Club, the star of the spring musical, homecoming queen in the fall, and the girl most likely to succeed according to the yearbook." Josie realized her crew was looking at her in amazement. She, herself, was surprised at how easily it was all coming back.

"So what did Little Miss Perfect say when she saw who she was going to be taping the show with?" Dottie asked.

"That's the strange part," Josie admitted. "I recognized her, but if she recognized me, she didn't admit it—at least not at first."

"Strange," Annette breathed, her eyes wide open.

"It is a little odd," Jill agreed.

"Why?" Dottie shrugged her well-developed shoulders. "You didn't say anything to her, did you?"

SIXTEEN

"Now I EXPLAINED to you all earlier. Courtney, as the celebrity of the show, has lots of obligations and reasons why she can't hang around the set constantly—Excuse me?"

"Nothing. Just muttering to myself," Dottie said.

Josie was just thankful that Bobby Valentine hadn't heard Dottie's comment concerning Courtney and her tendency to "hang around" this particular set. "Go on," she urged.

"Well, as I was saying, we frequently have to shoot around Courtney. This isn't at all an unusual situation. So if you ladies will just go on working in the background, I'd like to ask your boss here a few questions."

"Great."

"Fine."

"Where do you want me to stand?"

Bobby Valentine smiled at Annette. "Right over there." He pointed. "And you." He nodded to Jill. "If you would just work right there. To the left of Josie? Great."

"And where do you want me? Or are you afraid I'll fill up the screen?" Dottie asked.

"I don't suppose you could think of anything to do up on the ladder? It would add interest on another level. No? Well, then, maybe you can help that young lady . . . Ann—"

"Annette."

"Great. Lovely name. Like one of the Mouseketeers, right? The one who was . . . well, Annette. If you would just act like you're helping her hammer together that . . . uh, that beam or whatever it is."

Josie didn't know anything about television, but she sure didn't want her crew looking as though they were wandering around unoccupied or aimless during the workday, so she intervened. "Dottie, you and Annette get rid of the window frames on that side of the house and start demoing the walls. Jill, if you could pull the wires and top off the pipes around the perimeter? Great!" Once everyone was occupied, she returned her attention to the producer. "So what do you want to ask me?"

"If you don't mind, why don't we do two separate interviews? The show isn't completely blocked in and I'm not absolutely sure where these questions will be edited in."

"Fine with me. Where do you want me to sit?"

"I don't want you to sit. I want you to work and Courtney will come up to you, interrupt, and ask you some questions. Okay?"

"Sure. Do you want me to help them remove that wall?"

"No way. Our audience has been watching walls come down and go up for years and years. Let's think of something interesting. Something unique about the house . . ."

"I could be doing something with that sculpture."

"No. I don't think so. How about the canoe? It's coming down, right?"

"Yes, but not right now—"

"Hey, nothing is happening right now. It's all fiction. But you climb up the ladder and look like you're examining the . . . whatever is holding that canoe up there and I'll walk up as though I'm Courtney. Okay?"

Josie knew why she didn't want to do it, but she couldn't

think of a rational excuse not to, so she climbed up slowly and then even more slowly as she approached the top.

"Now, why don't you just put your hand . . . not that hand! The other one! Don't want to block that . . . uh, pretty . . . face! Okay! Okay! Just hold that position! How does she look?"

Josie jumped back. He knew Courtney was up there. "She . . . she . . ."

"The cameraman is trying to get your face in the picture." The statement came from Dottie, and Josie suddenly realized that Bobby Valentine was talking about her, not Courtney. "Maybe I should tie back my hair?"

"No!"

"Didn't you tell her? I thought that Henshaw kid . . . Chad . . . was supposed to tell everybody on the crew about their clothing!" The cameraman seemed distressed.

"I . . ." Annette was hesitant. "I . . . He told me and I told him . . . that is, I said I would explain to everyone else. I . . . Something happened and . . . I forgot."

"Okay. I will repeat myself. Everybody listen to me. We will be taping six shows. While each of you may not appear in each show, you will all appear in more than one, probably half of them, maybe more. You must wear the same thing for each day of shooting—"

"We—"

"What?"

"Guess you don't care how we smell, do you?"

"What's the big deal? Just put your jeans and T-shirt in the washer when you get home each night and—"

Josie was momentarily distracted. "Most of us don't live in houses with a washer and dryer in the basement." (She had a fleeting vision of the laundry room in her parents' basement. Like the rest of the house, it was color-coordinated; in this case turquoise, cream, and yellow.) "And even if we did, we work hard. Going home to do laundry is not exactly restful."

"Besides, we didn't know we were going to be seen in what we showed up in today for the entire series," Annette protested.

"Look, just try to wear something similar. Maybe we can make an exception with this series—after all, we all know how ladies are about their clothing." He looked up at four scowling women. "Uh, let's get going. Don't be afraid to really get into your work."

The hammering became louder. Josie knew that when those windows were pulled the sound would be deafening, but Bobby Valentine continued to give directions.

"I will walk in with the cameraman following me. The camera will pan the room—quickly—and then up the rungs of the ladder to where Josie is working." He turned all his attention on her. "I'll call out a loud hello and we'll take it from there. Okay?"

"I . . . uh . . . what if I say something stupid?"

"Not to worry. In the first place, you're a smart cookie and you won't. In the second place, nothing goes out unedited. Ready?"

"Yeah. I guess." She wasn't, but her nervousness about being on television was competing with the horror of being so near Courtney's body. She had to get down off this ladder as quickly as possible.

"Okay. Take one. Panning. Panning. Panning. Panning. Hi, Josie!"

"Hi, Bo . . . Mr. . . . Shit. You wanted me to say hello to Courtney, didn't you?"

"Sure didn't want you to say hello to Mr. Shit."

"Yeah. Sorry. Can we do that again? Take two?" she asked, inspired.

"Yeah, as Ms. Pigeon says, take two. Everyone's a producer these days. We'll start with the hello.

"Hello, Josie!"

She looked down at him and grinned. "Hello, Courtney . . . Miss Castle . . . Is it all right if I call her Courtney?"

"Everyone else in America does, why not you? Take three. Hello, Ms. Pigeon."

"Hello, Courtney." Josie found herself grinning foolishly down into the large lens of a video camera.

"Josie Pigeon is the founder, owner, and head carpenter at Island Contracting— What's that, Josie?"

"I said not founder. It was founded by Noel Roberts. He died and left the company to me."

"Well, I guess he was a real friend, wasn't he? So, Josie, why don't you tell us a bit about this house you're working on today? That canoe is an interesting thing to hang from the ceiling. Is it decoration or is something hiding in there? What was that?"

"Sounds like a window coming out of a wall—the easy way, Courtney." She was particularly proud of herself for remembering to speak to the dead woman, but she was having a difficult time not glancing over at the body. Then she had an inspiration. "You know, Courtney, this canoe is going to hang in the house after it's remodeled. Except for the sculpture by the fireplace, pretty much everything else is going to change. Maybe you'd like to see the blueprints?"

"Cut. Josie, Courtney is the one who decides in what direction the conversation is going. Just respond to her questions, please."

"Oh, of course."

"So is this canoe going to hang in the house once it's remodeled?"

"Yes."

"And is it the only original decoration that will remain?"

"Well, there's a sculpture next to the fireplace. It was created by a famous artist and will be in the new living room as well."

"Maybe you could come down from there and we could look at the blueprints for this project?"

"Sure, Courtney. That's a great idea." She heard some snickering from her crew, but maybe the audience would think it was just some sort of construction noise. She made some unnecessary noise coming down the ladder, trying to cover it up. "I think the blues are on the counter in the kitchen."

"Well, let's go look at them, shall we?"

Thank God! Knees shaking from stress, Josie started to walk toward the kitchen.

"Cut!"

She jumped and looked around. That hadn't been Bobby Valentine's voice.

"Keep going in that direction and those women will be in the next shot," the cameraman warned them.

Bobby Valentine stopped in his tracks. "I see what you mean, but we don't want to give the impression that Josie and Courtney are here alone. I mean, it doesn't hurt to have people in the background shots."

"Maybe they could be working out on the deck and the camera could sort of glimpse them through the window. You know, enough to see people—women—working, but not enough so that they can be identified later."

"Great. Good. Super. How about it, ladies?"

"Do you all mind?" Josie asked. She was beginning to feel very frustrated by this whole operation.

"We don't mind at all," Jill said, a smile on her face as she hurried out of camera range. Dottie, as usual, looked disgruntled. And Annette, spying Chad Henshaw carrying a load of lights toward the house, hurried in his direction.

"Josie, those blues are interesting and we'll be referring to them as we go through the other shows, but right now I want to ask you about your past, about what led you to be a carpenter in the first place."

"I . . . Courtney wanted you to ask me these questions?"

"Cut! I have a list here. It won't take long, but answer as briefly as possible and PLEASE remember you're talking to Courtney, as well as to thirteen or fourteen million viewers."

"Thirteen . . . Well, go ahead."

"Tell us a bit about your background. Where did you grow up, for instance?"

"I . . . I grew up in a small town, a suburb really, of Philadelphia."

"Really? And what led you into carpentry? And to this island?"

"Well, I . . . um . . . that's not easy to answer."

"Were there builders in your family? Did you have any particular role model?"

Josie laughed. "No, my family specialized in bankers and businessmen, not builders. I . . . Do you think I need to answer these questions? They're sort of private."

"Cut!" There was a scowl forming on Bobby Valentine's usually happy face. "Look, half of this stuff will end up on the cutting-room floor. But Courtney wanted these questions asked for background information and we're going to do it. And I don't know about you, but I'd sure like to get it over with."

"Fine. Take . . . whatever."

"Scene two. Take two. I'll ask the next question on this sheet. How many years ago did you begin your career as a carpenter?"

Well, that one was easy. "Almost sixteen years, Courtney."

"There are a fair amount of women in the building trades these days, Josie, but that wasn't true back then—"

"No, it wasn't. Oh, you hadn't asked the question, had you? Sorry. Cut."

"Keep rolling, we'll edit later. There are a fair number of women in the building trades these days, Josie, but that wasn't true back then. What did your family think of your decision to pursue such an unusual career?"

"I . . . They . . . I had an infant son at the time and he just loved hanging around construction sites. In fact, the crew I was working on then got together at lunchtime and made him the most wonderful set of blocks out of leftover hardwoods. He still has them and he's a teenager now."

"Cut! Look, that's all very interesting, but I don't think it's the way Courtney expected you to answer her question."

"Why?"

"She has lots of questions here about high school."

"Like what?"

"Whether you took shop classes."

"No. That's not a very interesting answer, is it?"

"Let's try the next one. Did you take home economics?"

"It was a required course when I was in high school."

"And did you do well?"

"Not really."

"What happened? Did the hems you sewed fall apart? Did you burn the hot chocolate? Stuff like that?"

"It's almost as though you were there to see it, Courtney." Josie tried to keep the annoyance out of her voice. After all, Courtney was dead. It was stupid to be angry at her. But she couldn't seem to help herself. "Just because I didn't get all A's like you did—" She realized what she was saying and stopped speaking.

Bobby Valentine was looking at her with a strange expression on his face. "So it's true. You and Courtney do have a past in common."

"I . . ." The camera rolled on, but she had no idea what to say.

"Let me ask you one more question, Josie. Do you know what happened to Courtney?"

"I . . ."

"Because she said you would."

"She said what?"

"She said if something happened to her, I should ask you about it."

Josie opened her mouth, but nothing came out. And the camera rolled on.

SEVENTEEN

"**T**URN OFF THAT damn camera!" Josie glared over Bobby Valentine's shoulder at the cameraman.

"Yeah, cut! Why don't we all take a coffee break? We can continue this later."

Josie wasn't accustomed to taking breaks before work had even begun, but she didn't see that she had any choice. "Just let me get my crew back in here working and we can find someplace more private to talk." She didn't wait for him to argue; she had a responsibility to the homeowners and her employees. She hurried out the back door to where the women were waiting for her. She had expected to find them idle. To her delight, they were prefabricating new frames for all the windows. She had a twinge of guilt; she should be working alongside her crew.

"How's it going?" Dottie asked, standing.

"Not well," Josie admitted. "Bobby Valentine knows that I grew up with Courtney."

Annette gasped, and Josie realized she had just explained more than she had planned to. "I . . . I can't imagine that my past has anything, anything at all, to do with Courtney's murder. I know I'm asking you to take my word for it, but—"

"Who else knows she's dead?" Dottie interrupted to ask.

"I . . . I didn't tell anyone. As far as I know, no one else knows."

"You should keep it that way," Dottie stated flatly. "And maybe we should all get together later to talk."

Josie stared at the other woman for a moment, taking her time to decide. "You're right." Annette's and Jill's faces also displayed concern. "I have to talk to Bobby Valentine and I won't tell him about . . . Courtney, but I hate to lose more work time. Would it be possible for us to meet for dinner tonight at the office? Pizza and beer? My treat."

"Sounds good to me."

"Me, too."

"Count me in."

Annette and Jill agreed with Dottie.

"Good. I'd better get going then. I'll be back as soon as I can."

"Don't worry about it. We'll go ahead and demo the south wall and then we can start framing in the second-floor addition."

"Great." With a new crew, there was always a moment when Josie realized that either she had hired the right people or she hadn't. This was the moment. And she had.

She left to find Bobby Valentine, knowing that she could depend upon these women to keep going.

Chad was near the front deck. "Mr. Valentine said he would be waiting for you in Courtney's trailer. It's the one with the show's logo stenciled on the doors."

"Thanks." She started toward the street and then turned back to the young man. "I hear you and Annette are dating."

"Uh, yeah."

"I don't want to be a busybody, but I think it's nice. I mean, that you two are seeing each other. You're both new on the island and it can be lonely." She realized she sounded like an idiot and changed the subject. "Courtney's trailer is the one with the logo on the doors? Is that what you said?"

Chad looked at her as if he thought she had lost her mind. "Yeah. That's the one. I . . . I'll see you."

"Yes. Sure." Why didn't she shut up? Her father had said she babbled like a brook when she was nervous—and after all these years she could still feel the sting of his comments. Well, she had more important things to worry about now. She continued on her way.

There were two trailers on the street, but only one carried the gold castle with COURTNEY CASTLE printed in a circle around it, and that one also displayed an open door. Josie climbed the two steps that hung from its side and called out, "Hello. Bobby?"

"Josie. Come on in. Close the door behind you."

She did as he ordered, again amazed by the interior of Courtney's trailer. But apparently she wasn't going to have a lot of time to look around.

"Sit down. I think we need to have an honest talk."

Josie sat on the edge of the plush chintz-covered couch. She wasn't going to get comfortable until she found out exactly how much he knew about Courtney's past—and hers.

But it seemed that he was the one who was going to ask the questions. "So, Josie Pigeon, how much do you know about all this?"

"I . . . To be honest, I have no idea what you're asking me. What do I know about the show? About why you're here? How you all found Island Contracting? I don't know anything. And I think I should be the one asking the questions and you should be providing the answers." She leaned back and felt something stabbing at her spine. Glad to have something to do in the awkward silence that seemed to be forming, she pulled out a pillow and examined it carefully.

"A gift from a fan. Courtney gets hundreds, thousands, every year."

Josie stared down at the pillow in her lap. She didn't know much about handwork, but this elaborately embroidered throw pillow displayed dozens of different (and complicated-looking) stitches in even more hues of threads. The part that had stabbed her was worked in metallic threads. It was Courtney's castle. But the words around the logo were different. " 'Courtney Castle's Crewel Work?' " she read, then turned and picked up another pillow. This one was needlepoint—that much she knew from the endless floral monstrosities her mother had worked on for years and years. The castle was the same (although slightly tilted), but the script around the seal read "Stencil with Courtney Castle." She looked up at Bobby Valentine. "This isn't Courtney's first show?"

"Not by a long shot. But we think she's finally found her niche. Or I suppose I should say that's what we did think."

"What do you think now?"

"I don't know what to think, frankly." Bobby Valentine looked her straight in the eye and Josie wondered if he was about to lie—or tell the truth. "You and Courtney grew up together."

She didn't know what he knew, but she didn't feel obligated to increase his knowledge. "We lived in the same town."

"I understood you were friends."

"Our mothers were friends."

"You went to high school together."

Josie remembered the question he had asked about home economics class. No reason to deny it. "Yes."

"And college."

"We started at the same college," she admitted.

"But you were never close."

"Bobby, I don't know what Courtney told you, but we hated each other."

He didn't respond.

"What did she tell you?" she asked.

"That you were good friends."

"What?" Josie squealed. "No way!"

"Well, not friends exactly. She said she was sort of your mentor. That you were one of those shy, awkward, unpopular kids—"

"Did she mention my adolescent acne?"

"I don't think so." He squinted at her freckled face.

"I was kidding."

"Oh."

"And isn't a mentor someone who supports another person, helps her along in life?"

"Sort of."

"Then Courtney wasn't mine. Believe me, she didn't want me to get ahead and she didn't help me to get ahead. Ever."

"She said . . ." Bobby Valentine stopped without revealing what Courtney had said.

"She said what? What about me? What about my relationship with her? And when did she say it to you?"

"Excuse me?"

Josie stuffed all the pillows behind her back and relaxed a bit. "Tell me," she demanded. "Tell me what Courtney said about me."

"Well, she said a lot, but not in any particular order. I mean, I just might have confused or forgotten some of the details."

"What did she say?" Josie repeated.

"Let me think. If I tell you how the story came out, maybe you'll understand why I'm sort of reluctant to tell you. It wasn't a cohesive tale."

"Do me a favor. I have work to get done. Just tell me the general idea and I won't blame you for leaving out the many details."

"Well, I don't think she told me anything about you when we were first talking about the project."

"How did you come to choose this job to feature on your program?"

"I don't remember. We're always looking for something unusual. A house of historical interest. A conversion of an industrial site into homes. A job that takes place in Hawaii in the middle of winter."

"You're kidding."

"About Hawaii? Nope. *Courtney Castle's Castles* has taped remodeling jobs in Maui, Honolulu, and St. Thomas—three winters, three shows. Why freeze when you can get a tan while you work?"

"I suppose. So, how did you find those jobs?"

"Well, we get lots of letters from people who think their remodeling job should be on television. Some think it would be interesting to get the publicity, some think they'll get special deals from workmen and suppliers if they're on the show. Others want free advice from experts."

"So you pick from the people who write?"

"Not always. We've been doing this show for almost four years. We have lots of professional contacts looking out for interesting projects."

"But this job. How did you hear about it?"

Bobby Valentine shook his head. "I don't remember exactly. It seems to me that we got a message from someone here in town. A neighbor maybe."

Josie thought for a moment before asking the next question. "Did you hear about the job itself or about Island Contracting?"

"Frankly, I don't know. But I do know that what makes this an interesting story is you and the women on your crew. I can't imagine any other big selling point, so I would assume that's what we heard." He gave her his intent "I'm telling the truth here" stare.

"But you don't know who you heard it from."

"No."

"Or who was contacted at the show."

"Well, come to think of it, that was probably Courtney

herself. I think I first heard about it from her. She was excited about the idea of an all-women contracting company. Thought we could sell it to a station for their fund-raising period. Financing like that is important for us. Our productions aren't produced by a single station, and while we have a few backers—a charitable foundation, a paint company, and a chain of hardware stores at present—we still need station support if we're going to keep producing shows. And the stations are always looking for something to put on during their fund-raisers that won't drive away the audience."

Josie wasn't interested in the financial woes of public television; she returned to the subject at hand. "So you think someone from the island called Courtney and told her about me."

"About Island Contracting. I know I didn't hear about you until fairly recently."

"But Courtney might have known about me earlier and just not spoken about it, right?"

"It's possible."

"Look, what sort of relationship do you and Courtney have?"

"If you're asking if we're lovers—"

Actually, she would love to know if that was true, but it really wasn't the question she meant to ask. "No. I mean, is she always honest with you?"

It was a simple question but it seemed to give him pause. "Courtney is talent."

"So?"

"Have you been around television people before?"

"I remodeled a house for a director and his . . . well, I always assumed she was his wife while I was working, but later I heard that his wife wanted the house as part of her divorce settlement. And he claimed she had no right to it as she had never seen it; his poor mistress had had all the wear and tear of remodeling. Weird."

"Compared to the ego of your average on-air personality, that's nothing. Courtney isn't the worst of the lot, but she has her moments. Well, all you have to do is look around this place and you know that. Her life story is here." He waved to the wall behind her, which was covered with awards and photographs. They were reflected in the mirrors across the way, but Josie hadn't had the time to examine them. "And the first thing Courtney does when anyone comes to interview her is go around this room and relate what she considers the fascinating high points of her life."

"I don't understand what that has to do with her honesty—or lack of it."

"It's not that this stuff is lies, it's more like it shows only the side of things that Courtney wants to present to the world. And that's kind of the way she lives. If there's something negative in her past, you won't hear about it from her. And that's the way she lives her life—with an emphasis on the positive. Which means she doesn't always tell the truth. Period."

"Oh." Josie thought that was interesting. "So you first heard about this project from Courtney, but you don't know how she heard about it. And, really, you don't know if she would have told you the truth even if she had told you."

"I guess you could put it that way."

"Do you think she wrote the note?"

"The one that was interpreted as being about her murder?"

"It's the only one I've heard of."

"I'm sure she wrote it. It was in her handwriting. But, Josie, it had nothing to do with her disappearance or anything. The note was just part of a piece of paper; the other half was found on the floor when the place was searched. The entire note was "Kill *Courtney Castle's Castles* segment three.' It was no big deal. Courtney was making notes about the show. She had decided to leave out one segment and put in another."

"What were they? The segment she wanted left out and the substitution?" Josie asked.

"The original segment was a short tour of the neighborhood, probably a comparison of all the similar houses. She was substituting a segment about the background and training of your workers."

"Which is why she wanted so many questions asked about that subject," Josie mused. "Did Courtney really have that much power? Did she choose what subjects you covered?"

"Hey, she's the talent."

Josie thought for a moment. He still hadn't answered her original questions. "So what exactly did she say about me?"

"She said that she had helped you and that you betrayed her."

"What?"

"She claimed you seduced her boyfriend." He looked skeptical.

"And you believed her story?"

"Hey, she's talent," he repeated.

EIGHTEEN

JOSIE HAD PICKED up three pizzas as well as two six-packs of Coors and one of Diet Coke. But even after a hard day no one seemed particularly hungry. Everyone had been talking about Courtney and what to do with her body since they walked in the door, still sweaty from work.

So far, they had consumed one pepperoni pizza, half of the cheese with extra garlic, and all the beer. Annette seemed to be a bit tipsy. Josie realized she had been serving beer to a minor and decided the only thing to do was to make sure Annette had a ride home—after they made some decisions.

If they ever came to an agreement. The women had repeated and repeated the details of the day. Their shock at the discovery of Courtney's body. Their panic when it looked like Bobby Valentine might discover their secret. The long afternoon, not talking about what was uppermost on their minds, waiting for this evening so they could.

"We need to come to some decision," Josie insisted. "Courtney cannot stay up there. She is going to start to smell soon." A giggle escaped her lips. "And she would really hate that." She felt another giggle bubble up and pursed her lips. Perhaps Annette wasn't the only woman who had had too much to drink.

"What do you suggest?" Jill asked quietly. Jill had been noticeably reticent, eating and drinking little, walking around the room examining the birdhouses that lined the small space.

"Frankly, I have no idea what to say. My instinct is to call the police—" Josie said.

"Good God. Why?" Dottie's flat voice interrupted.

"They're here to help us," Annette said.

"Bull."

"Well, I don't know how you were brought up, but my mother always said that if there was a problem I could go to the cop on the corner for help. Or dial 911," Annette added.

"Your mother may have been right for where you grew up. But the police on this island are notorious for arresting the wrong person. And I'm afraid the wrong person they arrest for Courtney's murder could be . . ." Josie paused. "Could be one of us."

Dottie looked at Josie. "Do you want to tell her or do you want me to?"

"I . . . It's your business. You should be able to keep it private if you want" was Josie's answer.

"Yeah, I should be able to. But in my life, what should be and what are are two different animals."

"I don't know what you're talking about, but you're entitled to your privacy," Jill said.

"She's right," Josie agreed.

"Yeah. But I think I should explain. Otherwise no one is going to understand why I think we should—or should not—call the cops."

"Listen, it's completely your decision." Josie had hoped it wouldn't come to this, but she understood what Dottie was up against.

"Okay. No point in beating about the bush. I was in prison."

Neither Annette nor Jill spoke.

"I think if you're going to say that much, you're going to

have to explain what put you in prison and how you ended up at Island Contracting," Josie suggested quietly.

"What put me in prison was stupidity and how I ended up here is Josie."

"Maybe you should tell them just a bit more," Josie said.

"Prison?" The word just reached Annette's consciousness.

"Yeah, I was there for assault. I beat up some idiot in a bar fight. Turned out his brother-in-law was a cop. I didn't deny doing it. The bastard deserved what he got. But I didn't deserve three years in prison. In some circles, punching that guy in the mouth would have been considered a public service."

"Why? Why did you do it?" Annette asked.

"Guy called me a dyke. Said working as a carpenter wasn't an appropriate job for a woman. He kept trashing me. And I got angrier and angrier and drank a bit too much. On the way out of the bar, he grabbed my breast and I slugged him—once or twice."

"And you were arrested?" Annette sounded horrified.

"Yeah. And a few months later convicted. I got six years. But served slightly less than three. I was released early because of good behavior—and because Josie was willing to hire me. But maybe you would like to explain about that."

"Well, it's a long story. I don't know whether you know the history of Island Contracting, but it was begun by a man named Noel Roberts and he tried to hire people who needed help."

"Women who needed help?"

"I'm not sure he set out to hire women, whether women just happened to need more help than men, or whether he was one of the only contractors who would hire women workers. It was the early sixties. There weren't many women in the business and the ones who were had a very difficult time finding jobs."

"What did he do? Put an ad in the paper asking for women

who needed help and were trained carpenters or plumbers or electricians to apply to Island Contracting?" Jill asked.

"No, he was more . . . what's the word? More proactive than that. For instance, I was pregnant and waiting on tables at a luncheonette here on the island when I met Noel. We chatted a few times when he came in to eat and one day he asked me to have dinner with him." Josie smiled, remembering that afternoon. It had been unseasonably hot. The air-conditioning hadn't been turned on yet. She had been seven months pregnant with swollen feet and sweating profusely as she worked. It had never occurred to her that Noel might be making a pass. She had accepted out of curiosity and because, in her financial situation, a free meal was something she couldn't pass up.

"It was at that dinner that he made his offer. I could come to work for him—in the office, if necessary, and bring the baby if I couldn't find anyone to take care of him—and he would teach me a trade and keep me employed and—this was the most important thing then—insured.

"I didn't even stop to think, I had agreed before I finished my salad." She had already been living in Risa's house but had never suspected that her landlady would be willing—in fact, thrilled—to sit with Tyler until he was old enough for day care.

"And over the years, I learned that Noel hired many women under similar, if not identical, circumstances. So when Sam told me about Second Chance—"

"What's that?" Annette asked.

"Second Chance is an organization dedicated to keeping recidivism rates low," Dottie explained.

"It's made up of people who believe that those who are convicted of a crime are less likely to end up in prison again if they are given a second chance to live a normal life. And that the first thing necessary for a normal life is a job. Sam's known about the organization for years."

"Sam Richardson? The guy you date who owns the liquor store? Why would he know about it?" Jill asked.

"He used to be a prosecuting attorney in New York City," Josie explained.

"Oh?"

"Yeah, in fact, he was involved with the group when he was in New York, and he still keeps in touch and gets their newsletters. So when he read that they were looking for placements for women who had been trained in nontraditional jobs—for women that is—he told me about it and I sent in Island Contracting's address."

"And when I was up for parole, I was put in contact with Second Chance and they sent me Josie's name."

"Most of the prisoners . . . people . . ."

"Call us prisoners. That's what we were."

"Well, most of them had been trained while they were in prison," Josie continued to explain. "But Dottie had been a carpenter before she was arrested, and, frankly, I thought I was lucky to get her."

"And I thought I was lucky to be here . . . until that snotty bitch was murdered."

"Why?" Annette asked.

"Look, I'm on probation. And one of the many terms of my probation is that I'm not supposed to be fraternizing with the criminal element—and I think you could probably call the person who killed Courtney Castle a criminal—so I just hope it wasn't one of you."

The words were spoken casually, but Josie knew the situation and knew Dottie was dead serious. "And that's why Dottie believes we shouldn't tell the police about Courtney's body."

"Yes. Not only am I the most likely suspect, but I think you could say that being a suspect in a murder investigation violates the terms of my parole."

Annette nodded. "You'd end up back in prison."

"Got it in one."

"I go along with Dottie." Jill spoke up. "I don't think we should tell them either. What do you think, Josie?"

Josie took a deep breath. "I tend to agree with you two. The police on the island are . . . well, they're not exactly competent. But we all have to agree to keep silent. If one of us doesn't go along, we're all in trouble."

"She's talking about you," Dottie said, pointing to Annette.

The young woman nodded seriously. "But it is illegal to withhold evidence in a murder investigation. I've seen it on TV."

"Yes, but, in fact, we've already done that."

Annette looked up at Dottie, her eyes opening wider. "You're right. I didn't think."

"Look, the truth is, you either believe I did it and then you should call the cops and we'll all be questioned and I'll be arrested. Or you believe I didn't do it and we shut up until the real murderer is found."

"Oh, I'd never think that you killed anybody!"

"Until a few minutes ago, you probably never would have thought that I'd been convicted of assault and spent three years in prison." Dottie's voice was surprisingly gentle.

"I guess that's true. But it's different. You were angry at someone for insulting you and you just hit him. You didn't murder him. And, besides, you have no reason to be angry at Courtney Castle. She didn't do anything to you."

"As far as you know," Dottie said.

"You were in prison for the last three years, what could she do?"

"Listen"—Dottie reached out and put a hand on Annette's arm—"you're a sweet kid. But you haven't been around much and I gotta tell you: You really don't know me. I mean, I appreciate that you believe in me, but, honey, what you've heard about prison is true. Everyone's got a sob story to tell and most of 'em are lies."

"Are you lying to me?"

"No. No, I'm not."

"Then I agree with you all. We shouldn't tell the police anything!"

Josie sighed, relieved. "Fine. We will keep the information to ourselves. But there's one other question. What are we going to do with the body?"

"We could just leave it up there and, when it starts to smell, climb on up and claim to have discovered it then. Of course, that doesn't really help us, does it? I mean, the police would investigate and Dottie would be arrested, et cetera, et cetera," Jill said, looking worried.

"We could hide the body, find out who the murderer is, and then turn both the body and the murderer over to the police," Annette suggested. "Just like Chad's mother does."

"Oh, yeah, and we could rent us a big barn and put on a show and raise money for the orphans." Dottie's sarcasm couldn't be missed.

"I'm just trying to help," Annette protested.

"And you are," Josie said firmly. "If you think about it, Annette has come up with the only solution that will keep Dottie out of prison. Anything else will mean calling in the police and they'll arrest Dottie, for parole violation if not murder."

"So what are we going to do with Courtney? Dump her in the ocean?" Jill asked.

"We can't do that!" Annette cried. "Someone might see us!"

"We can't do that because, on the off chance that this scheme to find the murderer actually works, we're going to have to provide the police with Courtney's corpse." Dottie was blunt.

"So we need to store her somewhere." Josie couldn't imagine where. "What we need is some sort of large refrigerator or a freezer. Can you tell if a body's been frozen after it thaws out?"

"Haven't the foggiest," Dottie answered.

"Well, if it got freezer burn . . ." Jill seemed about to giggle and Annette snorted.

Josie realized they were all tired and very close to hysteria. "Sam has a large refrigerator at the back of the store. I don't know how we could sneak her in there—"

"No way." Dottie was adamant.

"What's wrong with that? We can trust Sam."

"I'm not trusting anyone who was a prosecutor, I can tell you that right now."

"If it weren't for Sam, you wouldn't be here. You might not even have a job. You might not have gotten parole," Josie protested.

"You think he's going to break the law just to keep me out of prison?"

It didn't sound all that likely to Josie either. Maybe they could hide the body in his refrigerator without him knowing.

Jill seemed to read her mind. "How big is this refrigerator? Maybe we could sort of shove her in a place where she won't be found."

"I've got it!" Excited, Josie jumped up. "We can put it . . . her down in one of the freezers behind the Fish Wish."

"That's a restaurant?"

"It's the bait shop. And they have a freezer in the back of the store just filled with boxes and boxes of frozen moss bunker. We could put Courtney underneath. She'll be safe there for months—they don't get down to the bottom of that freezer until late August."

"And what are you going to do? Just walk in and ask

if you can use their freezer to store a famous television personality?"

"No, I thought maybe we could sneak in there in the middle of the night and put her away. I have the key to their back door. We're going to be adding a deck out back as soon as we finish this job."

"Then I guess we know what we have to do," Dottie said, getting up and stretching.

"What?" Annette asked.

"Go get Courtney and take her to the . . . what did you call it? The Fish Wish."

NINETEEN

THEY SPLIT UP and drove back to the work site in two cars. Josie made sure that Dottie traveled with her.

"It was good of you to talk about your past." She started the conversation as she steered her truck away from the curb. "I know it wasn't easy."

"Didn't have a choice, did I?"

"You could have lied."

"But you knew the truth."

"When you came to work for me, I told you I'd keep your secret."

"And you would, wouldn't you? You know, you're a good person. I haven't run into a whole lot of good people in the past few years." Dottie was silent for a moment. "You didn't sleep with that Noel person to get him to leave you his business, did you?"

Josie was shocked. "I . . . No, is that what you thought?"

"I didn't know. It did strike me as a possibility. I mean, most men don't just leave a business to a good friend."

"Noel wasn't most men."

"Look, I'm offending you and I sure didn't mean to. What I'm trying to say is thank you and that Noel Roberts left his business to the right person."

"I shouldn't get upset. You aren't the first person to wonder about my relationship with Noel and you won't be the last.

It's been a difficult day for us all." She stopped the truck for a group of giggling teenage girls, their blankets dragging on the road as they crossed to get to the beach. "They look like they're about to have a good time, don't they? Not a care in the world, as my mother would say."

"They're young. Wait until they get older. They'll do less giggling then," Dottie predicted.

Josie thought about Tyler. He was probably the same age as these girls. "I hope you're wrong," she said fervently.

"That Annette is just a kid," Dottie said.

Josie got the impression that the other woman wanted to change the subject. "Yes. In fact, I think she's the youngest carpenter Island Contracting has had. But I think she's going to work out."

"She knows what she's doing."

"She went to a vocational school upstate. Their graduates are working for other contractors on the island. Far as I know, everyone's pretty happy with them. Of course, the others are male."

"Women have to be twice as good as men to survive in this business."

"You know, I used to think the same thing, but then I ran across some truly incompetent women, so bad I had a hard time figuring out how they got their licenses, who trained them. And then I realized that there were men who wanted all those women to be bad carpenters or whatever because that confirmed their own prejudices. I've been a bit more careful about hiring people since I figured that out."

"Bastards."

"I won't argue with you about that," Josie said, remembering a few of the disastrous hires she'd made before she realized what was going on. It had been difficult for the company, but worse on the young women who, thinking they had the training necessary for a viable career, suddenly found themselves out the money it had cost them to be trained and without employment.

"What do you think about Jill?" Dottie suddenly changed the subject.

Josie was reluctant to discuss one worker with another. "She seems to be a good carpenter. And she's worked for four or five years. She wasn't hired straight out of school. And she had very good references from her last job. She worked out in the Pacific Northwest."

"She didn't want to tell the police about the body."

Josie thought about that for a minute. "Neither did I. Neither did you."

"And we both have good reasons for that. But Annette thought we should. If you think about it, you realize anyone who is innocent will think we should."

"I don't know about that," Josie answered slowly. "Maybe Jill just doesn't like authority figures or something." They had arrived at the house; Josie parked at the curb and both women jumped out before resuming their conversation.

"Like maybe she knows what they can do to an innocent person," Dottie suggested as they walked up to the front door.

"That's not necessarily so."

"Maybe not. But it's something to think about because there's one thing wrong with all this."

"What?" Josie asked, turning the key in the lock and pushing open the door.

"We all have to depend on one another. If one person goes to the police, we're all in trouble. That's what's wrong with this plan."

"Maybe," Josie said, walking in the door and flipping on the light switch. "But it looks to me like it's not all that's wrong with this plan."

"What else?"

"It looks like someone got to the body before us."

Dottie peered over Josie's shoulder. "Oh, shit."

There was a scrambling behind them and then Jill and Annette appeared.

"What the—"

But Jill's assessment echoed Dottie's. "Oh, shit."

The canoe was in the middle of the floor. Empty. The blanket that had been tucked around Courtney had been left behind.

"Turn off the light," Dottie hissed.

"What . . . Oh, you're right!" Josie reached out, flipped the switch, and plunged them into darkness.

"What are we going to do?" Annette's question came out as a whimper.

"Excellent question."

"Guess we don't have to worry about telling the police anything." Josie thought she heard relief in Jill's voice.

"Unless the police are the ones who found the body and took it away," Dottie suggested.

"How would they have known about her?" Annette asked.

Josie had been looking around. "I don't think it was them. If the police had found her, they would still be investigating— or if not, they would have hung that yellow scene-of-the-crime tape around the place." In the past, she had illegally crossed that tape more times than she wanted to think about.

"So who was it?" Annette persisted.

"Could have been one of those television people," Jill said.

"But wouldn't they have called the police?"

"Maybe they have a good reason not to," Josie suggested. It was dusk and there was ample light to examine the room, but that would change as soon as the sun set. "Maybe we should look around—but don't touch anything! Whoever moved the body might have left a clue to his or her identity, and if we don't find it before it gets dark, it would be nice if it was still here in the morning."

"What are we looking for?" Jill asked.

"Clues!" Annette sounded excited. "Pieces of fabric that might have been ripped from clothing as someone dragged the body across the floor. Hairs. Cigarette butts. Maybe even a glove or something like that!"

"Or if we're really lucky, a small pile of the perpetrator's DNA."

"I don't think . . . You're kidding me, aren't you?"

"I am. And I shouldn't be," Dottie said. "As the boss says, let's search. We don't have a lot of time to lose."

"Where do we start?"

"With the canoe," Josie said with more assurance and authority than she was feeling. "How was it taken down? Is there anything in it? Any sign of how Courtney was killed?"

"Excuse me?"

Josie looked at Dottie. "It would be interesting to know how she was killed, wouldn't it?"

"I don't know about everyone else, but I thought we knew how. At least, I thought you knew how it was done. You were up there so close to her for such a long time."

"There was no sign—"

"No gunshot wound?"

"No knife sticking out of her chest?"

"No long, thin cord tied tightly around her neck?"

"I didn't even see any bruises." Josie answered their questions. "She was covered with a blanket. Well, not exactly covered. It wasn't over her head or anything like that. It was lying across her from her feet up to her chest—and tucked in neatly. Almost as though she had been asleep. But she wasn't sleeping," she added quickly before Annette could jump to another conclusion. "I'm sure she was dead. She was . . . well, I'm sure she was dead." She glanced around the room.

"Look, there's nothing here that we didn't put here. One of

us might recognize something that doesn't belong, something that has been moved, something different. All we can do is look."

They looked. Fifteen minutes later they had nothing. No clues and no ideas. The canoe had been hung from the rafters by a metal chain attached to large metal hooks screwed into beams across the ceiling. The hooks were still there. The chain was piled neatly in the bottom of the canoe. Island Contracting's policy was to keep a neat workplace. It impressed the customers and saved time in the long run. Nothing, as far as anyone could tell, had been moved. Since the house was unoccupied, there was a lot of dust around. Now that layer of dust was full of scuffed footprints and other marks of human habitation. There was no way of knowing which, if any, had been made by whoever had removed Courtney's body.

It was getting dark. They were going to be forced to turn on the lights or leave. Josie picked the last option. "Time to go. If there's anything here, we've missed it—"

"Shut up! Someone's outside."

"Get down! Shh!"

At Josie's order, the women dropped to the floor

"Do you think it's the murderer?" Annette sounded terrified.

"Shh!"

"Josie! I know you're here. Where are you?"

She recognized the voice and stood. "Everything's all right. It's Sam."

"Who?"

"Her boyfriend, stupid!"

Josie ignored her crew's comments. "Sam. We're in here, Sam!"

"Who's we? Did you have some trouble with the electricity? Why are all the lights off?"

"We . . . we didn't want anyone to know we were here. I'll explain later," she added.

"Fine. Are you ready to go?"

"Wh—"

"You were meeting Tyler and me for dinner."

"Oh, I forgot! It's late! Tyler must be starving!"

"Tyler is fine. I fed him an entire pizza with the works and he's gone home to watch videos."

Josie instantly reverted to mother mode. "He's had pizza two nights in a row. And he watches videos at that store all day. Shouldn't he be out getting some fresh air?"

"He's fine. We ate at a table on the boardwalk. He's had his daily allotment of air—and cheese. I, on the other hand, am starving."

"Oh, Sam . . ."

"We'd better get going now that we've finished up here." Dottie spoke up.

"Yeah, good night." Jill picked up the hint.

"See you in the morning," Annette added, sounding a bit doubtful.

"Why doesn't Dottie drive the truck and Jill the Jeep," Josie suggested. "Annette can ride."

"Okay."

"Good night."

"Good night. Thanks for everything." Josie realized they all wanted to get out of there as soon as possible. She felt the same way. "You must be starving," she said, looking up at Sam with a smile on her face.

"I am. Good night, ladies." He waited until they were alone and then put both hands on Josie's shoulders and turned her toward him. "What is going on here, Josie?"

She had a question of her own. "How did you know I was here?"

"Your truck and the Island Contracting Jeep are parked out front. I even know that you were at your office earlier."

"The same way, right?"

"Your truck was parked outside. Anyone could tell you were there."

"I never thought about that." Josie spoke slowly.

"So are you going to tell me what's going on now? Or do you want to wait until we get to the restaurant?"

Josie decided that wasn't the time to tell him that she had already eaten. "Let's go to the restaurant. We can talk there."

And she would have the entire drive to decide just how much she was going to tell him.

TWENTY

JOSIE GOT INTO Sam's antique MGB. "Do I need to go home and change? Where are we going?" she asked, peering through the windshield.

"How about Basil's new spot? I'd like to try it and he won't care what you look like. Although you look very nice," Sam lied diplomatically.

"I didn't know his new place was open yet."

"You've had other things to think about. It opened last week. I hope we can get a table."

Josie didn't answer. Sam was just making conversation. They both knew Basil would fit them in someplace.

"I saw the menu when Basil was placing his wine order. This should be an interesting meal."

"I don't remember exactly what he was planning. I know he was talking about a Southwestern theme emphasizing fish on the menu—or was it Thai?" She was momentarily diverted. She'd eaten earlier but, in fact, was always hungry. And Basil's meals were always worth relishing.

"He couldn't make up his mind. So he decided to try a multi-cultural approach. All the main courses emphasize fish, but the recipes are Thai, Tex-Mex, Caribbean, American Southern, Cajun, French, even a bit of English—Basil thought he needed to provide fish and chips for families who want to eat with their children."

173

"Interesting."

"As is his selection of wines. If I buy a bottle of good Chardonnay, will you at least tell me a bit of what's going on?"

Josie opened her mouth to protest and then shut it again. Sam knew her. He knew she wouldn't have been leading her crew around that house long after the workday had ended unless she had a good reason to be there. And he knew there was something odd about doing it in the dark. She leaned back against the soft glove-leather seat (original equipment) and closed her eyes. "Yes. In fact, I'd like to ask your advice. Just don't tell me we should go to the police. We already decided against that."

It was dark; her eyes were closed. She didn't see Sam roll his eyes. "You're making me very nervous" was all he said.

"Join the crowd." She opened her eyes as the car made a sharp turn. "Are we already there?"

"Yup. But I don't see anyplace to park. Is that car coming or going?"

It turned out to be leaving and they slid easily into the spot vacated by the big white Lincoln Town Car. They both got out, and as Sam locked the doors, Josie stared up at the bright sign over the long one-story building. A KETTLE OF FISH was spelled out in green neon light. They walked under the sign and through a door decorated with an imaginative underwater scene.

Josie looked around curiously. Island Contracting had remodeled two of Basil's five restaurants, but he had bought this building recently and decided to go through this season with what he called "a little minor decorating."

What was minor decorating for Basil would have been considered a major project by almost anyone else. The walls had been painted with white gloss paint and displayed fish, not the normal stuffed variety, but the type found in galleries in SoHo, fish formed of every material: glass, pottery, fabric, metals, painted on paper, made from paper, and displayed on paper. The effect was unique, modern, and chic. Just the sort of environment to attract the type of people who work in the media, she realized, spying Bobby Valentine at a large table with three members of his crew.

"What's wrong?" Sam asked as she hesitated.

"I . . . I was wondering if there's a table free. But . . . not too close to Bobby Valentine."

"Why are you avoiding him? I thought you all were getting along just fine."

"We are, but . . . Well, I thought we were going to have a chance to talk."

"And you don't want him to overhear what we're talking about?"

"Exactly."

"No problem. We'll just tell Basil—"

"You'll just tell Basil what?"

He was right behind them. They turned and were confronted with a remarkable sight. Basil Tilby had outdone himself. His long legs were encased in dark green slacks. His shoes were silver. He had on a T-shirt of the same shade as his pants, but his jacket was a work of art. Fashioned of canvas, it had been painted with mythical creatures of the deep. Aquarius poured water from a large urn across Basil's shoulders. Mermaids swirled about his lapels. Josie was speechless.

"We'd like a table, but preferably on that side of the room." Sam pointed away from Bobby Valentine's party.

"No problem. Most of my customers prefer the other. Let's see . . . How about that small one by the window?"

"Perfect." Sam looked around. "Is this the smoking area?"

"No, all smoking is done on the enclosed porch."

"Then why is that the most popular side of the room? This is just as charming and it has a view."

"That side has become our own little media hangout."

"We noticed the people from Courtney's show there."

"They've been here every night since we opened. And where they go on the island, crowds follow, as Josie knows by now. I can't complain. I've never had a restaurant become popular so quickly."

"Has Courtney shown up recently?" Sam asked, sitting down across from Josie.

"Nope. But the crowd keeps hoping and her producer says she'll be here any day now."

"Really?" Josie felt she had to say something.

"Yes. How is it working with her?" Basil asked, handing her a menu written on a large white piece of paper shaped like a life preserver.

"Great!"

From the expression on the men's faces, she realized her response had been just a bit too enthusiastic. "Although it would be nice to be interviewed by her instead of Bobby Valentine pretending to be her."

"Is that what's going on now?"

"Yes, it's called working around her."

"Only, of course, she's not around," Basil suggested.

"No, not anymore."

"I hate to interrupt, but watching Tyler wolf down pizza was a real appetizer. I'm starving. What do you suggest?"

"Everything is good. Everything is fresh, but the penne al mare and filets de daurade à la julienne de légumes are my personal favorites."

"I'll have the penne," Josie said.

"And I'll have the sea bass," Sam said. "Now what about wine?"

Sam's last question required a serious discussion with Basil, and Josie looked across the room at Bobby Valentine. He seemed to be enjoying himself, eating some sort of pasta and drinking what looked like a martini as he chatted with the cameraman, the woman who set up the lights, and someone she didn't recognize.

Josie stared and wondered if he knew about Courtney's death. If so, he didn't seem terribly distressed. Did that mean he really thought her disappearance was normal? Or was he just a good actor?

"You're staring."

Startled, Josie looked back at Sam. "I . . . I guess I'm sort of curious about the TV people," she admitted.

"I'm a little surprised you don't get enough of them during the day."

Sam's tone of voice was odd and Josie frowned, then grinned as she realized what she was hearing. "You're jealous, aren't you? You're jealous of Bobby Valentine."

"I know it's foolish—"

"Oh, Sam, don't say that! No man's ever been jealous over me."

"That's a compliment. It means you're trustworthy."

Josie suspected it meant she rarely had one man in her life and never two at once. But she wasn't going to admit that to Sam. "You'll understand more when I tell you what's going on, but . . ."

A young man, wearing a conventional suit but sporting a tie shaped like a fish, brought the wine Sam had ordered and began the elaborate opening and tasting process that Josie sometimes found so irritating. This was one of those times. Until . . .

"You're so lucky to be working on a television show," the young man gushed. "They're fascinating, aren't they?"

"Well . . ."

"I've been changing my station every night to make sure I wait on them. Just listening in on their conversation is an incredible opportunity. That producer—"

"Bobby Valentine." Josie supplied the name.

"He told me to call him Bobby," the young waiter said proudly.

"You were saying . . ." Josie prompted.

"And pouring wine," Sam reminded him.

"Oh, sorry." He poured a bit and offered the glass to Sam. Sam tasted, nodded, and smiled. "Fine."

While their glasses were filled, Josie encouraged the waiter to chat. "They're interesting people, aren't they?"

"Yes, especially Courtney. I thought she was just another carpenter, but she's done everything! All those different types of shows . . ."

"What sort of shows?" Sam stopped sipping long enough to ask.

"Lots of things! A painting show—not the stuff you hang on the walls, but the type of things you put in the walls—"

"Faux finishes." Sam offered the correct term.

Josie, as always, amazed by the depth of Sam's knowledge as well as curious about who he might have dated who knew these things, asked a question. "She did a show about faux finishes?"

"Yes. It was very successful, according to her. But she even talked about her failures. She said she hosted some sort of needlepoint show that was a complete disaster."

"Really?"

"Yes, she said sewing just wasn't her thing, that she would leave it to the less artistic types."

"Very cool of her," Sam commented, smiling.

Josie was suddenly reminded of fifth grade. The second week of school Miss DeFrancisco had announced that they were going to elect class officers: a president, a vice president, a secretary, and a treasurer. Courtney had, of course, run for president. But her opponent had been an unknown quantity: a new girl who had, only a week earlier, moved to town from Southern California. The girl claimed to have met many famous actors and rock stars—Bruce Springsteen among them—and, using these supposed connections as any seasoned politician would—had won. When the results were announced, Josie had been thrilled, covertly glancing across the room to where Courtney was seated, hoping to spy a tear trickling down her pale cheek, or at least a grimace. But Courtney had leaped from her seat, hand out, to congratulate the winner.

"I guess the best man won," she had said, and then giggled. "The best woman, I should say."

But Josie had seen the blush on the winner's embarrassed face and known Courtney's barb had met its mark. And, for some reason, the new girl had become less and less popular as the year went on.

She wasn't listening to what their waiter was saying.

". . . and she never refuses to sign an autograph. She signed a photo for me the first night they were all here and the next night she signed one for my father. He's a big fan of *Courtney Castle's Castles*."

"Wait a second. Where did you get all these photographs?"

"Courtney herself. They're publicity photos."

"She carries them with her?"

"Yes. Well, not exactly. They were in a large briefcase, but I think someone else on her staff actually carried them."

"Doesn't that seem a bit conceited?"

"She's a celebrity. That's what celebrities do."

"Oh, I guess. I haven't known a whole lot of celebrities." Josie picked up her wineglass and took a sip. "Do they come in here a lot?"

"Every single night since we opened."

"Really?"

"Yeah. You can go get an autographed photo if you want."

"But Courtney's not here."

"No, but I noticed the briefcase lying on the floor."

"You mean they pass out her photos even when she's not here?" Sam asked.

"Yeah, nice, huh?"

"Do you wait on them every night?" Josie asked.

"All except for the first night they were here. I hadn't figured out how to trade stations then."

"And when did Courtney disa—stop coming in?"

"A few nights ago. It was weird."

"Why?"

"Her crew was planning to have some sort of celebration for her. Champagne was ordered. Basil was planning a special dinner. Then she didn't show up."

"You're kidding!" Josie exclaimed.

"Nope. They waited for over half an hour, then Bobby insisted everyone drink the champagne and eat. It was odd."

"And she hasn't been here since then?" Josie asked.

"Nope. And that's strange, too, because Bobby was sure she'd be back. He said she never, ever missed a day of shooting."

"Really?" Then he had lied to her. Josie smiled and drained her glass.

TWENTY-ONE

THE WAITER WAS called away to another table and they were left alone. "I think you have a lot to tell me," Sam said, glancing down at his watch.

"I have no idea where to begin," she said honestly. Or how much to say, she added to herself.

"Why don't you start by telling me where Courtney is."

"Where she is? Why do you think I know?"

"Just an impression I got when you and the waiter were chatting."

"How? What did I say?"

"It wasn't what you said but what you didn't say. You wanted to know when she stopped coming here and what Bobby Valentine said. You didn't ask if anyone knew where she had gone."

"Oh."

"I know you, Josie. You were quizzing that young man. If you hadn't known where she is, you would have asked him."

"Do you think he noticed?"

Sam smiled. "Nope. I think he was absolutely thrilled to talk about Courtney."

"Yeah, he was, wasn't he? It's weird how much people like to talk about her."

"It's because she's a celebrity. Some people love getting

181

close to celebrities; it makes them feel that a bit of that fame rubs off on them."

"I suppose."

"So where is she?"

"I don't know."

"Josie . . ."

"No, it's true, Sam. I did know, but now I don't."

"Then I'll change my question. Where was she?"

"In—" A waitress arrived carrying steaming plates and Josie stopped speaking. It took a few minutes—and two refusals of freshly ground pepper and one for fresh shavings from a chunk of Parmigiano-Reggiano—to regain their privacy.

"So where was she?" Sam repeated his question.

"She was in the canoe hanging from the ceiling of the living room." Her food smelled wonderful. She didn't want to answer these questions. She wished Sam would leave her alone and let her eat.

"Courtney Castle was hiding in a canoe hanging from the rafters of the house you're remodeling? I can't believe that!"

"It isn't exactly like that," Josie admitted. "You see, she was dead . . . is dead."

Sam looked at her, reached for his wineglass, changed his mind, and folded both hands in his lap. "Say that again."

"She's dead, Sam. Someone killed her. I think," she added.

"You *know* she's dead, but you *think* someone killed her."

"I know she's dead. And someone must have killed her. She didn't climb a ladder up to the canoe, get in, cover herself neatly with a blanket, and die. Besides, we put the ladder there. Later, we put the ladder there later." She took a deep breath and tried again. "There was no ladder up there. Someone on my crew put it there, and climbed up, and looked inside. And there she was. Am I making any sense at all?"

"Are you hungry?"

Surprised by the change of topic, she looked down at her plate. "It looks delicious, but I did eat earlier. Why? Do you want to leave?"

"No, I'm starving and this looks wonderful. I want to eat it while you tell me the entire story—from the beginning to the end."

"I . . ."

"And you shouldn't leave anything out, Josie. Because it sounds to me like you might be needing my help—and I can't do anything unless I know everything."

Josie sighed. "Okay. You're right. Just let me get my thoughts together." She sipped her wine, sighed again, and began the tale.

"It started when she didn't show up. I didn't know what to think. Bobby acted as though it was nothing. He said Courtney went off and did things—fund-raising, stuff like that—all the time. I didn't give it another thought, frankly. At least, not until I climbed the ladder and found her."

"Josie—"

"Sam, just hear me out. I'll tell you everything. That is, everything I know."

"Fine. Why don't you start with why you climbed that ladder?"

"Because Dottie told me Courtney was up there!" Josie continued, telling him of her crew's discovery and how she had been forced to stay up there with the dead body while Bobby Valentine, pretending to be Courtney Castle, had interviewed her. "It was creepy."

"I can imagine. Did you get the impression that he knew she was up there?"

"I thought about that, but I have no idea if he did or not. I know he wasn't in a position to look in while he was talking to me. I'm sure of that."

"But he could have done that before, right?"

"I guess."

"And what about later?"

"Yeah, he might have come back later and looked in, but . . . Do you think he took her down?"

"I suppose. The canoe was on the floor when I picked you up there. Did you take it down or did you find it that way?"

"Found it that way."

"And she wasn't in it."

"No, it was empty. Except for the blanket."

"The body was gone, but the blanket was left behind?"

"Yes."

"That's interesting."

"Why?"

"Whoever moved her didn't use the blanket to do it."

"Obviously, but so what?"

"It might not mean anything, but it might mean that whoever did it came prepared with some means of transport."

"Or maybe they just picked her up, plunked her in one of the wheelbarrows out back, pulled a tarp off the wood back there, tossed it over her, and rolled her away." Josie picked up her fork and stuck it in her pasta. Excellent!

"Good point. So go on with the story. What happened between the time you did the interview on the ladder and I arrived at the house?"

"We worked."

Sam put down his fork and looked at Josie. "You mean you left the body alone?"

She heard the disapproval in his voice and hesitated. "Well, not exactly alone. We were shocked, of course, but we discussed the situation and decided to do nothing until we could spend some time alone and discuss the problem. We took away the ladder, of course, so no one could get up to the body."

"You thought that by ignoring it, it would go away." He saw

the expression on her face and stopped speaking. "I'm sorry. Of course you didn't. It's just that this whole story is a bit hard to understand. Go on. When did you find the body?"

"In the morning."

"And what exactly did you all do once you found her?"

"Well, we talked about it . . . about her, of course. Everyone climbed up the ladder and looked at her. That is, I think everyone did."

"But you're not sure?"

"No, I guess not."

"What exactly did you all do?"

"Well, after a very uncomfortable interview with Bobby Valentine, pretending to be Courtney, we went back to work."

"Inside the house?"

"No. It would have been difficult to work with it . . . her . . . Courtney's body hanging over our heads. We had a lot to do in other parts of the house."

"So you all stayed away from the canoe for the rest of the day?"

"Yes."

"No one went in that room?"

"Well, that's not true. We probably all went in there at one time or another. I know what you're thinking, Sam, and you're wrong. No one could have moved the body without someone else knowing."

"That wasn't what I was thinking, but why don't you explain why not."

"Because it was up in the canoe and getting that canoe down to the floor without dumping it"—Josie suddenly had a vision of Courtney's body—"her out would have been impossible."

"And would that matter? After all, she's already dead. Or do you mean that it would make a lot of noise and attract attention?"

That wasn't what Josie had meant, but she was willing to accept his suggestion. "Yes. Exactly."

"But one person could have brought the canoe down from the ceiling?"

Josie thought back to the elaborate pulley system that held the canoe up. "Yes, I think so. Someone strong though. It isn't one of the new fiberglass affairs, remember, it's handmade from wood. I haven't lifted it myself, but it probably weighs a couple hundred pounds. We had one when I was a kid, and it weighed at least that much." She stopped talking and picked up her fork, hoping Sam would give her a chance to eat. For once she wasn't hungry, but she had just had a flash from her past, a memory startling in its clearness. She and Courtney had been members of the same Girl Scout troop (at her mother's insistence) and one entire miserable weekend they had been paired by their troop leader for the annual camping-canoe trip. Courtney's older brother had required the family's new sleek fiberglass vessel and so the pair of thirteen-year-old girls had paddled up and down the Delaware River in the Pigeons' handmade craft. It had been awful. Too heavy to carry around rapids, the boat had been repeatedly smashed against rocks and fallen limbs. Courtney, her hair tied back in a navy and white bandanna that matched her outfit of trim white poplin shorts and Brooks Brothers' navy polo, had been stonily silent, obviously appalled to be parted from the clique of popular girls and their up-to-date sporting goods. Josie had struggled to make the best of it, but her eyes had been filled with tears more than once and she had been so miserable that even her mother's relentless angry comments about the damaged canoe couldn't minimize the relief she felt when the trip had finally ended and she was safely home.

"Did anyone else come into the house after you discovered Courtney's body?"

"I suppose so. The television crew is in and out all the time."

"How many people are there with the show?"

Josie thought for a minute. "Five most of the time. Bobby Valentine, of course. And a cameraman—no, two cameramen although one is a woman. Someone is always running around setting up some sort of equipment—I suppose he could be a third cameraman—and there's the intern. The one Annette has a crush on."

"Anyone else? Deliverymen or the like?"

"I don't think so. No one I remember."

"Okay. Tell me about the rest of the day."

"There's nothing much to tell. We worked. The camera crew worked—"

"Doing what?"

"Actually, I don't know. But they seem to stay very busy."

"Did they do any more taping? More interviews?"

"No. Is that odd?"

"Frankly, I don't know. I once dated"—he glanced up at Josie, who had frequently accused him of having dated someone in every possible profession—"a television producer. But she worked for a major public television station and that may be different from freelancing for public television, but all I know is that she seemed to always be busy."

"Really." Josie was jealous. She was always busy, too, but wearing dirty overalls and T-shirts, not wearing Armani and lunching at 21. "Oh, the Rodneys stopped by."

"Why?"

"I haven't the foggiest."

"Did you get the impression that they knew about Courtney?"

"No. They didn't say anything about it."

"And I think we can be sure they'd mention your hiding a murder victim. Which leads us back to my first question.

How did you know she was murdered? Is it just because of the place you found her? Or did you see a wound?"

"I didn't see anything. In fact, she looked wonderful."

Sam squinted at her. "Wonderful? You're sure she was dead?"

"I'm sure."

"And she wasn't pale or anything?"

"Actually, she looked like she was wearing makeup." Josie thought for a minute. "You know, I think she was. She had on eye shadow. And probably blush and lipstick."

"Really?"

"Of course, Courtney probably hasn't been seen without makeup in public since she was in eighth grade."

"Unlike some women we know and love." Basil appeared at their table, a small plate in his hand. "I hope you two are enjoying your meal."

"Definitely."

"It's wonderful." Josie agreed with what Sam said.

"The chef is still experimenting with new things. Try these, a variation on shrimp toast. And, if you don't mind, I'll get myself a drink and join you."

"Have a glass of our wine and sit down," Sam said.

"Let me say good evening to my most famous guests, then I'll get a glass and be right back."

"Your most famous guests?"

"Yes. The staff of the Courtney Castle show. I want to talk to you about them and I'd rather they didn't overhear anything."

Josie almost choked on her food. This was what she had been hoping for!

TWENTY-TWO

THE DAY'S EVENTS and two dinners had taken their toll; Josie was exhausted by the time she arrived home.

"I'll give you a call tomorrow," Sam said, glancing up at the lights burning in the windows on the second floor. "Looks like Tyler is still awake."

"I think he said something this morning about having a friend stay over." It seemed like years ago. She looked up at Sam. "I figure if he has friends over they'll reciprocate and he will stay with them. I love having him home, but . . ." She didn't have to finish the sentence. They had agreed that Tyler should remain ignorant of their sex life and thus it was impossible for them to spend the night together while he was home. It had only been a few weeks, but she missed their closeness.

"Good thought." Sam leaned over and kissed her good night. "I'll stop by early tomorrow. I want to think about this evening. Your story was incredible enough, but I sure don't know how it fits in with what Basil said."

"So I'll see you early tomorrow?"

"Yup. I'll bring doughnuts."

"Make that crumb cake."

"You got it." A few more kisses, then he returned to his car. Josie heard the engine start as she opened the door and climbed the stairs to her home.

Her apartment door was locked—a pleasant surprise. She

had asked Tyler repeatedly to lock it if he planned on falling asleep or showering before she arrived home. He usually ridiculed her suggestion ("Ma, you're paranoid. I'm not a small kid. What do you think is going to happen? Are you worried that someone will walk in the door and abduct me?"). Since that was just one of the scenarios that kept her awake at night, she only smiled stiffly and repeated her request. And, son of a gun, he had remembered.

Of course, she always had trouble finding her key. She dropped her bag on the floor with a loud *clunk*, but before she could find it, the door opened.

"Hi! Mom! Hi!" Her son and a boy she didn't recognize were standing before her, foolish smiles on their faces.

"Hi, sweetie," she answered, too tired to remember how much her son hated her calling him that.

But tonight Tyler seemed genuinely happy to see her. "Mom, this is Eric Swanson. His uncle owns Family Video."

Josie offered her hand to the young man. "Nice to meet you, Eric." She turned back to Tyler. "It's been long day and if you two don't need anything, I'd really like to get to bed."

The young men assured her that she was extraneous, and she headed off to her bedroom. She showered and fell into bed, too exhausted to worry about Courtney's death and where her body had gone.

But she woke up worried about Tyler. The summer wasn't turning out as she had planned. She always worked hard, year round when she could get the contracts, but spring and summer were Island Contracting's busiest months and working from sunup to sunset was normal. Tyler, though always busy with some project or part-time job, had been home in the evening, ready to spend time with his mother. This year things were different. Tyler was working many evenings, and when he wasn't, there always seemed to be a friend of his around.

He thought he was grown up, but she knew better. He still needed a mother. She had to find a way for them to spend more time together.

She drove up to the work site and hopped out of her truck. The television vans were still there, but there was no sign of Sam's little sports car. Oh, well, he was probably at the bakery, picking up crumb cake and coffee. At least that's what she hoped.

Still thinking about Tyler, she was startled by a loud voice calling her name. "Hey! You! Pigeon!"

It was a man's voice. And he sounded angry.

Josie turned around, trying to find its source. "I don't see . . . Oh, there you are. I didn't know who was talking."

"What's wrong with her, Howard? She on drugs or something?"

The couple next door stood on their front deck. By the expressions on their faces, Josie guessed they weren't there to enjoy the beautiful morning. Oh, lord, as if she didn't have enough troubles . . . Josie put a smile on her face and walked toward them. "Good morning," she started hopefully, trying to remember whether any of the work scheduled for today was noisier or dirtier than usual.

"We need to talk." Howard didn't return her smile.

"Right this minute." His wife ditto.

"I'm sorry about the noise—"

"We're not concerned with undue noise," Howard stated.

"Although they could keep it down a bit, Howard," his wife added.

Josie tried again. "The dirt. There's always lots of dust during the demolition phase, but I assure you that's almost over—"

"It's not the dust," Howard informed her.

"The windowsills have been filthy, Howard. Just filthy. We don't come to the beach to breathe dirty air."

"The trucks—"

This time his wife spoke up first. "They make a lot of noise and their exhaust is awful, just awful, Howard. There's no reason such a small job should require so many trucks—"

"It's not the trucks," he said, interrupting his wife.

Nothing would be gained by losing her temper—but Josie did it anyway. "So what the hell is it?"

"Don't get snippy with me, young woman. I . . . I happen to be friends with the owners of this house—your employers, I must remind you—and I'm sure they would be interested in knowing what is going on in their home."

Shit! They knew about the murder! "Going on?" Josie repeated, stalling for time. How much did they know?

Howard frowned and spoke one word. "Inappropriate."

That was one way of looking at it. "I guess," Josie said weakly.

His wife was less succinct. "I thought maybe we could force ourselves to accept the dirt, the noise, all the commotion from the television people and the press and all, but when I saw what was going on . . . Well, I don't think you should expect people to put up with that type of thing. Almost in our own backyard."

"I'm sorry, but I don't see what I can do about it."

"You don't see . . . She says she doesn't see, Howard!"

"I hear her, Cheryl. I hear her."

"The world is going to hell in a handbasket. That's what my father always said and he was right," Cheryl continued to rant.

That was one of the frequently used parental phrases when Josie was growing up also. But this wasn't the time to reminisce, she realized. Josie started again. "I am very sorry, but what's happened has happened. I really don't know what I can do other than find out whose fault—"

She was caught off guard by Howard's change of topic.

"What is the name of the contracting company remodeling that house?"

On the other hand, at least she knew the answer to this question. "Island Contracting. There's a sign in the front yard." She pointed over her shoulder.

"And who is the owner of Island Contracting?"

"I am."

"And ask her how that happened, Howard. I heard that a man left her the company. And why would he do that if they hadn't been having an improper relationship? Ask her about that, Howard."

"Don't change the subject, Cheryl. We're talking about how she runs her company, not how she *came* to run her company!"

Josie had to think that one through. "Noel and I were just friends. He didn't leave me Island Contracting because we were lovers, he left it to me because he thought I would run it the way he wanted it run."

"That's not what we hear, missy."

"Cheryl—" her husband started, but she wasn't going to be interrupted.

"We hear that you and this Noel person were more than friends. A lot more. So much more that you had a son by him!"

Josie was stunned. She had no idea what to say. "I . . ."

"Acting as though you inherited the company because you were the best person for the job! How stupid do you think we are? What do you know about being a carpenter?"

"Cheryl . . ."

"I am an excellent carpenter. And you have no right to talk about things you know nothing about. Everyone on the island, everyone who knew Noel . . . or knows me . . . everyone would tell you that what you're saying is completely untrue. Completely!"

"And beside the point entirely," Howard roared. "Miss Pigeon, what are you going to do about that slut you have hired?"

"That slut?" Josie was stunned. "What slut?"

"She hired more than one slut, Howard! You heard her admit it! Who knows what those women are doing when we're not watching!"

Josie realized what was going on—or at least enough to ask the correct question. "What did you see?"

"We saw one of your carpenters with one of those television people!" Cheryl crossed her arms and stepped back as though she was a lawyer who had just finished an elaborate closing argument.

"Who?"

"The young one," Cheryl said. "In fact, you could say the young ones. That girl on your crew and that boy who came along with Courtney Castle."

"Annette and Chad?" Annette and Chad were the problem? Josie was so relieved, she felt faint. These horrible people didn't know about the murder! They were talking about Annette and Chad! "What about them bothers you?" she asked quietly.

"Well, that slut and that—"

"Annette is not a slut." Josie spoke firmly, and it seemed to have an impression on Howard.

"That may be. But we're not concerned with her morality here. What she does on her own time is, naturally, her own business. But you should be concerned about what she does while you are paying her, don't you think?"

"Well, I . . ."

"If I were you, I wouldn't want to be paying people to have sex."

"I'm not doing that!" Josie protested.

"Howard, you are, as always, missing the point completely!"

Cheryl inhaled and aggressively stuck out her rather large breasts encased in shimmering turquoise polyester. "The point is not what they were doing! The point is where they were doing it!"

"Well, I don't know!" Her husband seemed to be alarmed by her statement. "They—"

"They were doing it practically on our property! That is the point!"

Howard quickly added his agreement. "My wife is right. That's the point! She—"

"Annette." Josie supplied the name.

"Okay, Annette, if you insist. Annette was supposed to be working, doing what you pay her to do, and she was over on our property necking with that young man!"

"That's all? They were necking and you're upset about that?"

"You are missing the point, young lady! They weren't working—"

"Perhaps Annette was on a break," Josie suggested. "She is allowed two fifteen-minute breaks a day as well as half an hour for lunch. What she does during that time is her own business—although, of course, she is not supposed to be trespassing on your property."

"Exactly! That is exactly the point we've been trying to make!" For the first time this morning Josie saw a faint smile on the other woman's face.

"I always warn everyone who works for me not to trespass," Josie lied. She hadn't, in fact, thought it was necessary. The women who worked for her were well trained and intelligent. They knew they shouldn't be wandering around on property that belonged to others. "I'd be happy to remind Annette of that particular policy, if you like."

"And what about the young man she was with?" Cheryl asked.

"Look, he's not my problem. You're going to have to talk to Bobby Valentine—he's the show's producer—if you want Chad Henshaw warned."

"We know who Bobby Valentine is. We had him over for cocktails just the other night." Cheryl was smug. Josie got the impression that Cheryl considered this a social coup.

"Well, he's the one to talk with about Chad. And I don't know what he can do. Chad isn't an employee. He's a summer intern. He's not paid. You can't fire a volunteer, can you?"

"You know nothing about it. Summer interns may not be paid, but they get college credit for what they do. That's probably important to him."

"Maybe. All I know is, he's not my business. Period. As I said, I'll remind Annette not to trespass on your land."

"That's all you're going to do?"

Josie was beginning to find these people—and this conversation—tedious. "What in heaven's name do you want me to do? Fire her?"

"Yes. Get her off the island." Cheryl's answer came out as a shriek.

"Are you nuts? For necking with a young man on your property? What the hell is wrong with that?" Josie realized her voice was rising and she was in danger of screaming back. "You must be completely crazy. You—"

Howard interrupted, his voice booming deeply over the soprano rantings of the two women. "You are right. We are over-reacting. You just remind that young woman to stay on her side of the property line and we'll all be fine. Come along, Cheryl. Live and let live, as I always say." He grabbed his wife's arm and propelled her off the deck and back into their home.

Josie was left standing on the sidewalk, her mouth open.

TWENTY-THREE

DESPITE THE ADVICE of health gurus, the American Medical Association, and her mother, Josie believed that problems were best dealt with under the influence of lots of caffeine, starch, and sugar. Sam, straight from the bakery, brought all three in large quantities.

"I should wait until my coffee break, but—"

"It's breakfast," Sam urged, opening a bag and handing her a large rectangle of cake covered with thick, powdery streusel topping.

Josie noticed he was carrying three bags. "How much did you get?"

He chuckled. "I love a woman who loves her food! Don't worry. There's more than enough. Three slabs of cake and it's all for you and your crew. I have a toasted bagel in the car to munch on when I get hungry."

Probably without butter or cream cheese. Josie loved this man, but she didn't share his taste in food. "Sam, something strange happened this morning."

He was instantly alert. "Something to do with Courtney's murder?" he asked quietly.

"No, nothing that serious, but it's . . . I . . . I'm in an awkward position. You see, I sort of had a run-in with the couple next door." She explained what had happened, then was disappointed in Sam's response.

"Sounds to me as though they're making a mountain out of that molehill everyone's always talking about. I know she hasn't worked for you long, but what do you think about Annette?"

"She's a good carpenter. But she's young and in love and—"

"What I was asking—and I should have put the question more clearly, I admit—was do you think she will do what you tell her to do?"

"I don't see why not. She knows I'm the boss and I haven't seen any signs that she has trouble with that fact."

"So warn Annette not to neck with her new boyfriend on the neighbors' property—or in their sight—and don't worry about the . . . What are their names?"

"Cheryl and Howard. I don't know their last names."

"Well, then, don't worry about what Cheryl and Howard think."

"You're right. I've had problems with cranky neighbors before. I guess I just let this upset me because of everything that's been going on around here."

"Understandable." Sam looked down at her. There was a serious expression on his handsome face. "Josie, I had trouble sleeping last night. I kept thinking about what happened here yesterday and wondering how I could help."

She beamed. What a nice man!

"So I called this woman I mentioned to you yesterday. The one who worked for public television."

"The one you used to date." The smile had vanished from her face.

"Yes. I didn't tell her about your problem, of course. But I did explain that I was interested in learning more about Courtney Castle."

"And does she know her?" Josie didn't know whether she wanted him to answer yes or no.

"Yes, and she has access to tapes of all the shows Courtney has been on in the past."

Now that was interesting. Josie perked up. "Really?"

"Yes, and she offered to get some for us."

"Really? That's nice of her. I've been wondering about Courtney. Apparently she's terribly popular. It's hard to imagine anyone wanting to kill her. The more we find out about her at this point, the better."

"I thought the same thing. Anyway, she'll be down this afternoon, early if the traffic isn't bad, and—"

"She's going to deliver the tapes in person?"

"I suggested she FedEx them, but she said something about getting away for the weekend and volunteered. I thought it was very nice of her."

"It will give you both the opportunity to catch up," she said shortly.

"Josie . . ."

The arrival of Josie's crew prevented her from making a jealous fool of herself. "I have to go. When do you think I can see the tapes?"

"Tonight. I'll call you as soon as Sondra arrives with them."

"Sure." Sondra—not Sandra, not Sandy, but Sondra. Didn't Sam know any women who weren't rich, thin, and chic? Any women other than herself? she added mentally. "If you can't get me here, call the office. The machine is on there and I'll be checking in this afternoon. I need to spend an hour or so figuring out overtime so I can write paychecks."

"I'll call you as soon as I have them." He kissed her quickly and was off. Josie went over to her crew. They had all had an evening to think over the events of the day before, and from the looks on their faces they had all found it a sobering experience.

"Sam brought fresh crumb cake. Why don't we have some before we start," she suggested.

"Okay," Annette agreed listlessly. It was the most enthusiastic response from the three.

"In the house," Josie added, seeing a van of television people pull up to the curb.

"Good idea. One more perky greeting from that Valentine guy and I just might woof my cookies." Dottie scowled and stomped off.

They all followed, waiting impatiently while Josie unlocked the front door.

The canoe still sat in the middle of the floor. There was a pause while the women all looked at it. Then Josie took a deep breath, stomped across the bare wood, stepped over the side, and plopped herself down on the caned seat at the back of the boat. "Anyone want some crumb cake?" she asked, holding up the white bakery bags.

Dottie snorted and then one of her rare grins appeared. "Well, what the hell. I do. You've got guts, boss. I'll give you that. Real guts."

"Thanks. Anyone else want some?"

Annette and Jill glanced at each other and then at the food, but whatever their feelings about the situation, greed won out. In a few minutes the women were seated around the canoe, eating and talking quietly.

"I didn't think we'd get much done if we had to pussyfoot around this thing all day," Josie stated flatly, then stopped. Why were her parents' corny expressions slipping into her speech so often these days? "I mean, what the hell. She's dead and gone and we have to go on with our work and . . . and all," she ended rather weakly.

"You know, you're right. Nothing we do can bring her back," Annette said rather tensely, taking her first bite of cake.

"True," Jill agreed, stopping eating long enough to wipe up the drift of confectioners' sugar that had fallen on her ample chest.

"I think the best thing we can do is just get on with our work—and cooperate with the television crew, of course," Josie said.

"Oh, I was supposed to tell you." Annette spoke up, her mouth full of cake. "Chad said that Bobby Valentine wants to interview each of us individually again today. Apparently they're interested in hearing about our training. He said it would take less than half an hour apiece. But he wanted your permission, Josie. I was supposed to say something about it first thing this morning."

"Oh, well, what do the rest of you think?"

"Fine with me," Dottie said. "Just as long as they ask about my work and not about my personal life. That's no one's business but mine."

"You should tell him that before the interview starts," Josie suggested. Not that she thought it would necessarily make a difference. "And remember the interviews are edited. If you don't like a question, you can refuse to answer and they can just cut it out."

"Are you sure?"

Josie looked up. The last question had come from Jill, which surprised her. As far as she knew, Jill had nothing to hide. Unless . . . Jill had something to do with Courtney Castle's death. "I'm sure," she answered, reaching for another square of crumb cake and trying to remember the information on Jill's application form. She didn't remember much, so it probably had been unremarkable. She didn't remember where Jill had been born, but she had trained as a carpenter in Buffalo, New York. She'd left there for the suburbs around Portland, Oregon, where she'd worked for a number of years before arriving on the island in the late spring. There were undoubtably other details, but this was all she remembered. If any of it related to Courtney, she sure didn't see how.

"Where did Sam rush off to?" Dottie asked after a rather long silence.

"He . . . well, to be truthful, he went back to the store to wait for an old friend who's arriving on the island sometime this afternoon." Josie didn't see any reason to mention the sex of this old friend or to change the phrase "old friend" to something more appropriate, like "old flame." She frowned.

"Someone you don't like?" Jill asked.

"Someone I don't know," Josie replied honestly.

"Maybe you can get away while we're being interviewed and meet him," Annette suggested.

"Maybe. But it's time we got to work. I do need to talk to you all. I was going to speak with Annette privately, but I think this could concern all of you.

"The couple next door complained to me this morning that Annette and Chad were on their property—"

"We weren't!" Annette protested. "I know better than to trespass on anyone's private property!"

"I'm not accusing you of anything. I'm just telling you what they told me." God, she really was beginning to sound like her mother.

"They told you that Chad and I walked on their property? When? Did they accuse us of leaping over the split-rail fence that divides their property from this one?"

"No, they didn't say anything like that. If you must know, they accused you and Chad of making out on their property. It's your business what the two of you do, and I know you're a hard worker and probably were with Chad during a break, but—"

"But they were lying."

"I . . ." Josie looked at Annette. She was obviously indignant. Could she be telling the truth? "Really? Why would they lie?"

"I have no idea. But Chad and I were never on their property. And we weren't necking—or anything like that—on their property or on this one."

"Are you sure?"

"I'm sure. We are . . . well, we do like each other, but we're not kids! We're not necking in the bushes, for heaven's sake. We both have our own places to live. Jill and I share a place and Chad has his own apartment over a garage. It's big and private and . . . everything."

"Look, I believe you." What Annette said made sense. "But—"

"But what?"

"But why would they make something like this up?"

"They're nuts." Dottie interjected her opinion. "They're always peering over that stupid bayberry hedge at the end of the property to see what's going on."

"Really? Maybe they're interested in our work. Or in possibly hiring Island Contracting in the future. I probably should have been nicer," Josie said.

"They're not interested in Island Contracting for any reason," Dottie said. "They're fascinated by the TV people. They watched and watched and thought of excuses to come over here while Courtney was around, but now they've lost interest."

"Unless . . ." Josie began slowly.

"Unless what?" Jill asked quickly.

"Oh, nothing."

"Well, Chad and I didn't do anything improper, and even if we had, we sure wouldn't have gone next door to do it," Annette repeated. "And I'd be happy to go over there and tell them that if you want."

"No. Let's just leave it be and get to work. We're going to fall behind if we don't watch out."

They all knew what to do and Josie was relieved when the work resumed and she could take some time to think. She didn't understand what was going on. She hadn't known Annette for long, but the young woman's argument made sense. Why would she and Chad be necking, here or next door, when they both had places where they could be alone together? On the other hand, why would Cheryl and Howard lie about it? Could it be that they had mistaken two other people for Annette and Chad? It was the only possible answer. She decided to worry about something else.

Naturally, the first thought she had was of the woman now, presumably, on her way to see Sam. Sondra. Blond, she decided. Slim, of course. (They all were.) Well educated and well connected. (She was, after all, working in a very competitive medium.) Well coiffed, well dressed, skin that looked as though it lived in a spa and was only taken out and worn on special occasions. Josie was becoming seriously depressed. Because even if Sam actually believed this woman's story that she was coming to the shore and would find it convenient to drop off the tapes, to Josie it sounded like an excuse to renew an old acquaintance—and possibly to kindle an old flame.

It's dangerous to stop paying attention to what you're doing when you work with heavy equipment. Josie picked up a piece of molding and slid it against the back of the table saw but didn't hold on tightly enough as she lowered the blade. The wood shattered and pieces flew in all directions. A splinter slit her left wrist. She turned off the saw and leaned back. She was lucky she hadn't been seriously injured. But the molding had been a special order and would be expensive to replace. Damn, damn, and triple damn. Nothing was going well today!

She straightened, kicked the lumber aside, and slapped her hands together. She had the supplier's number back at the office. The sooner she replaced this piece, the better. She stuck her head out the back door. "I've got to go back to the office for a few minutes. Anyone need anything there or on the way?"

"We were just talking about ordering some lunch," Jill said.

Josie realized they were reluctant to ask their boss to run errands for them. "If you get something from the Deli Delight, they would have it ready and waiting for me to pick up in less than half an hour. I know it's early for lunch, but it would save time later in the day."

"We'll order stuff that can wait around for a bit," Dottie promised.

"Good. Then an Italian hoagie with the works for me and tell them I'll be by to pick up the order in about twenty minutes. See you."

Howard and Cheryl were entertaining Bobby Valentine on their front deck. Josie assumed they were regaling him with the tale of Chad and Annette's misdeeds. She walked faster, hoping they either wouldn't see her or would ignore her presence. No such luck.

"Josie! Ms. Pigeon. Did that young woman tell you we want to interview your carpenters this afternoon?" Bobby Valentine called out.

"Yeah. It's fine with me. Gotta run." Josie waved and dug around in her pockets for the keys to her truck. For once, they were where she thought she had left them. She hopped in the truck, started the engine, and roared off down the road. She'd go to the office and then pick up their food at Deli Delight for lunch and be back in no time at all.

And, surprisingly, everything worked out the way she expected it to. Except she returned to work with more to think about. Next door to Deli Delight was Le Château, the only French restaurant open for lunch on the island. And there, going into the front door of Le Château, were Sam and a woman who could only be Sondra. Josie had been wrong. She wasn't tall, thin, blond, and chic. She was tall, thin, brunette, and definitely chic, wearing clothing Josie couldn't find in a store, couldn't afford if she did, and wouldn't look good in anyway.

She spent the rest of the afternoon depressed.

TWENTY-FOUR

SAM HAD LEFT a message at Josie's office. It was brief and to the point. He had gotten the tapes. Why didn't she come over to his house when she was done with work and he'd cook dinner and they could go through them together.

She had wasted most of her day. She had worried about Cheryl and Howard. She had wondered about Sam and his ex-lover. She had thought about where Courtney's body might have gone and who might have moved it. She had wondered exactly what Sam and his gorgeous ex-lover were doing.

Then she had tried to put up a wall while listening in on Bobby interviewing her crew members. Dottie had started out characteristically abrupt, verging on rude. Surprisingly, after a while, Bobby Valentine had appeared to charm her, and by the last question they had been chuckling together over something one of them had said. Jill had been less susceptible to Bobby Valentine's charms although he began the questioning by flattering her. (Had his "Wow! I haven't met many carpenters who look this gorgeous!" been more than a bit insulting to the rest of them? Josie thought.) Jill had merely nodded and waited for the questions to begin. She hadn't warmed up. She had been polite, professional, and cold. Annette had been a nice contrast. Young, bubbly, obviously thrilled with the possibility of being on television, she had chatted on and on, full of enthusiasm for her job, her life, the house they were remodeling. Bobby Valentine had been smitten. Her interview had exceeded the total time he had spent with the other two.

When the interviews were finished, Josie had watched Chad help another young man roll wires and put lights and microphones and things away. Then she had started to wonder again what Sam and Sondra had been doing all this time.

Josie had taken the time to go home and change before heading to Sam's house at the north end of the island. Her closet didn't provide anything as chic as the wraparound silk blouse and linen capri pants Sondra had worn to lunch, but her jeans were clean, her yellow-and-white-striped oxford-cloth shirt pressed, and her green plastic flipflops only a few weeks old.

Sam lived in a small ranch house tucked into the dunes at the exclusive north end of the island. He and Josie had been remodeling it over the years; recently they had installed some rather elegant outdoor lighting. It was still light out, but Sam had turned on the display and Josie smiled as she hopped from her truck and walked up the wooden boardwalk to the deck that encircled the house. She peeked through the screen door into the living room. Sam was stretched out on one of the twin couches, a remote control in one hand fast-forwarding through the channels on the large TV, which stood to the left of the fireplace.

"Sam?"

"Josie, come on in." Sam slid his lean, jean-clad legs to the floor, stood, stretched, and smiled. He was tall and tan, his sandy hair falling over his glasses and into his eyes, and Josie was instantly glad they were having this evening together. She might even have forgotten about Sondra if the woman herself hadn't appeared in the kitchen doorway, a tray in her hands.

"I found some munchies," Sondra announced, walking into the room. "You must be Josie. I'm Sondra."

"Hi." Josie looked over at Sam. "I thought you were going to be cooking."

"The grill is warming up," he explained. "Sondra volunteered to prepare some appetizers while I got these things organized for you. There's a lot here, but you should be able to scan them in a little over an hour."

"Sam's spent the last few hours going over the tapes, getting them in order, tossing out the duplicates and the ones that don't show Courtney. I'm afraid I just grabbed from a pile in the tape room, and some of the ones I brought weren't at all useful or relevant," Sondra added, putting the tray down on the cherry coffee table.

"It was very nice of you to bring these," Josie said, remembering her manners.

"It wasn't a big deal. I was coming down for a long weekend anyway. And it's been great seeing Sam. He and I go way back." Sondra beamed at Sam. Sam beamed back at Sondra. Josie reached out for a gourmet potato chip.

"We put the tapes in chronological order, and the first one is in the player. I've marked the rest of them. They're on the coffee table," Sam explained. "You might want to get started while I cook dinner. There are about three hours of tape here. But Sondra and I found that once you get going, you can start zipping through fast-forward. You'll see for yourself."

"Great." Not thrilled that this would leave more time for Sam and Sondra to reminisce, Josie sat down on the couch Sam had just vacated and pressed play on the remote.

And found herself in the early eighties with a very perky, very curly Courtney Castle. Once again Josie wondered what she would look like if she went to Courtney's hairdresser.

"Good evening. Welcome to *Crafty Times with Courtney Castle*." Courtney as a brunette was sitting on a bench with what looked like a million stuffed animals scattered around her. "Today's show is called 'Stuffies for All,' and we're going to meet Janie Jones, creator of this plethora of absolutely adorable toys, and she's going to tell us how to make them ourselves. . . ."

Josie watched about fifteen minutes of this show before pressing fast-forward and heading to another *Crafty Times with Courtney Castle*, to a show entitled 'Stenciling for All.' She pressed the fast-forward button again and found a Courtney in a new environment with shorter, flatter, lighter hair.

Josie leaned forward and squinted at the screen. Courtney, wearing denim overalls, was actually sitting on a bale of hay in what appeared to be a garden-variety barn. "Welcome to *Country by Courtney*," she announced, smiling broadly. "Today our topic is apples and we're going to make apple butter and apple chutney, see cider being pressed during a short field trip, and then learn all about those absolutely appealing Appalachian apple dolls . . ." Josie pressed fast-forward.

"Welcome to *Country by Courtney* . . ." The hair was the same, but the overalls had been replaced with jeans and a gingham blouse. "On this show we're going to be talking about corn. Corncob pipes. Corn stacks to decorate your home for Halloween. Corn relish . . ."

Josie pressed again. And again. And again. Through *Country by Courtney* and "Rhubarb, the First Sign of Spring in our Garden." Through *Country by Courtney* and "Beans from the Vine and Bush." To *Country by Courtney* and "Give Peas a Chance," where she switched from fast-forward to eject.

The next tape contained another show, another Courtney. Blond this time, still curly but less bubbly. Although perhaps the topic and the set lent themselves to a more conservative tone. "Hello, I'm Courtney Castle and this is the first show of *Crewel with Courtney*. Now some in our audience will understand me when I say there is really nothing cruel about crewel . . ."

Josie couldn't hit the button fast enough.

Apparently she wasn't the only one. On this tape, at least, *Crewel with Courtney* had a very short run. The next transformation was entitled *Decorate Your Castle with Courtney Castle*. Courtney was moving into her own now. Her hair was golden and worn in a polished style reminiscent of those popularized by the Breck girls of Josie's childhood. She was dressed in an elegant navy suit and looked right at home in the English chintz drawing room, where, apparently, the opening of the show took place. There was an entire tape filled with three hours of this show and covering topics from "Swags for Every Room" to "Tassels to Go" to "Damask and the Den."

From the general to the specific. The next tape was of two different shows: *Stencil Your Castle with Courtney Castle* and *Faux Finishes in Your Castle with Courtney*. Josie didn't take her thumb off the fast-forward button until she arrived at the end.

She was putting the final tape in the machine when Sam appeared in the doorway. "Three minutes to dinner," he announced. "We can eat in here, but if you'd like to take a break, it will take only a minute to set up out back."

"Out back," she said. "I'll just use the bathroom and join you."

Sondra and Sam were enjoying goblets of something fruity and dark red on the deck off the kitchen. They were deep in a conversation about someone skiing in Aspen when Josie appeared.

"You look tired. What can I get you to drink?" Sam asked. "Sondra made sangria. Do you want a glass?"

"It's delicious, but it can be lethal," Sondra said. "Remember the time we got so drunk at my apartment when I was living down in the Village and neither of us could remember the name of the restaurant where we were supposed to be meeting one of your colleagues?"

Sam laughed. "Sure. We were with that producer and his girlfriend. He kept insisting that we were planning to go for sushi and she was positive we had made reservations at some Thai place."

"I'll have the sangria," Josie announced. Perhaps it would help her get through what was beginning to seem like a long evening.

"And I'll get it for you while Sam apologizes for telling you you look tired, and then, after you've had a glass and are feeling mellow, I'll apologize for talking about people you don't know in front of you." And with this Sondra stood and trotted back into the house.

Sam looked at Josie and grimaced. "Sondra's right and I'm sorry."

"She's nice," Josie said, hoping the admission didn't sound as begrudging as she felt.

"She is. I hope John knows how lucky he is."

"John?"

"Her fiancé. She's meeting him here tomorrow. His family has that big pink stucco house down near the beach."

"She's engaged?" Josie was beginning to like Sondra more all the time.

"Yup. Getting married in a few weeks. I was invited to the wedding—with a date. It's in the city. I was hoping you'd be able to go with me. We could stay with Mom," he added. "Or maybe a suite at the Plaza?" he added, a wicked leer on his face.

"How do you know I won't be in jail for murdering Courtney Castle?" was Josie's reply. She didn't mean to be overheard, but Sondra had returned, a full pitcher of sangria in one hand, a clean goblet in the other.

"So you hate her, too, huh?" Sondra asked, pouring the wine and handing the glass to Josie.

"I sure di—don't like her." Josie was prompted to change her words by a gentle kick in the shins. She was thankful that soft Italian loafers were Sam's preferred choice of footwear.

"That's true of most people who work with her for any length of time." Sondra took a sip of her drink.

"Sondra was telling me about Courtney while we went through the videotapes this afternoon," Sam explained, opening the grill.

A delicious scent wafted in the air, but Josie was interested in something other than food. "What about her?" she asked.

"Well, as you saw on the tapes—" Sondra started.

But Josie interrupted. "Explain the tapes first. They didn't make a lot of sense to me. Was Courtney the star of all those shows?"

"Yes, but—"

"Then why didn't I ever hear about her?" Josie interrupted impatiently. "I mean, I may not watch a lot of public television, but I watch some. And I see promos for upcoming shows. Generally, I know a fair amount of what's on."

"But you only see the shows broadcast by your public station. There are hundreds of stations all over the country and they put different shows on the air. Most of those shows come from the public broadcast network feed; the local stations pay to put them on the air. And some of the shows originate at the station themselves; those shows have a fairly limited distribution.

"Most of the shows you saw on those tapes were locally produced and distributed to a very small audience," Sondra explained. "They may not have been seen by more than a thousand people—maybe fewer."

"Why are there so many different shows?" Josie asked.

"Because, up until this last show—*Courtney's Castle* or whatever she calls it—she was a complete failure."

"You're kidding!" Josie was thrilled.

"Actually, I'm wrong. If she had been a failure, she would never have gotten to anchor all those different shows. Courtney, in the vernacular of my business, is talent looking for the proper vehicle. That is, she was until now."

"I don't understand exactly," Josie admitted.

"That's because I'm not explaining very well. Maybe I should tell you a bit more about my chosen field."

Sam served the meal and, Josie's appetite having returned with the news that Sondra was engaged, they ate while Sondra talked.

"You see, television is a very mobile business. People move from station to station and from job to job within the station. They move up, they move out, they move laterally. It's the norm. Courtney's career has been fairly typical of someone who doesn't make it big right away. You may not have been paying attention to the call letters at the beginning of the shows you just watched—"

"No, not at all."

"Well, the first few tapes were done at a small station in North Dakota."

"How did Courtney end up in North Dakota?"

"Who knows? Getting your first job—your foot in the media door, so to speak—can be difficult. If you're smart—and lucky—you decide where you want to work after graduation and figure out a way to get an internship there. Then you network like mad and hope that someone will remember you when you need a real job."

"In North Dakota?"

"Doesn't seem likely," Sondra admitted. "Usually people go after the jobs at the bigger stations, either New York,

Boston, L.A., or Washington. She probably tried those and when, surprise, surprise, they weren't enthusiastic about hiring a young person with limited experience right out of college, she looked elsewhere. She probably got a job the way the rest of us did: off the bulletin board in the mass-communications department at college. Who knows? It's probably not important. What is important is that someone gave her a chance to anchor a show."

"More than one show," Sam said.

"Yes. Well, that says something, too, of course."

"What?"

"Probably that she managed to blame the lack of success of the earlier shows on something or someone other than herself."

"Sounds like Courtney hasn't changed much since she was a kid," Josie said.

"Well, go on, tell her what else you know," Sam suggested.

TWENTY-FIVE

"**W**ELL, I DON'T know anything, but I can guess. Both from the situation and from knowing Courtney—"

"You actually know Courtney?" Josie couldn't help but ask.

"Yes, for a couple of years, in fact, but that's jumping ahead in the story."

"Go ahead," Josie urged.

"As I was saying, those tapes show that someone—or more than one person—was willing to give Courtney a few chances to succeed as an on-air personality. There are three different shows bearing the call letters of the PBS station in Fargo, so someone there was working to find something that would work for her—"

"Just for her?" Sam interrupted with a question. "Doesn't what you're saying imply that the . . . on-air personality is solely responsible for the success of the show? Surely the topic, the production, other things I don't know about, are at least partially responsible?"

"Yes, but what we see in those tapes—and they're certainly only part of the story—is that Courtney survived and the shows didn't."

"And you think that means someone was promoting her, not blaming her for the shows' lack of success," Sam said.

"Yes. And then after those three shows, she moved on and

tried again. Two more shows with short lives—not terribly surprising if you consider the joke about crewel embroidery she used to open one of them. And then, suddenly, success."

"When? I only got through the first four tapes—skimming them really. What's on the last one?" Josie asked.

"The first few shows of *Courtney Castle's Castles*. A show whose time had come apparently. As far as I know, it was popular from the very moment it went on the air. Of course, remodeling shows have been on for years, but never with a woman in charge. My guess, having lived through a nightmarish remodeling of a loft years and years ago, is that many women believe things in their own home would have been different if a woman had been in charge of the work." She smiled at Josie. "Well, you probably know more about these things than I do."

"Island Contracting does get some jobs because the employer or homeowner is a woman and she thinks we're more likely to listen to her—without putting her down—than some of my male colleagues. And, frankly, it's true." Josie glanced over at Sam and blushed. "But that's not what we're talking about here. Go on."

"For whatever reason, the show was a success from the first. Courtney doesn't know a damn thing about building or remodeling, any more than she did about embroidery or interior decoration or . . ."

"Or making apple chutney?" Josie suggested.

"Lord, maybe she knows more about it than that. Courtney is a dreadful cook. No one who has ever been forced to eat anything she's cooked would ever suggest a show called *Cooking with Courtney*. She is one of those people who should stick to takeout. Period. But I digress—as I always do," Sondra said, laughing at herself.

"You were talking about *Courtney Castle's Castles*," Sam reminded her.

"What is there to say? It's been picked up by all the major PBS stations across the country as well as lots of the smaller ones. And it has made her a household name."

"Are you connected with the show?" Josie asked.

"Not really, but a friend of mine was the original producer of the show."

"You said he introduced you to Courtney," Sam prompted.

"Exactly. He gave a big cocktail party the night the show premiered on the New York station. And he introduced her to me."

"Did you like her?" Josie asked.

"Not really. My friend didn't say anything about what I did to Courtney. He just said something like I'd like you to meet my good friend Sondra. She practically ignored me. She was—as she always was then—busy sucking up to the important people in the room. She thought I was insignificant and treated me accordingly. I don't find that a particularly appealing trait."

"But you got to know her better later on," Sam said.

"And didn't like her any better, as you well know. I thought you had retired. Aren't you supposed to stop asking questions all the time?"

"Sorry. Tell it your own way."

"Well, as Sam says, I did get to know her better, at first by hearsay and then in person. You see, my friend, her producer, and she had an argument. Well, they had lots of arguments. They argued about everything from the size of her dressing room and staff to the way the show was produced. Eventually he either quit or was fired. The story depends on who is telling it. So I heard every single detail of their feud. And then Courtney came to me and asked me if I would produce her show."

"Take the place of your friend?"

"Yes, but don't be horrified. It happens all the time. My

friend wouldn't have cared. He might have thought I was crazy after listening to him enumerate the disadvantages— hell, the miseries—of working with Courtney Castle, but he wouldn't have held it against me if I'd said yes."

"Which you didn't," Josie guessed.

"No. I'm old enough to let a few mistakes go by. But I did tell her I would work as a consultant on the show for the rest of that season—provide continuity when new employees came and the like. To tell the truth, I don't know how I let her talk me into it. I knew she was a manipulative little bitch. I should have had more sense."

"So it didn't go well."

"A disaster from the get-go."

"Why?"

Sondra shook her head, obviously disgusted with herself. "It was stupid. She wanted more airtime. She wanted staff— staff, for heaven's sake. We're talking public broadcasting, not network television. There isn't a lot of extra money to toss around. People send in donations to keep their favorite shows on the air; we owe it to them to be responsible. But Courtney was the star and she wanted to be treated like one. The very second my commitment was over I was out of there. And thrilled to be gone, I can tell you."

"That's when Bobby Valentine took over?" Josie asked.

"No, Bobby was there when I was around. How do you know him?"

"He's the producer on this project," Josie explained.

"You're kidding! If you'd asked me, I would have said he'd be long gone before now!"

"Why?"

"Courtney and he were always fighting. When I wasn't say- ing no to one of her outrageous, egotistical ideas, he was."

"These days he's saying yes," Josie said. "You should see

Courtney's trailer—makeup table, couches, exercise equipment. It looks like it belongs to a rock star."

"And Bobby Valentine is her producer? You're sure?"

Josie nodded. "Yes."

"Amazing. She must have gotten to him."

"What do you mean?" Sam asked.

"Blackmail!" Josie exclaimed. "She blackmails people, doesn't she?"

Sam leaned forward. "Does she?" he asked Sondra.

"Not that I know of. She gets what she wants, but she does it by manipulating people. It's more subtle than blackmail, but just as effective in the long run. And legal."

"Sounds like Courtney," Josie said, leaning back in her chair and flinging her napkin down on the table.

"Sam told me you grew up together."

"Yes."

"Is that why she chose your company to feature on her show?"

"I . . ." Josie stopped and thought for a moment before answering. "To tell you the truth, I don't know the answer to that question."

"She's nice."

Sondra had gone off to her fiancé's house, and Josie and Sam were saying good-bye in the street next to the Island Contracting truck.

"You didn't expect to like her, did you?"

"No. I always feel inadequate next to your old girlfriends," she admitted.

"That problem is in your head."

"I know. But I can't afford the years of expensive psychotherapy it would take for me to get rid of it," she added with a grin.

"Good. I like you just the way you are." He reached out for her. "Do you have to go home?" he asked after a few minutes.

"You know I do. In fact, I should be there now. I don't want Tyler to worry."

"I love your son, but I sure wish he weren't too old for sleepaway camp," Sam said, giving her one last kiss and opening her truck door for her.

"Maybe next summer we can arrange for him to be a counselor," Josie said, starting the engine. She took off down the street with a final wave out the window. The island was only seven miles long; in less than ten minutes she was climbing the stairs to her apartment. Tonight the door wasn't locked and she was surprised to find Tyler sitting on the couch, apparently engrossed in a magazine dedicated to mountain biking.

"Hi, Mom."

"Hi yourself, sweetie. Aren't you up a bit late?" Damn. In less than a dozen words she'd broken two rules of mothering an adolescent: she'd referred to her son by a nickname *and* she had suggested he didn't know how to take care of himself properly.

However, Tyler either didn't notice or didn't mind. "I can sleep late in the morning. I'm on the late shift tomorrow."

"Good. I'm going to shower and get into bed. I'm beat."

"Uh, Mom . . ."

She recognized that tone of voice. Something was up. She glanced down at the magazine Tyler still held. "You want to spend your money on a new bike?"

"No, it's serious, Mom."

Josie sat down on the couch without another word.

"I . . . Well, I've been doing something you're not going to like . . . and I have to tell you about it because of something I know . . . Oh, hell, just press the play button and see for yourself."

Apparently she was going to spend the night the way she had spend the evening: watching videos. She leaned back and then sat up straight with a gasp. "Tyler!"

"I know, Mom, we'll talk in a minute. There's something here you have to see. There's a reason." His voice was pleading.

"It better be a good one. Because, generally speaking, I don't think watching X-rated videos is a good mother-and-son type of activity. I . . ." The opening credits were more than brief and they were into the meat of the picture in seconds. Josie didn't know whether to laugh or lecture. Then she sat up. "Do you know who that looks like?"

"It is. Jill Pike. The woman who works for you. Her hair is a little longer, but it is her." He glanced over at his mother. "We can keep watching, but—"

"You wanted me to see her."

"Yes. I thought you should know. Considering the disappearance of Courtney and what people in town are saying . . ."

But Josie had other things on her mind. "Tyler, where did you get this video?"

"Well . . ."

"I thought the reason you could work at that place was that it was a family store, that it didn't carry videos like . . . like this one." She waved at the now blank TV screen.

"That's true. Really, Mom."

"So where did this come from?"

"Well . . ."

Josie had a hard time not smiling; he looked adorably sheepish. "Well what?" she said sternly.

"Both stores are owned by the same person and the videos are ordered together. Nothing of this type is supposed to come into Family Video, but if you ask the delivery guy nicely, he sometimes mixes up the orders."

"Tyler . . ."

"I didn't do it, Mom. One of the kids I work with did."

"The young man who was here last night."

"Yeah."

"And you were watching this last night?"

She watched him struggle. Was he going to tell the truth or not?

"No. We watched a different one then. But I saw this one a few days ago."

Josie was silent for a minute. "I don't want this type of thing in my house," she said quietly. "It demeans women and . . . and I just don't like it."

"Sorry. I won't do it again. Mom?"

"What?"

"Are you going to fire her?"

"Jill? Of course not."

"Did you know about this?"

"No, I had no idea. But she's a good worker, a good carpenter. I'm glad to have her working for me. I wish I hadn't seen this, though."

"Why?"

"Because I have to let her know that I know about it. It's the only way to keep our relationship honest. And I sure hate to have to bring it up. It will probably hurt her."

"Yeah, I guess. But I had to let you know, didn't I?"

"You did. Thank you." She reached out and ruffled his red hair. "And you know what?"

"No."

"If I ever find you watching this stuff again, you're grounded."

TWENTY-SIX

AS SOON AS she woke up, Josie called Jill. They agreed to meet at the office half an hour before the workday was scheduled to begin. Josie could hear Jill's nervousness over the phone. She fed the cat, wrote a quick note to Tyler thanking him for showing her the video the night before and reminding him to return it to the store, and started down the steps.

Risa was waiting at the bottom.

"*Cara,* I not sleep last night."

"What's wrong?" Josie asked, instantly concerned.

"I think about you and your work and that television show."

Josie smiled. "I appreciate your concern, Risa, but I really have to go now. I have a meeting before work."

"*Cara . . .*"

"We'll talk tonight."

"*Cara,* that producer, that Roberto Valentine—"

Josie stopped. "What about him?"

"He was here last night. He was looking for you. He said it was important."

"Did he say what was important?"

"No, just that he must see you and talk with you. That it was important," she repeated.

Josie thought for a moment. Did Bobby Valentine know

Courtney was dead? Did that mean he knew where the body was located? "Did he say anything, anything at all, that would give you a clue as to what he wanted?"

Risa repeated her statement. "It was important."

"Well, I'll be sure I see him as soon as possible. What's this?" she added as Risa handed her a large paper bag.

"With that man running around talking about important things to say to you, and little Tyler looking so serious and worried, I start to get upset myself. So I bake. I calm down."

Josie opened the bag and peeked in. "Biscotti! Risa, thank you!"

"I have a bag for Tyler, too. I think you not do much home cooking this season."

Josie hugged her. "You're the best, and you know Tyler prefers cooking from your home to anything I might produce. I've got to run. Thank you! Thank you!"

Josie got in her truck, started it, and plunged her hand into the bag of biscotti. Her overalls were getting a bit tight, but no sane person would turn down Risa's cooking. She munched all the way to the office.

Jill was perched on the front porch rail of the office for Island Contracting. Swinging her legs, her long hair moving in the early morning breeze, she didn't look much older than Tyler. Then Josie remembered the video.

But the face that looked up at her wasn't that of a naive young woman with nothing on her mind. Josie got the impression that Jill had passed a difficult night.

"Hi."

Jill's response was a surprise. "You know, don't you?"

Josie decided to be honest. "About the films—the tapes—yes, I do. My son and his friend . . ."

"I can guess." Jill jumped down and slid her hands into the pockets of her jeans. Josie realized for the first time that Jill's clothing was always a size or two too large. It was, she now realized, an attempt to camouflage a remarkable body. "Do I get two weeks' severance or doesn't that apply?"

Josie was taken aback. "What are you talking about?"

"You're firing me, aren't you?"

"No, why would I fire you?"

"Because of the video."

"No way. What you did before you came to Island Contracting is your own business."

"I lied on my application."

"Well, yes, but . . ." Josie stopped herself before she admitted that particular activity could be considered an Island Contracting tradition. "You probably thought you had a good reason to," she finished her sentence.

"But it says on the bottom of the third page of the application that inclusion of inaccurate information is grounds for dismissal."

"Does that sound like me?" Josie asked, smiling. "It's just a standardized form." She thought for a moment. "Maybe I could cover that bit up with Wite-Out."

Jill's face brightened and she laughed. "You probably shouldn't. That would be almost like asking people to lie to you. Don't you want to know about the people you hire?"

"Sure, but our hiring practices are a bit different from most contractors'. One of the founding principles of Island Contracting is to help people. A lot of people make mistakes, but not a lot are helped to correct them. We do that."

"Like Dottie."

"Exactly."

"But things are different right now."

"You're talking about Courtney."

Jill nodded. "Yes. Let's face it, as soon as the police find out she was murdered, Dottie will be a prime suspect."

"You're right, of course. But no one knows she's dead."

And Josie hoped she would be able to figure out who the murderer was before anyone did.

"But once the word about my past is out, Dottie won't be the only suspect. I can just see the headline 'Porn Queen Suspect in Murder of Courtney Castle.' "

"Porn queen?" Josie repeated the phrase.

"Yeah, like Cleopatra, Queen of the Nile, or Elizabeth, Queen of England. I've always wondered what royalty had to do with skin flicks."

Josie was silent.

"You want to know why I did it, right?"

"Look, it's your business and I don't want to be nosy, but . . ."

"I did it for the same reason most everyone does. So I could eat and keep a roof over my head and pay my car insurance—and save enough money to learn a trade.

"You see, I wasn't a good student and even though I graduated from high school, I didn't have any marketable skills. Hell, I was so stupid, I didn't even know what a marketable skill was. But I had taken a shop class my last semester of my senior year—I think my adviser stuck me in that because I needed the credit to graduate and he figured I wouldn't have to know anything to pass that class. But after the first week I was hooked.

"I love everything about being a carpenter, from the way the wood smells and feels to the kick I get out of slamming nails into wood and building something from nothing. Unfortunately, I discovered this love a little late in my education. If I'd been smart, I would have flunked yet another class that semester. Then I could have returned in the fall, taken some classes in carpentry, and gotten some qualifications under my belt. As it was, I discovered that the only qualifications I had were under my shirt. Sorry, bad joke."

"So you got a job acting in skin flicks," Josie said, repeating the term Jill had used.

"Well, not at first. But it took me less than a month to learn two things: If I was going to be a carpenter, I needed some formal training and getting trained would take more money than I was making working at the mall. Actually, I was working in a T-shirt shop and it was my boss who suggested I apply for a job at a modeling agency on the other side of town. I knew it wasn't legit—that they were looking for women to do nude stuff—but I didn't think much about it. The money was good and I figured I'd do a few films, get the cash to go back to school, and that would be that. The pay was great. I did three of those lousy films and made enough money to live and go to tech school for a year."

"Was it awful?" Josie asked.

"Making the films?"

"Yes."

"A little embarrassing at first. But you get used to anything and the films I was in were pretty tame compared to many these days. The problem is that while thinking about my future, I didn't think about the future."

"What do you mean?"

"I forgot that those films would be around for a long time, that I would always have to wonder if someone recognized me."

"Like Tyler. Has it happened before?"

"No. At least, not that I know of. I suppose someone might recognize me and not say anything. You know, not want to admit to watching things like that and all."

"What you did . . . It wasn't illegal or anything, was it?"

"No. I wasn't a minor and what I did was just run-of-the-mill porn, not snuff films or anything horrible like that."

"So it's just that they were embarrassing. That's the only reason you hide the fact that you did them."

"Look. Be honest. If I had listed star of porn videos: *Ample Assets, Born to Bop,* and *Vegetarian Meat*—"

"What?"

"*Vegetarian Meat.* Apparently the producers were aiming for distribution in the California New Age market."

"You're kidding."

"That's what I was told."

"Was it . . . um . . . different from the other two?"

"There were some windchimes hanging in the background and we did it on a zafu."

"A what?"

"It's this round pillow that people sit on when they meditate—it may be comfortable for that, but for what I was doing, give me the average bed pillow any day of the week. Other than those things, it was same old, same old. You know." Jill paused. "But you didn't answer my question."

"Would I have hired you if I had known about the movies?" Josie thought about the question. "I can't think of any reason not to. I mean, you had the qualifications to do the job and the experience." She paused.

"But things are different now that Courtney's dead." Jill spoke what she thought Josie was thinking.

"Does that have anything to do with your films?" She asked a second question when Jill didn't answer the first. "Did Courtney know about them?"

"She may have."

"Why do you say that?"

"Well, you know those interviews that Bobby Valentine did yesterday?"

"Yes."

"Twice he referred to me as the photogenic Ms. Pike."

"But he was filming you."

"Yes, and he said something about that, too: how much I

seemed like someone who was accustomed to being before the camera."

"Could he have been referring to anything else? Have you done any more legitimate film work?"

"Nope. Not a bit. Those videos and whatever is shown on *Courtney Castle's Castles*. That's it. I wondered, you know, if I should tell someone about the films once I heard about the television show."

"Why?"

"Because once you're on TV, you're not exactly the same anonymous person you were before. It did occur to me that I might be recognized."

"Good point. So you thought about telling me about your past when you heard about Courtney's show."

"To be honest, no. I did think about telling either Courtney or Bobby Valentine though. I actually tried to bring up the subject with Courtney. But she said she was too busy to talk. That she had to meet someone."

"When?" Josie asked, surprised when Jill didn't continue.

"That morning. The morning she interviewed you."

"Really?"

"Yes. In fact, I think I may have been the last person to see her alive."

"Well, not the last person," Josie said. "The last person to see her alive was her killer."

"The person she said she had to meet," Jill said.

"Sounds like it to me," Josie agreed, wondering just who that person could have been.

TWENTY-SEVEN

JOSIE SLAMMED HER hammer against the two-by-four, wedging it into place. They'd been working for two hours without a break. It was hot, her arms and shoulders ached, and sweat was pouring down her forehead. She smacked the board one more time, and with a loud crack, the last piece fell into place. The women sighed and then laughed a bit.

"Time for lunch." Josie pulled a filthy bandanna from her pocket and wiped the sweat off her forehead. "There's a giant thermos of iced tea in the back of the truck. Anybody want to run to the deli?"

Fifteen minutes later four very tired women were sitting on the dock, large sandwiches on their laps, passing around a giant bag of Chee•tos. There was a gentle breeze off the water, and Josie, busy consuming her year's allowance of fat in one sitting, took a break, leaned against the silvery wooden rail, and closed her eyes. She'd been up early and then worked hard all morning.

"The world is your oyster, but you'll never crack it lying on a mattress."

The words were spoken in a shrill, familiar voice. Josie reached into her past and identified it. Naomi Van Ripper. Josie opened her eyes and looked right into the stern face of the librarian. "We're on our lunch break," she said, and then

231

regretted the explanation. She didn't have to justify her actions—or those of her crew—to anybody.

"Then you are free to speak with me." It wasn't a question.

Josie sighed. No reason to be rude. "I suppose."

"Privately."

Josie stood up and stretched. "Okay. But I'll have to eat at the same time."

Dr. Van Ripper looked down at the food in her lap, and for a horrible moment Josie was afraid politeness was going to force her to offer to share. "Not exactly a healthy repast, is it? Very high-calorie."

"I burn a lot of calories," Josie said, standing up for herself. "If you want to speak privately, maybe we'd better go back to the house."

"It will be filthy, but I suppose that can't be helped."

"Remodeling is dirty work." Josie led the way up the path. She walked briskly and was maliciously pleased to hear Naomi Van Ripper panting with the effort of keeping up.

But once they were inside, the librarian reasserted her dominance. "What is that thing?" she asked, pointing to the well-wrapped sculpture still sitting by the fireplace.

"It's art. The owners asked us to be especially careful with it."

"Oh. Is it sturdy?"

"It's made from steel . . . What are you doing?"

"Sitting down. If it's made of steel, it certainly won't be damaged by my weight."

Josie wasn't inclined to argue. "I hope not." She leaned back against a pile of Sheetrock and pulled her sandwich from its greasy wrapping. "Why are you here?"

"I thought I had explained. I need to speak with you."

Josie took a big bite of her sandwich. A large ruffle of ham fell from her mouth and into her lap. She reached down, dusted it off, and popped it in her mouth.

Naomi grimaced.

Josie took another bite and reminded herself that anger would accomplish nothing. She chewed and waited for the other woman to speak.

"I had an interesting conversation with Courtney."

"When?"

"What difference would that make?"

"I'm just . . . you know, curious."

"I don't know. A few days ago. Apparently what she said is true, otherwise you would know all about it."

"I have no idea what you're talking about," Josie admitted. "What did Courtney say about me . . . that you think may be true."

"She said you maintain absolutely no contact with your family. Disgraceful."

Josie had opened her mouth to answer before the final, condemning word. But when she opened it again, she found she had no idea what to say. It had been years since she had thought much about her family. Because she had trained, carefully trained, herself not to. "You don't know anything about it. They chose not to have contact with me." She knew she sounded like a stubborn child, inarticulate and angry.

"Why, I happen to know a lot about it. I speak with your mother at least once a week and I frequently see your father at the hospital."

Josie noted that some things didn't change. Apparently her mother still visited the library for a weekly pile of books. That didn't surprise her any more than her father's dedication to his job as hospital administrator did. She had assumed that their lives had gone on without her, but the reality of that fact was surprisingly painful. "They complain about me?" she asked, suddenly unable to eat another bite.

"No, they're more dignified than that. But everyone in town knows how much you hurt them."

"I hurt them! What about how they hurt me?" She was

shocked into saying more than she planned. "I needed them! I was desperate! I can understand their shock, but to abandon me and my son—their grandson—like they did! How dare they claim to be the ones who were hurt? How dare they?"

"That's not—"

"I never talk about them," Josie continued. "You just ask my son. I have never, no matter how much they hurt me, I have never, ever, ever said anything against them. They left me stranded with no money, no insurance, no nothing. But I created a life for myself and I brought up Tyler alone. And I've been a good mother and he's a good kid. And you can ask every single person I know—you can ask my son. I have never, ever complained or criticized my family. Ever. Never."

"I don't believe I accused you of that particular failing."

"You said everyone in town knew that I hurt my parents!"

"Not this town. Your hometown. The town you grew up in."

Josie heard a bit of compassion in Naomi Van Ripper's voice, but she heard the words also. "So my parents have been complaining about me? Telling everyone they meet that their daughter is a dreadful person?"

"No. I doubt if they have said more about you than you claim to have said about them."

"So you're just assuming I hurt them! What do they do? Wander around with pitiful expressions on their well-groomed faces? Did my father rip the Father's Day poster I made him in fifth grade off his office wall? Are they ashamed of me and my life?" Josie realized that she was going to begin crying if this conversation went on much longer.

"Josie, I believe you misunderstand the situation. If your father doesn't have your poster on his office wall, it's because he doesn't have an office. He was forced to retire many years ago. Fifteen or sixteen. Right after you left college."

Josie was stunned. He had barely been in his fifties then.

Her workaholic father retired early? "I don't understand. Why did he retire? He was so young and he loved his job."

It was Naomi Van Ripper's turn to be surprised. "You don't know, do you?"

"I don't know what? What are you talking about?"

"Your father had a stroke. Right after you vanished. At least, that's what we thought when we pieced the story together later."

But Josie was focusing on the original statement. "My father had a stroke? Was it serious?"

"Very. He was in the hospital for months and then in a rehabilitation facility for almost a year. He speaks now and can use his upper body, but he can't walk."

"He's paralyzed? He stays in bed?"

"Heavens, no. He uses one of those scooters and gets around just fine."

"But . . . but he can't work like that. And golf. He can't play golf or tennis, can he?" When her father wasn't working, he could usually be found playing one of those two games at the country club.

"No, he can't. It's been quite a change for him, but your father is a strong man and he has managed just fine—to all outward appearances, that is."

Josie knew what that meant. Brought up in a family where "No one wants to hear what's wrong with you" was a constant theme, and "Keeping yourself to yourself " was considered a virtue, outsiders wouldn't have any way of knowing to what extent her father was suffering. "When did it happen?"

"The stroke?"

"Yes, the stroke."

"Years ago. I told you."

"But when? Exactly."

"Three days before Christmas your freshman year of college—your only year of college apparently."

Josie didn't even hear the second half of the statement.

"Are you sure? I mean about the day. Exactly. Are you sure it was three days before Christmas? Not a day later?"

Dr. Van Ripper took being accurate very seriously. "Let me think about it. As I recall, you were due home the day before Christmas Eve."

"I was, but how did you know that?"

"Your mother was in the library the week before trying to find a recipe for some sort of cookie you liked. I don't remember exactly, but I think it was something made with peppermint. She said she had never made them."

Josie slowly nodded her head. "They were made from pink and white dough, twisted together and shaped like little candy canes. Our next-door neighbor used to bake them for Christmas when I was a kid, but then she moved to Florida. My mother always said they were just too much trouble to make." She looked at the librarian. "Are you sure she was going to make them? For me?"

"That's what she was planning. To surprise you, she said."

"It would have amazed me," Josie admitted. "But about the stroke. Are you sure it happened the day before I was to come home?"

"Yes. I was one of the last people to see your father that day. It was snowy and I took a longer than usual lunch hour to pick up a few last-minute gifts. I should have walked—you should always walk when you can, of course—but I was hoping to find a large stockpot for my sister-in-law and I didn't want to have to lug it halfway across town on foot, so I ended up driving around downtown looking for a place to park. I had just about given up when I saw your father get into that big black Mercedes he always drove. Funny how you remember things when tragedy strikes, isn't it? Later that night, when I heard the news, all I could think of was how healthy and happy he had looked, tossing the wrapped gifts he was carrying into the passenger seat and waving for me to take his spot when he left. I called out a greeting, of course, and he replied, saying something about how it would be a good Christmas because you would be home." She nodded to herself. "He looked wonderful. Who would have known?"

"He said that? That it would be a good Christmas because I would be coming home?"

"Yes, I think his exact words were that you would be home tomorrow. So, you see, that *was* the day he had the stroke. Is the date very important?"

"Yes. To me, it's very important." She thought for a moment before continuing. "He almost died. That's what you said, that he almost died."

"Yes." Dr. Van Ripper paused for a moment, then added meaningfully, "And no one from town ever saw you again."

"I . . ." There was just too much for Josie to assimilate. Everything she had thought, every hurt, every angry moment, had been, apparently, based on an untruth, a misunderstanding. She had no idea what to think. "I don't know what to say. You . . . You and everyone in town . . . You don't understand what happened. How . . . this all got started." She looked around at the torn-apart house. The life she lived now, the life she had created for herself, was, if she could believe this woman, based on a misunderstanding.

Dr. Van Ripper was staring at her and Josie realized she should say something. She grasped at the only topic that didn't seem to matter very much at the moment. "You mentioned Courtney. What does she have to do with this?"

"It was Courtney who told me that you still have no contact with your family."

Josie tried to focus on the topic at hand. "I don't think she and I spoke about that."

"Perhaps not, but she has spoken with your family."

"When? Recently?"

"My dear, just because you chose not to keep in touch . . ." She didn't end the sentence.

"You mean other people did."

"Others, yes, and Courtney was prominent among them."

"You did say that she always came to the library to visit when she was in town, but I'm sure she didn't visit my parents the same way. Of course, her mother and my mother are probably still close."

"Yes, I'm sure they are. I don't want to upset you more, but there are people in town who are of the opinion that Courtney has become something of a substitute daughter."

"For my parents?" Josie realized she sounded stricken. It was almost as though she had discovered she actually did have a family only to have it taken away from her once again.

"Yes. Things have been difficult for them, of course. And since you chose not to be around—for whatever reason—they have come to depend on Courtney more and more."

"Is that what they say?" Josie asked. Something didn't sound right here. Unless things had changed dramatically, her parents weren't likely to be complaining about their lives—or their daughter's choices. Of course, she realized, things had changed dramatically. A lot had happened. She had changed. Why wouldn't they have done so also?

She remembered the last time she had spoken with her mother. She'd called right before leaving school, thinking that the announcement of her pregnancy would be easier on the phone, that they could use the night to get over the shock and then the three of them could sit down and talk it through once she arrived home. Looking back, she knew it had been a cowardly thing to do, but she had been young, scared, and, she had to admit, stupid.

Her mother's response to the news she had blurted out abruptly had been straightforward—or so she thought at the time. She had said nothing. After a few minutes of silence on the other end of the line, Josie had asked to talk to her father.

Her mother had finally spoken. "I'm sorry, dear, but under the circumstances, your father will not—cannot—speak with you. I'm very sorry, dear, but you're going to have to . . . take care of . . . yourself by yourself. Your father . . . I . . . Your father and I have a lot on our plates just now—"

Josie had hung up without listening to more. That was the last time she'd spoken with either of her parents. Over the years she had replayed the conversation again and again. She had wondered about each and every word of rejection. It had never occurred to her that the circumstances her mother was referring to were something that had happened at home, not her pregnancy.

"Josie, you're becoming a bit absentminded, dear. It's not an attractive trait."

It was true. She was getting absentminded. She needed to find out more about Courtney. She needed to ask questions this woman might be able to answer. She took a deep breath and opened her sandwich again. She would think, worry, mourn her relationship with her parents later. Right now she had to find out who killed Courtney Castle before her murder damaged the life Josie had—whether prompted by necessity or a foolish misunderstanding—worked so hard to create.

TWENTY-EIGHT

"**S**O DID COURTNEY visit my parents the way she visited you at the library?" Josie asked.

"That's a dreadfully imprecise question. Are you asking if she visited as frequently or, possibly, whether or not she talked as intimately to them as she does to me?"

"Both, I guess."

"Naturally, there's no way I can compare my visits with those Courtney paid to your parents, but I believe she saw them frequently."

"And they talked about me."

"I don't know that."

"You said Courtney told you I didn't have any contact with my family," Josie reminded her.

"Yes, that was recently, when she and I spoke here on the island. At home, I quite frankly don't remember her mentioning you or your family. She talked mainly about the television shows she was on. She's been very successful, you know."

Josie thought about the tapes she had watched the night before. Not, she knew, so very successful until recently. But she wasn't there to trash a dead woman. "She did a lot of different types of shows. Did she ask your advice about her career?"

"She asked my advice about everything." It was obvious that Dr. Van Ripper was proud of this fact.

Through the open doorway Josie could see her crew picking up their tools and preparing to return to work on the addition. They were a great bunch of women, responsible and energetic; she owed it to them to solve this murder before it damaged the lives of innocent people. "Really?" she asked aloud. Talk, talk, talk, she chanted silently.

"Courtney worked very, very hard for her successes. But she made time to return home at least once—and sometimes twice—a year, and we always talked about how her career was going. She had things planned out from the time she graduated from college, you know."

"Really?" Well, it had worked the last time.

"Yes. There were changes, of course. She had hoped to make it to a network and anchor a newscast, and I think a show like *Today* or *Good Morning America* would certainly have benefited from her talent. But she changed her mind after her first job in public television."

"Really?"

"Yes, I remember how it happened. She had been working out west somewhere for about a year and she spent the first week of her annual vacation in New York City, visiting the networks and deciding if she wanted to work for one of them. She came home quite discouraged."

"They didn't want her?"

"Heavens, no! I can't imagine such a thing!" came the indignant response. "But she was upset by the greed and self-importance she found there . . . Excuse me?"

"Nothing." Josie had mumbled something about how it sounded like Courtney would fit right in, but on second thought she decided that silence was best.

"She knew then and there—talking with me in the library reference room—that she would dedicate her life to public broadcasting. She wanted to share herself with the public. That's the way she put it."

"Very generous of her."

Dr. Van Ripper looked up sharply. "You always were jealous of Courtney."

"I . . ." Why deny it? Josie just shrugged. "So Courtney decided to work for public broadcasting."

"Yes, and, as the network of such shows as *Masterpiece Theatre* and *Julia Child's Kitchen*, I certainly thought she was making an excellent decision. It is the correct place for her to be. And that's important when you choose your career."

"Definitely."

Dr. Van Ripper looked around. "You think this is the correct place for a young woman who had all your advantages to end up?"

Josie took a deep breath. Her red hair began to become slightly static; people who knew her would be aware of her rising anger. "Yes, I do. I am a hard worker. I am successful. I have a useful trade and I use it to help people. I am proud of what I do and I believe that anyone would be. Including my family." The last words came out of her mouth before she had thought them through. But she heard them and realized, surprised, that they might possibly be true. "This is an excellent place for a young woman who was brought up with many advantages to end up," she concluded, smiling sincerely.

The librarian seemed startled. "Well, perhaps."

"But let's get back to Courtney. Did she talk to you about her personal life?"

"You mean men?"

"Yes."

"No. Of course, I knew she had many admirers, many, many admirers, but she didn't talk about them. We usually discussed her career."

Josie frowned. "Do you know a lot about television?"

"Well, no, but I am very interested in the subject, and my sister happens to be very involved in charitable work, and the foundation she runs is a major donor of funds for public television."

Bingo! She'd known it. Courtney was not the type of person to stay in touch with an elderly librarian just for old times' sake. She had gotten Naomi Van Ripper to do much of her high school research many years ago. And she had used her—or her connection to her sister—to move up in public television. Suddenly, Josie felt tired and old and, above all, deeply sad. She folded the wrapping over the remainder of her sandwich and got up. "I'm glad we could talk, but I have to get back to work."

"I hope, Josie, that I have given you something to think about. Perhaps you should reconsider some of your decisions. Your parents are getting old. And there might be other people in town who would be happy to see you."

"You've given me a lot to think about," Josie replied seriously and honestly. "Thank you very much."

"Well, I'm glad. I'll be seeing you around. Courtney invited me to visit the set anytime I please."

"Do that." Without another word, Josie turned and walked out of the house, back to her crew.

Tyler was asleep on the couch when Josie entered her apartment. She looked down at him and smiled. He was beginning to grow a beard, but she could still see the little kid he had been. She sat down in the chair across from the couch. Urchin, Tyler's little brown Burmese cat, jumped into her lap and the two of them stared at her son. After years of worrying about the consequences of raising him without any family other than herself, it was possible that she would present him with grandparents sometime in the near future. Would that make him happy? Improve his life? She had no idea. It was the same problem she'd had for the last seventeen years of motherhood. She never knew if her decisions were right, if what she was doing was good for her son.

She was still deciding whether or not to contact her parents when Tyler's eyes opened and he smiled at her. "Hi. Why didn't you wake me up?"

"I just got here," Josie lied. "Have you had dinner?"

"No, and I'm starving." He sat up and stretched. "Is there anything in the house?"

"I don't know." She got up and headed over to the refrigerator. The last time she had looked, this morning, there had been a half-gallon of milk, some diet soda, a quart of orange juice, and a full complement of all the things that seemed to grow in there: bottles of catsup and mustard and jars of mayonnaise, jam, and pancake syrup. If she had eggs, she could produce a cheese omelet. Or, perhaps, if that package of hot dogs hadn't been consumed yet . . . She pulled open the door, ignoring the magnet and shopping list as they dropped to the floor. "What the . . . ?"

A bright blue casserole sat on the top shelf.

"It's that tortellini salad you like so much. Risa said she made extra."

"I don't know what we'd do without that woman," Josie said honestly, pulling the casserole from the refrigerator.

"She also sent up bread and a bowl of those great burnt peppers." Tyler got up and started opening drawers and grabbing silverware.

"She really takes care of us." Josie glanced over at her son before she continued. "She's almost like a member of the family, a relative."

"What do you mean? She's better than a relative. You and I don't cook this well!" Tyler said.

Josie realized that his concept of family was limited to the two of them. What would happen if she expanded that concept? What would happen if, after all these years, she called home and explained her side of that last phone call? Her misunderstanding of her mother's statements? She frowned.

But Tyler's concerns were more immediate. "Hey, do you want orange juice, beer, milk, or diet soda?"

"Diet soda. Cream soda, if there is any. Or else . . ." She noticed the tiny flashing light on her answering machine as she spoke. "Did you check for messages when you came in?"

"Oh, yeah, I forgot to tell you. That Bobby Valentine called. He said he needed to speak with you. He said it was . . . uh, urgent."

Josie glanced at her son. At least he had the grace to look embarrassed. "Urgent, hey?" She sighed. "Did he leave his number?"

"Yeah, it's the first message. The second was from Sam. He said he was calling to say hello."

Josie rolled her eyes. It seemed that dinner would have to wait.

Bobby Valentine hadn't just insisted on talking to her. He had insisted on seeing her. Immediately. And he wouldn't tell her why. Not, he had said, on the phone. He was in Courtney's trailer. He needed to see her there. Immediately.

If he hadn't sounded so worried, she would never have left home without eating. Now, banging on the aluminum door of the trailer, she regretted that decision. If it was so important that he see her, why wasn't he answering the door?

"For heaven's sake, shut up! Do you want everyone in the neighborhood to know we're here?"

Well, if they hadn't heard her banging, they probably got the point when she screamed. She would have made more noise if she hadn't been grabbed from behind and pulled toward the darkened trailer.

"What the . . . ?"

"Stop kicking me, damn it!"

The door fell open, smashing into the wall behind it, and Josie and Bobby Valentine fell into the trailer, crashing into furniture and landing in a tangle on the floor.

"Damn. Damn. Damn. What the hell do you think you're doing?"

"Me? You attacked me. You asked me to come here and then you attacked me from behind!" Josie rolled away from him as she spoke. "Turn on the lights and tell me why I'm here before I call the police!"

"Shut up. Shut up. Shut up. Shut up." Bobby Valentine scrambled to his feet and, ignoring his own injunctions about silence, slammed the door, and switched on the overhead light. "Look, damn it! Look!"

He pointed.

She looked. And looked again. "What the hell is that?"

"Courtney . . ."

"It's not Courtney." Josie walked across the floor to the exercise bike. "It's a wig. Courtney wore a wig?"

He walked over to the mirrored wall and pressed a tiny button she hadn't noticed before. A door sprang open and a hidden shelf appeared. Three wig stands stood on it. Two had identical Courtney pageboys. One was bald. The third wig was sitting on the seat of the exercise bike, not a strand of hair disturbed by the move.

"You called me here because one of Courtney's wigs is out of place? I'm missing my dinner for hair?"

"Courtney is dead."

Josie looked at him, walked over to the wig, and examined it. "There's no blood on it." She glanced around the room, relieved by what she didn't see. "There's no body." She looked up at him. "Why do you think she's dead? And why did you call me here to see this?" She wanted to add one more question. What did Bobby Valentine actually know?

"Courtney is never, ever seen without one of those wigs."

"You're telling me you think she's dead because . . . because these three wigs are here and she isn't?"

"I am telling you that if these three wigs are here and she isn't, she is dead."

"She wears one in the shower? When she sleeps?"

"No, of course not. But you don't hear water running, do you?"

"So? Maybe she's sleeping somewhere. Maybe she's gone for an evening swim. I can think of a million places she might be." A wooden canoe in the middle of the house wasn't one of them.

"You don't know Courtney. She takes her hair seriously. Very, very seriously. If her wigs are here and she's not, she's dead."

"Maybe she has another one. And she's at a party someplace wearing it."

"No. Courtney has had her wigs made by a woman who lives in Queens for longer than I've known her. That woman made her three wigs, those three wigs. There's only one explanation. Courtney is dead."

"And her wig walked back here?" Josie realized she sounded sarcastic. But he had taken her away from an evening with her son for what seemed like a foolish reason. Now, if he had seen Courtney's body, like she had . . . She leaned forward and looked at him. Bobby Valentine was frantic.

Josie made a quick decision, took a deep breath, and plunged in. "You know, don't you? It's not just a guess with these wigs and all. You know that she's dead."

Bobby Valentine let out a long relieved breath. "Yes. Yes. And . . . you do, too?"

It was a question. "Yes. I saw her body."

"Thank heavens!" The relief was visible. His entire body seemed to relax. "So where is she?"

"What?"

"Where is Courtney? Where is her body?"

TWENTY-NINE

"YOU DON'T KNOW where Courtney's body is?" Josie asked.

"Not at this minute. No. Do you?"

"No." Josie frowned. "When was the last time you saw her?"

"The day before yesterday."

"In the canoe?"

"Canoe? What canoe?" Bobby Valentine grabbed her shoulders. "Did you toss her in the bay, for God's sake?"

"Let go of me!" Josie pulled back and heard the sound of her shirt ripping. "Let go!"

"What the hell is going on?"

"I—"

"He—"

"Sam, what are you doing? Stop that!" As the words slipped out, Josie realized exactly what Sam was doing. He was, to her complete amazement, punching Bobby Valentine in the nose.

"Josie, call the police," he shouted back.

"Damn it! Would you please stop hitting me?" Bobby Valentine, the younger and clearly stronger man, pulled himself free and started slugging back.

Josie, in a panic, grabbed the first thing her hand met and threw it at the two men. There was a crash and then an incredible smell filled the air. But the fighting stopped.

Sam was leaning against one wall of the trailer, breathing heavily. Bobby Valentine stood in the middle of the floor, fists clenched, eyes flashing, and nose running. "What did you do?" he asked Josie.

"Yeah, what was that?"

The two men were looking at her as though *she* had done something wrong!

"I . . ." Josie looked down at the floor. She had broken a large bottle of some sort of smelly oil. "Bath oil?"

"Probably massage oil," Bobby Valentine explained. "The bath oil would be in the bathroom. Courtney believed that daily massages kept her sane. At least that's what she said. There's a portable massage table stashed under the couch."

"Daily massages?" Sam repeated the words as he rubbed his knuckles.

Josie thought it was time to get back to the point. "Why did you come in here and start punching?" It was so unlike Sam to do something like that.

"Why do you think? I walked in and this man was grabbing at you. Look, your shirt is in shreds! What did you expect me to do?"

Josie and Bobby Valentine both looked at her ripped sleeve. "Well, not exactly in shreds," she said.

"You thought I was assaulting Josie?" Bobby Valentine sounded as though he could hardly believe it.

"You were grabbing her," Sam stated stubbornly.

"He was upset. He thought I had put Courtney in a canoe and floated her out to sea," Josie explained. Truth be told, she was thrilled. Sam had fought for her! He had been protecting her . . . well, her whatever!

Sam kicked a piece of broken glass across the room. "I guess this means you know Courtney is dead." He looked up at Bobby Valentine.

"Yeah. Good thing, too, because if she was alive to see what we did to this place, she would have killed us."

The oil was liberally splashed on both the flowered chintz armchair and couch; it was also forming a large patch on the Berber wool wall-to-wall carpeting. (Courtney had chosen these furnishings, Josie suddenly realized. They reminded her of her mother's home.)

"It's new and it's something she's always wanted. This trailer was Courtney's pride and joy," he continued.

Sam had been walking around, looking at everything. "It should be," he commented. "I never thought public broadcasting paid well enough for people to afford things like this. It's not a perk, is it?"

"A perk? You mean something that's provided for her by the company? No way! We do everything on the cheap. The salaries are low, ridiculously low, in fact. And we survive on free work provided by our internship program."

"Then who pays for this? Or is Courtney Castle independently wealthy?"

"It's donated. Like the food we eat. Like the T-shirts the crew wears. Et cetera, et cetera."

"You're kidding!" Josie looked around. "Is stuff like this normally donated to public broadcasting people?"

"I can answer that one," Sam said. "No. Not usually. Right?" He looked at the producer for confirmation.

"Never. At least not that I know about."

"Who provided all this junk?" Sam asked.

"That I don't know," Bobby Valentine answered.

"I thought there was always on-screen credit for donated items," Sam said.

"Sometimes. But it's not required. We're very careful to credit two groups of donors. First, of course, donations that are made because the donor is looking for an on-screen credit. You know, like those travel and accommodation credits you see on most of the shows on television. And we always credit anything that might look like a conflict of interest."

"What do you mean?" Sam asked.

"Well, if we use a brand-name piece of equipment during a show—a donation, right—well, we make sure the credit goes out on the air because the viewer has seen the brand name and we want to be sure that it is understood that we're not endorsing the brand but using it because it was free."

Sam nodded.

Josie had another question. "What about publicity? Personal publicity? When brands are mentioned, does that mean those things were paid for? Not donated?"

"No way! Do you think actresses pay for those dresses they wear to the Academy Awards? Famous people are always being given things. That's just the way it is."

"Who paid for this trailer?" Sam asked.

"I really don't know. We're not putting up a trailer company credit at the end of the shows, so it must have been a private donation, that's all I know."

"Could you find out?"

"I could ask around. See what the scuttlebutt is."

"Great."

Josie didn't see why Sam was so interested in who paid for the trailer. They had just discovered that Bobby Valentine knew Courtney was dead. There were, it seemed to her, a lot more important and immediate concerns. "So where did you see Courtney?"

"I thought you said he knew she was dead. You mean, you don't have a body? Again?"

"Sam, you make it sound as though I've somehow been negligent in losing Courtney. I keep telling you it had nothing to do with me. I left her hanging in the canoe."

"The canoe that is . . . that was . . . in the living room, the one we did the interview next to?"

"Yeah. In fact, she was in there when you were asking all those questions."

"How long did she hang there?" Bobby Valentine asked.

"Less than forty-eight hours as far as I know."

"You think she was moved from someplace else after she was killed?" Sam asked.

"I didn't say that." Josie thought for a moment. "But I see what you're getting at. She disappeared two days before. I suppose she was probably up there until Jill found her."

"Jill? She's the pretty one with the chest, isn't she? Why was she up there?" Bobby Valentine asked his second question before Josie had time to answer—or protest—the first.

"She was figuring out a way to get the canoe down without damaging it. She was doing her job, and I don't think—"

"If you didn't know the body was up there, then when— and where—did you see it?" Sam asked Bobby Valentine.

"Last night. It . . . was here." He pointed at the oil-soaked chair. "Just sitting there . . ."

Sam nodded. "Sure, rigor would have started to wear off . . ." he mumbled to himself. "How was she killed?"

"I haven't the foggiest. I mean, I didn't see any blood or anything," Josie said.

"How was she killed?" Sam directed the same question to the producer.

"I . . . I think she may have been hit on the head." Bobby Valentine started to look a bit pale and sat down in the makeup chair before he continued. "I didn't look as closely as I should have," he admitted, his voice a bit shaky.

"You came in here and found her. It must have been a shock," Sam said slowly.

"Not a shock. Not at first. You see, I didn't know she was

dead. I came in after work. . . . I wanted to check her answering machine for messages. And I didn't turn on the light or anything. I . . . She was in the chair. I was surprised . . . thrilled . . . relieved to see her, I guess. And then, almost immediately, I realized she wasn't all right. Well, that she was dead."

"How closely did you look at her?" Josie asked, remembering how reluctant she had been to do the same thing.

"I . . . I moved her. I didn't mean to. I went up to her and . . . I guess I touched her on the shoulder. I don't remember exactly."

"You were in shock," Sam said. "It's completely understandable. Go on."

"Well, I think I may have pushed her a bit. Anyway, she fell over and . . . I saw a large lump on her temple. No blood. But it was certainly ugly."

"I didn't see a bump," Josie said. "But . . ." She looked across the room at the wig on the exercise bike. "It could have been hidden by the wig, couldn't it?"

"It probably was," Bobby Valentine said. "She loved that thick wave that came across her forehead. The injury was right underneath."

Josie nodded.

"What are you thinking?" Sam asked her.

"When she was up in the canoe, one of the things I noticed was that she was made-up and her hair was in perfect order. Maybe that was to disguise the injury. Do you think that's possible?"

"Well, whether that was the motivation or not, it seems to have been one of the end results. None of you touched her when she was up there?"

"I don't think so," Josie answered. "No one said they had. And it was a little creepy."

"What did you do, run tours?" Bobby Valentine must have realized how he sounded. "Sorry, I'm a bit upset."

"Not surprising," Sam said.

"Everyone on the crew did look up there," she explained. "But I don't think anyone touched her."

"Let's go back to when you discovered the body here," Sam asked Bobby Valentine. "After you found out that Courtney was dead, what did you do?"

The producer snorted. "I headed for the nearest bar and got drunk."

Sam frowned. "You went down to Gallagher's?"

"If that's the name of the fake Irish place down by the five-and-dime, the answer is yes."

"Good description. It's owned by a man named Smith. He calls it Gallagher's because he wanted people to think of it as that friendly little Irish place on the corner, but the name is the only good thing about it," Sam commented.

"Yeah. He serves off-price brands while claiming they're top-shelf. But it did the trick. I was plastered."

"And when did you return here?" Sam asked.

"I came back this morning. And she was gone." Bobby Valentine put his head in his hands. "I was hung over. For a moment, I wondered if I was going mad. If I had imagined the entire thing. That was wishful thinking, I guess."

"There was no sign of her here this morning?" Sam asked.

"None."

"What about the wig?" Josie asked.

"What wig?"

Josie pointed. "That one."

They all stared at the blond wig, which was still, despite the fight, sitting on the exercise bike.

"It wasn't there this morning," Bobby said.

"You might not have seen it," Sam suggested.

The other man seemed to consider the question. "I think I

would have. I came in the door and I looked around. Frankly, I felt like shit. Not just the hangover, but I was terrified of seeing Courtney again. Her body, that is." He stood up and walked over to the doorway. "I didn't come in any farther than I needed to be to close the door behind me. And, frankly, I didn't even look around until I had the door closed. Then . . . Then, frankly, I was thrilled to death that the body was gone. I told you. I couldn't believe my eyes. I thought I was dreaming or seeing things. And when I realized she was really gone, I got out of here as fast as possible."

"But you came back——" Sam started to say.

"Are you sure about the wig?" Josie asked at the same time.

"The wig. I really think I would have noticed it from here."

"Why did you come back this evening?" Sam asked.

"Wait a second, Sam." Josie got up and stood by Bobby Valentine's side. "You didn't move from this spot?" she asked.

"No. I'm sure of that."

"And Courtney was sitting . . . placed . . . whatever in that chair last night?"

"Yes."

Josie frowned and then walked over to the chair he had indicated.

"Why did you return here this evening?" Sam repeated his question.

"I couldn't stop thinking about her. About Courtney. She appeared and then disappeared. I . . . I wondered if she would do it again."

"You thought she might come back?" Josie had been circling the chair and she stopped to ask the question.

"It might sound stupid, but I didn't know why she was here in the first place." He shrugged. "So I thought it was possible that she might come back."

"But she didn't." Sam's voice was flat.

"No. Her hair did, though."

For one horrible moment Josie thought Bobby Valentine was going to giggle.

Then he put his head in his hands and began to cry.

THIRTY

JOSIE AND SAM waited patiently for Bobby Valentine to recover his composure. Then . . .

"Why did you call me?" Josie asked.

"I didn't know what else to do." Bobby Valentine glanced over at Sam. "Did you hear about what Courtney said about Josie?"

"That if something happened to her, I would know about it—or something like that," Josie explained.

"Yes. Yes, exactly. Do you know what she meant by that?"

"I haven't the foggiest."

"Are you under the impression that she meant something sinister?" Sam asked.

"What do *you* mean?" Josie asked him.

"I'm asking if it was a 'If I'm found dead, Josie Pigeon is the person who killed me' type of comment," Sam explained.

"Yes, it was," Bobby Valentine answered.

"Wait a minute! How did that subject come up? Do you chat about murder during casual conversation? Or was Courtney obsessed with her own death?"

"It was weird," Bobby Valentine admitted, walking over to the wig and looking at it carefully. "I mean, you're right, Courtney was not the type of person to contemplate her mortality. It was the first day we were here on the island. She was slightly hyper—"

"What sort of hyper?" Sam interrupted to ask.

"You know, excited. Frankly, I thought it was this place."

"The trailer?"

"Yeah, she'd been wanting a customized trailer for years and years. She'd planned it and talked about it. Everyone who knew her had heard about how much she wanted something like this. And then it was finally hers."

"It meant that much to her?" Josie asked.

"Yes. This type of stuff meant the world to Courtney."

"So you were talking about the job or whatever," Sam prompted again.

"Yes, and somehow the conversation turned to people dying."

"Like accidents on the job?"

"No. Maybe. I really don't remember. I was surprised."

"I should hope so. After all, Courtney was accusing Josie of a future murder, after all," Sam said.

"Well, that's true, of course. But I was surprised that she knew Josie Pigeon. It was the first I'd heard of a connection between the two of them."

"Really? She didn't mention knowing Josie when this whole thing began?"

"No way."

"Do you happen to remember when you first heard about Island Contracting?"

"A few months ago."

"From whom?"

"Courtney, I think."

"Do you think she could have known about Josie for a while without mentioning her?"

"Definitely. Courtney only told me what she wanted to tell me."

"And who did Courtney hear about Josie from?"

"No one seems to know the answer to that one." Josie answered Sam's question.

"Maybe we could go through her papers and find out?" Sam suggested.

"Ha. You didn't know Courtney. She was a disaster when it came to keeping records. Drove me nuts," Bobby Valentine said.

"Josie has the same problem. Must have been something in the water when they were growing up," Sam said with a smile.

Bobby Valentine looked as though he didn't believe it. "You two don't seem to have all that much in common. That librarian lady said you've always been different."

Josie frowned. She had just had a thought that seemed significant. But the idea of Naomi Van Ripper talking about her like that had driven it right out of her mind.

Everyone stood around without saying anything for a few minutes. Then Sam asked another question.

"Do people ever pay or give things to get on the show?"

"No way. We're not a sleazy operation. If that has happened, I can promise you that I knew nothing about it." He looked over at Josie. "You didn't offer anyone anything to be on the air, did you?"

"Of course not! I wouldn't do that even if I could afford to, which I can't." She yawned. The adrenaline was subsiding and she was beginning to realize just how exhausted she was. "I've got to get up early tomorrow. And I'm only going to get . . ." She glanced at her watch and gasped. "Four hours of sleep if I leave right now. Which is what I'm going to do!"

"God, I had no idea it was so late," Bobby Valentine said, looking down at his Swiss watch.

"I gather that wig is significant," Sam said.

"Courtney never appeared without one of them on."

"If no one objects, I'll just take it home with me," Sam said, using one finger to pick up the wig.

"Fine with me—" Josie's comment was interrupted by a yawn. "Sorry."

"Are you awake enough to drive home?"

"I'll be fine. And I'll be home in less than ten minutes."

In fact, with a little late-night speeding, ten minutes later she was in bed. She fell asleep wondering what had been said tonight that had seemed fleetingly significant.

She woke up with a horrible ringing in her ears. She really had to find the time to replace the doorbell. By the time her feet hit the floor, Tyler was doing his bit to increase the noise level.

"Ma! You've got company."

Josie grabbed a robe and pulled it over the T-shirt she slept in. She ran her hands through her hair to smooth it down, vaguely expecting Sam. But Annette and Chad stood in her living room, holding hands, nervous expressions on their faces.

"Hi."

"We're here too early," Annette said.

"We wanted to talk to you before work started," Chad explained.

"It's important," Annette added.

"Let me get dressed," Josie said, and hurried back to her bedroom.

When she returned to her guests a few minutes later, the room smelled deliciously of coffee. "Who . . . ?" She spied her son near the coffeemaker watching the fresh brew drip into the pot. "Oh, Tyler, thank you so much. That's just what I need." She reached for a mug and then remembered her manners. "Can I get you both some?"

"Tyler already offered us some, thanks," Chad answered. He and Annette were still standing by the door.

"Come in and sit down," Josie suggested. "I know Tyler is going to leave in just a few minutes. He . . . runs a couple of miles every morning," she lied, inspired. "Thanks for making the coffee, but we don't want to keep you, sweetie."

"Sweetie's just leaving. Nice meeting you two," he said to Chad and Annette. "Bye." With a wide grin on his face, Tyler left the apartment.

"Does he run in plastic flipflops?" Chad asked.

"His running shoes are downstairs," Josie explained, ignoring the fact that a pair of size-ten Nikes lay in the middle of the living room floor.

"We need to talk to you," Chad explained again.

"We're here to tell you the truth," Annette added.

Josie sipped her coffee. "About what?"

"We . . ." Annette looked at Chad and didn't continue.

"We were together on the property next to the house you're remodeling." The young man spoke up.

"Together? You mean you were . . . making love? Outside? On the ground? In the middle of the day?"

"No, of course not. We had only known each other then for a day or two," Chad explained.

"And we wouldn't do something like that outside . . . in the middle of the day . . ." Annette was becoming flustered. "Would we?" She looked at Chad for confirmation.

"No." He took her hand again.

Josie thought they were charming, but it was taking quite a bit of time to tell their story. "So what were you doing? What did Cheryl and Howard have to complain about?"

"It wasn't what we were doing, Ms. Pigeon. We were just kissing. Really. It was perfectly innocent. But we talked about it and, well, we were afraid that we might have been on the next-door neighbor's property."

"And yesterday we checked, and . . . we were. Josie, we're really sorry. When we told you we hadn't been there, we really didn't think we were lying!"

"I believe you." Josie took another sip of coffee. "I hope Cheryl and Howard didn't see you on their property again."

"We were very careful," Annette said.

"Well, actually they may have seen me the day before yesterday," Chad admitted. "Remember I told you I was going to check it out?" He looked at Annette, who nodded lovingly. "Well, I did. I went over to where you and I had been sitting and realized that, in fact, we were probably off the work site."

"When did you go?" Annette asked.

Josie seemed a bit preoccupied.

"In the afternoon sometime. I wanted to check it out before we went to dinner."

"And that's why you told me we should look at it yesterday morning!" Annette beamed, apparently proud of Chad's forward thinking.

"Exactly."

Josie realized they were expecting a comment from her. "So you went back together yesterday morning." She suspected that Howard and Cheryl had been given a perfectly adequate excuse to complain about all this trekking back and forth across their property line, but she appreciated that Chad and Annette were trying to help and so didn't mention it.

"Yes. And Chad was right. Where we were sitting was right over the property line! Josie, do you think we should go over and apologize to them?"

"For what?"

"Trespassing!"

"I wouldn't bother. Every time we see or speak to them, they just find something else to complain about," Josie said.

"But we're really here to apologize to you. For putting you in such an uncomfortable position," Chad asserted.

"Yes." Annette nodded vigorously. "We're sorry. We really are."

"It's okay." Josie put down her mug, thinking it was time for them to leave. But they didn't seem to agree.

"We're really sorry," Annette repeated.

But Chad had other things on his mind. "Ah, Ms. Pigeon . . ." He stopped and looked over at Annette. "I'm going to tell her," he said.

Annette sighed. "I will. I did it."

"Did what?" Josie asked, hoping they would get to the facts as soon as possible.

"I told Chad about Courtney."

"What about Courtney?" Josie asked, suspecting that she knew the answer.

"That she's dead. And gone. I mean, that her body is gone."

Josie sighed. She should have known this was a secret that wasn't going to be kept. "So?"

"I'm so sorry—"

Annette was going to begin another round of apologies when Chad interrupted. "I've been thinking about all this quite a bit," he began.

"Really?"

"Yes. I don't know if Annette told you, but my mother has investigated many murders. And actually solved them." Josie thought he sounded a bit amazed by this fact. "So I've had some experience with this sort of thing. And I've taken both Introduction to Psychology and Sociology 101 at Cornell and have some limited knowledge of human behavior."

"Really?"

"Yes. And I have some thoughts." Chad plunked himself down on the couch, rested his elbows on his knees, and rested his chin on his knuckles.

"Really?"

"Yes. You know, I think murder is usually committed for one of two reasons. Either personal gain or revenge."

"Really?"

"Yes, Chad's been explaining it all to me," Annette jumped in enthusiastically. "You see, the person who killed Courtney either benefited from her death or hated her so much that he or she could not bear to live in a world where she lived, too. So..."

"So we need to look at the people Courtney knew. Someone either had something to gain from her death or else hated her. Gain or hate," Chad said. "Gain or hate. That's what I think causes most murders."

Josie looked at the earnest young man and nodded slowly. "You may have a point there. But it might have been the result of a combination of those things. Not gain or hate, but gain *and* hate. And you know what? I think those two things got Courtney killed. And I think I know who killed her."

THIRTY-ONE

JOSIE WENT STRAIGHT to Sam's store. As she turned the corner, she spied his little MGB parked on the street and sighed with relief. She knew who had killed Courtney. But she didn't know what to do now. She sure hoped Sam would.

Sam was in the store, but it wasn't open for customers until nine-thirty. Josie had to hammer on the door to get his attention.

"Josie, I didn't hear you. I was back in my office." Sam looked at her face as he unlocked the door and let her in. "What happened? What's wrong?"

"Sam, I'm so glad to see you! I know who did it! I know who killed Courtney! I—"

"Josie, maybe you don't want to—"

"Sam, didn't you hear what I said? I know who killed Court . . . Oh, damn. What is he doing here?"

"I tried to tell you," Sam said as Chief Rodney walked down the aisle between cases of expensive wine and English gin. He was grinning.

"Miss Pigeon. You were saying something I would be interested in hearing, I believe."

Josie looked at Sam. "What is he doing here?" she asked again.

266

"Your boyfriend and I have been making plans for the Island Police Association Benefit. Now what's all this about our emcee?"

"You mean Courtney?"

"Yes."

Josie was silent for a few minutes. "She's dead."

"How do you know that?"

"I saw her dead. I mean, I saw her when she was dead. Her body."

"You saw a dead body and you didn't bother to call the police, Miss Pigeon?"

"I . . . It . . . I mean, she disappeared before I could do that."

"You didn't think you should come down to the police station and tell me that you saw a dead body that somehow slipped away while you weren't looking? You didn't think I would understand?"

"Would you have?"

"No way, José. And no way to you, Josie!"

"You know, if Josie doesn't cooperate with you, you have nothing except a missing television personality," Sam said flatly.

"I—" Josie started.

"And she's not going to say anything at all until you agree to listen to every word she says and do whatever she thinks you should," he continued, refusing to allow Josie to finish her sentence.

"I think . . ."

"Well, do you agree to that?" Sam asked.

Josie looked up at Chief Rodney. From the expression on his face, she decided it would be stupid to drive even one mile over the speed limit for the rest of the summer.

"Do you agree?" Sam repeated.

"Fine. Fine. But you better have a body or some rock-hard evidence, Miss Pigeon. You better have enough for me to make an arrest and get a conviction."

Josie grimaced. "Well, I can't promise anything—"

"Just tell us what you know," Sam said.

"Not much," Josie began. "But if you think logically about what I'm saying, I think you'll realize that I'm right and . . . that I'm right."

Chief Rodney sighed long and loud. "I suppose," he said, saying the words slowly and looking at Sam, "it's a bit early in the day for a drink."

"I could get you a cup of coffee and put a dollop of brandy in it," Sam offered.

"Make it a double dollop and I won't drag your girlfriend off to jail without hearing the entire story."

Josie scowled and tried to figure out exactly where to begin.

"Maybe you should start with finding the body," Sam suggested, heading for the area where liquors were displayed.

"Yes. When did you find the body?"

"It was a few days ago. But I didn't find it."

"Just who did find it?"

"My crew. Someone on my crew," Josie replied.

"You telling me there's a conspiracy of silence here?" Chief Rodney growled.

"There's no conspiracy," Josie answered before realizing that almost half a dozen people keeping the knowledge of a crime from the police was, most likely, exactly that.

Sam seemed to be thinking the same thing as he rushed over with a steaming and alcoholic drink in his hand.

"Start when the body was discovered," he prompted. "I'm sure the chief will let you tell the story in your own way."

Apparently the chief would let her do what she pleased as

long as Sam kept a steady stream of alcohol and coffee coming his way. So Josie got on with it.

"I didn't find Courtney. My crew did. She was hidden in
the canoe that was hanging from the ceiling in the living
room of the house we're remodeling."

"When?"

"A few days ago. But the body disappeared that day, too."

"Let's start at the beginning again. You—or someone on
your crew—discovered Courtney in the canoe hanging from
the ceiling. Am I correct in assuming that she was dead?"

"Yes. Of course, yes." Josie described how Courtney had
looked, being sure to mention how her hair had covered part
of her forehead—which she now knew to be significant—and
went on to explain her interview up near the rafters, how the
women had continued to work that afternoon, all acutely
aware of the body on high, and how they had decided to meet
at Island Contracting's office for dinner to make a decision
about what to do.

"Who suggested leaving the body where it was and heading down to your office?" Chief Rodney asked.

"I think I probably did, but that doesn't matter," Josie told
him. "Just listen to what I'm going to tell you and you'll
understand."

"You damn well better be right, Mizz Pigeon." He sprayed
his sarcasm.

Josie continued her story as he wiped his spit off his shirt.
"So we went to the office and tried to figure out what to do
about Courtney's body. We did think of calling the police,
among other things." She was fairly sure no one in the store
would think much of their decision to freeze Courtney along
with most of the island's bait supply. "But when we returned
to the house, the body was gone."

Chief Rodney grunted, and from the expression on his

face, Josie got the impression that keeping his promise not to interrupt was causing him some pain. She continued the tale.

"We knew the body was gone right away. The canoe was on the floor, but the blanket that had been covering her was still there. We . . . um . . . we didn't know what to do."

Chief Rodney made a sound that could have been a gulp or an expletive.

"So we didn't do anything. And Bobby Valentine said that Courtney was always going off and doing things and suddenly no one seemed to care that she wasn't around. So . . . well . . . Look, the truth is that I knew you would suspect my crew members if you knew Courtney had been murdered. None of them had any reason to kill her, but some of them are especially vulnerable, so I thought if I figured out who killed her myself, I would tell you about it and . . . and that would be that." She glanced at Sam, who was staring intently at the police chief.

"You thought I would arrest Dorothy Evans," Chief Rodney said flatly.

"I thought it was a good possibility. And so did she. You see, Dottie—"

"Josie, he knows about Dottie's record," Sam said. "It's one of the terms of her release and her parole."

"Oh. Dottie's a wonderful person," Josie assured him.

"I realize that, Miss Pigeon. I realize that."

"The chief was telling me earlier that he introduced Dottie to one of his officers, a relative, and he asked her out on a date," Sam explained.

Josie was momentarily diverted. "And she refused, right?"

"Yes. But the Rodney men do not take no for an answer. At least not until it's been said at least a half-dozen times," Chief Rodney added with a surprising amount of self-deprecating humor.

"Go on with your story, Josie," Sam prompted. "What happened next?"

"I guess the next thing that actually happened was that I got a call from Bobby Valentine. But that's not . . . I'm leaving out things."

"Well, we sure don't want you to do that," Chief Rodney said as the beeper on his belt began to squawk. "Goddamn. Someone better have a real good reason for bothering me now." He read the message. "Mind if I use your phone, Sam?"

"Feel free."

Josie moved over to Sam as the police chief headed to the phone on the checkout counter. "How am I doing?" she asked.

"Frankly, not well. I know more of the whole story than the chief and I have no idea what the hell you're getting at—or who you think killed Courtney."

"Sam, I thought you'd figured it out. Howard and Cheryl—well, I suppose only one of them actually killed her, but certainly they were both involved in the coverup and in moving her from place to place. . . . Where's he going?" she added as the police officer bounded for the front door.

"Got to go. That call was from one of your workers, Miss Pigeon. Seems Bobby Valentine and some man from the neighborhood are trying to kill each other on the lawn in front of the house you're working on."

"I still don't get it," Sam said, getting into the driver's seat of his car while Josie plunked herself into the passenger seat.

"What don't you get?"

"Why Howard and Cheryl? And, more important, how did you figure it out?"

"Think, Sam, from the very beginning of this project, some unknown neighbor was involved. It was someone from the island, a neighbor, who told Courtney about the house—and about Island Contracting."

"And Howard and Cheryl are those neighbors?"

"Yup, and I'll bet if we look into it, we'll find that Howard and Cheryl are the owners of that damn house. I was stupid. I should have insisted on speaking with the owners. I guess the job just fell into our laps and I was so thrilled to be asked to be on television . . . Funny, I thought I was immune to that sort of thing," she mused, interrupting herself.

"What sort of thing?"

"Oh, believing that being a celebrity—even if only for a day—was important. You know, believing that the parents at Tyler's school would think more of me if I'd been on television."

"Well, as long as the show you're on isn't *America's Most Wanted* or *Cops*, you were probably right. We are living in a culture that values celebrity."

"I know. That's probably what motivated poor Howard and Cheryl—that, and greed, of course."

Sam yanked on the steering wheel and directed the car into a space at the curb. "Why don't you tell me about this before we get to the house?" he suggested.

"Sure. It won't take very long. You see, Cheryl and Howard wanted to be famous. So they got in touch with Courtney Castle and told her about the house they owned on the island. They were smart enough to realize that they needed to provide an added inducement for Courtney to choose their project. This isn't the Bahamas; there's no reason to come here to do a show because of the weather. So they hired Island Contracting. We're unique enough to interest viewers."

"Good point." Sam nodded.

But Josie was still putting together the pieces. "Come to think of it, I'll bet anything that, once we look into it, we'll find out that the convenient schedule change of our other early-summer job had something to do with Cheryl and Howard."

"Sounds likely."

"Okay, so as I was saying, Cheryl and Howard told Courtney about this interesting house and the company that was going to remodel it. And then to clinch the deal they offered Courtney a customized trailer—the trailer of her dreams—if she would use their project for her television series."

"So the trailer was a bribe."

"Yes. And since they had bought the house under a corporate name rather than their own, Public Broadcasting wouldn't make the connection. Because it must have been unethical for them to give her the trailer in exchange for getting their house on the air."

"Definitely. And it must have cost them a fortune," Sam said, thinking of the laws that governed the giving of gifts.

"They were going to sell their house for an inflated price and be on television as well. I guess it was really important to them."

"Being on television?"

"Yes, the first time I met them, Howard talked about Cheryl getting ready for her television appearance—picking out the right clothes and everything. I didn't think it was significant at the time. I figured she would just wander over and expect to be on television. And I didn't think that would happen." She grimaced. "The truth is that I was busy worrying about what I was going to look like on television and not thinking much about anyone else."

"So what went wrong?"

"I suspect Courtney had never seen them before. Cheryl and Howard are one of the tackiest couples you would ever want to meet. I'll never forget the shocked expression on Courtney's face when she met them for the first time. I think Courtney either refused to give them airtime or else suggested they change their style. It all fits together, Sam. Cheryl and Howard were going to be segment three of the show, the segment about the neighborhood. But Courtney met them and decided no way."

"And wrote the note that said 'Kill *Courtney Castle's Castles* segment three,' " he added.

"Exactly. The murder must have happened when she told them she was canceling their appearance. They were furious."

"Of course."

"And one of them picked up something heavy, slugged her with it, and killed her. Probably a piece of that damn sculpture." She pulled on a lock of unruly hair. "I doubt if they actually meant to kill her."

"And then they hid the body in the canoe?"

"Yes. Probably hoping we would find her and get blamed. They had already bragged to me about their connections on the island. If they know the island, they know the Rodneys aren't awfully likely to arrest the correct person for any crime other than speeding."

"But why did they move the body from the canoe? They were the ones who moved it, am I right?"

"Yes, their plan wasn't working out. They left the note in the trailer, and when Bobby Valentine called the police—as I'm sure they thought he would—no one was arrested. They probably realized they had a problem when that happened. We knew the body was there. But we weren't talking. I guess that spooked them and they waited until the house was deserted in the evening, took down the canoe, and removed Courtney. I imagine they would have dumped her in the bay, but that wasn't a safe option once the island started buzzing with talk of a possible dredging."

"So there they were, stuck with a body that was going to start to decompose," Sam said, nodding.

"Yes, there aren't a lot of refrigerators or freezers on the island where you can stash something that large and not expect it to be found right away."

"Sounds as though you've done a bit of thinking about this yourself," Sam said.

"Uh, yes. But that's not important. What's important is that I overheard Bobby Valentine arguing with someone when I was on the phone with you the other day. He must have been arguing with Howard. And that's probably when Cheryl and Howard decided to pin the murder on him."

"So they put the body in the trailer where he would find it."

"Yes. But they panicked again and moved it. They probably thought he would tell someone about it, and when the body vanished, he would be arrested. That's why they returned with the wig and left it there."

"Josie, you may be right about all this. It makes a certain amount of sense. But I don't see what happened that caused you to suspect them."

"Annette and Chad."

"Excuse me?"

"I never would have thought of Howard and Cheryl if they had just shut up. But they kept complaining about Annette and Chad being on their property and I suddenly realized why. Annette and Chad weren't doing anything wrong. Howard and Cheryl were concerned about being seen moving the body, so they were upset when Annette and Chad slipped over their property line looking for a place to be alone. It must have seemed to Cheryl and Howard that whenever they planned on moving a body, there was a young couple necking in the bushes close by. Close enough to see what was going on. If they had cared to look."

"Which they didn't," Sam guessed.

"When you were young and in love, would you have?"

"Even at this advanced age, I'm likely to be so involved in the person I love that I don't notice a whole lot going on around me," Sam said, pulling Josie over to his side of the car.

"Sam, don't you think we ought to get going? We don't even know if Howard or Bobby won the fight."

"Remember, I've had some personal experience there. And, frankly, I'd place my money on Bobby Valentine any day."

THIRTY-TWO

SAM AND JOSIE were enjoying a rare day at the beach. Labor Day was just around the corner and they both felt the need to relax and catch up on their reading. He had brought a pile of *New York* magazines and some *New Yorker*s. They lay by his side as he dozed in the sun. Josie had a trashy novel in her lap, but she was reading a letter.

Sam opened one eye and peeked out. "What's that?"

"A note from Dr. Naomi Van Ripper."

"A doctor . . . Are you all right?"

"I'm fine. She's not a medical doctor. She's the librarian from my hometown. Remember?"

"Of course, she was Courtney Castle's friend. Why is she writing you?"

"To lecture me."

"About what?"

"My personal relationships."

"She has a lot of nerve. Her close, personal relationship with Courtney turned out to be a lie. Courtney was using her to get to the money her sister's foundation was giving out, if I remember correctly."

"Yes. But Dr. Van Ripper got something out of the relationship, too. She got to schmooze with a celebrity. And we learned just how far people would go for that at the beginning of summer." Josie sat up and stared off at the hazy horizon.

"Strange that she was in town at the same time Courtney was here. Or wasn't that a coincidence?" Sam asked.

"Not at all. We talked later. It turned out that Courtney invited Dr. Van Ripper here to see just how successful she had become with her own show and her new trailer and all. And possibly Courtney knew Dr. Van Ripper would be able to fill me with guilt for being a dreadful child. And Courtney loved making me miserable. Always did. But you know what amazed me?"

"What?"

"Courtney was still mad about her boyfriend getting me pregnant. She wanted to embarrass me and she set up the interview questions to do just that. After all these years, she was still angry."

"But she didn't know you were on the island when she planned this show, did she?"

"Probably not. But the first thing she found out about Island Contracting would have been the name of its owner. She must have been thrilled. She thought she was going to get her new trailer, a great series of fund-raising shows, and revenge for an old wrong."

"Instead she ended up in a Dumpster down by the commercial fishing pier."

"Yeah. It was typical of Howard and Cheryl that they didn't even think of an original place to dump the body." She paused for a minute. "I was relieved when they confessed."

"I understand it wasn't exactly a confession. Each one blamed the other long and loudly down at the police station, is what Chief Rodney told me."

"Sounds like them. They aren't exactly a loving couple."

Sam reached over and took her hand. "I don't want to pry, but have you thought more about contacting your parents?"

"I've been thinking about it for weeks and weeks," she admitted quietly. "And I . . . I was going to talk to you about it."

"Does that mean you've made a decision?"

"I called."

"You called your home? Your parents' house?"

"Yes. I spoke with my mother."

"How was she? How was the call?" Sam seemed to be having trouble knowing what question to ask.

"She . . . she said she and my father were thrilled to know that they had a grandson and . . . they were hoping we . . . the four of us . . . could get together soon."

"And is that what you want?" Sam asked gently.

Josie looked from the horizon to all the happy families on the beach. "I don't know if what I want is even possible," she answered quietly. "But I know that I have to see them again. I have to discover what is possible."

"And Tyler? What does he think about your decision?"

"I haven't told him anything about it. He goes back to school next week. I'm going to drive him there and stop off to see my parents on the way back here."

"You're not going to tell him about them?"

"Not yet. I've thought about it. But, Sam, Tyler is happy and well adjusted. If he misses having an extended family, it doesn't show. I want to resolve any problems I have with my mother and father before introducing them to one another."

"They'll love him, Josie. Everyone loves Tyler. He's a remarkable kid. You've done a fine job raising him."

"Thanks. I wonder how he's doing?"

"Now?"

"Yeah. He and that other kid from Family Video entered the sandcastle competition that the lifeguards sponsor every year. They left home at dawn with buckets, shovels, trowels, and assorted tools. They were really enthusiastic. They're convinced they have a good chance of winning."

"Really? What's the theme this year?"

"Theme?"

"Yes. There's always a theme. A few years ago it was monsters from the deep. The guys who won created a fifty-foot-long sea monster. The fins sticking up from the spine were Coors bottles. I went to see it because they had been dashing in and out of the store for almost eight hours buying twelve-packs. Since it's illegal to drink alcohol on the beach, I always wondered where they stopped and imbibed on the way. Or if they just dumped out the contents. It was a pretty impressive sand sculpture."

"Let's ask the guard what the theme is." Josie looked up at the handsome young man sitting high above them in the lifeguard's chair.

"Good idea."

"I'll do it. You look so nice and relaxed." Without waiting for an answer, Josie trotted off. A few minutes later she was back.

"Well, what is it?" Sam asked.

"What I did on my summer vacation," she answered, gathering together towels, suntan lotion, and reading materials.

"Where are you going?"

"The lifeguard recognized me. Those guys have walkie-talkies and they communicate with one another. There's a rumor going around that Tyler's sandcastle is one of the best. The judging is done. He thought maybe Tyler and his friend had won a prize."

Sam stood. "Let's get going. I always enjoy seeing your son win awards."

The Annual Lifeguards' Benefit Sand Sculpture Contest had attracted entrants along almost three miles, and Josie and Sam had walked for almost an hour before they found Tyler.

From the time he was two years old, her son had thrived on attention, so Josie wasn't surprised to discover that his sculpture had attracted a crowd. She just wished it would part and let her see what he had done.

Sam, tall enough to peer over some of the spectators' heads, reported that Tyler had won an award. "Most creative," he announced.

"That sounds like Tyler. But, Sam, what is it?"

He was laughing so hard, he couldn't answer.

Josie decided motherhood had some privileges and she pushed her way through the crowd. And stopped dead when she saw what her son had done.

"What the—"

"Mom! Hi, Mom! What do you think?"

Her son was jumping up and down, his red hair gleaming in the sunlight, the smile on his face almost irresistible.

"What do you think?" he repeated.

Josie looked at the sand sculpture. The sand had been piled up and carved into an intricate sculpture representing the healthy way her son had spent his summer vacation: with a television set complete with a remote control and a pile of current videos.

"What do you think?" he asked a third time.

"I think I'm glad you're such a creative person. And that I'll miss you when you go back to school."

His response astonished her. In front of his friends and neighbors on the island, Tyler Clay Pigeon reached out and gave his mother a big, sandy hug.

Both of them blushed to the roots of their bushy red hair.

"Great! Cut! Did you get that on tape?"

"What the hell?" Josie pulled away from her son. "What are you doing here?" she asked, astonished to find Bobby Valentine in the front of the crowd, a cameraman on one side, a young lady carrying lights and reflectors on the other.

"Working on a new show. Beaches of the world. Actually, it's going to be a series of ten shows and the first is going to feature this contest. I can see it now. We open with a shot of the sand television screen Tyler made. We'll run our credits across it. It'll look great!"

"That's a good idea," admitted Sam, who had joined them. "This will be the first show in the series?"

"Sure will. We're starting filming in the north . . ."

"And traveling south as the weather gets colder," Josie said.

"Yeah." Bobby Valentine looked surprised. "How did you guess?"

"I've spent a little time around people in television," she answered, a big grin on her face.

If you liked this Josie Pigeon mystery,
don't miss any of the others:

SHORE TO DIE
The First Josie Pigeon Mystery

PERMIT FOR MURDER

DECK THE HALLS WITH MURDER

by
VALERIE WOLZIEN

Published by The Ballantine Publishing Group.
Available at your local bookstore.

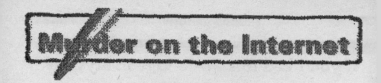

Murder on the Internet

Ballantine mysteries are on the Web!

Read about your favorite Ballantine authors and
upcoming books in our electronic newsletter
MURDER ON THE INTERNET, at
www.randomhouse.com/BB/MOTI

Including:

- What's new in the stores
- Previews of upcoming books for the next four months
- In-depth interviews with mystery authors and
  publishing insiders
- Calendars of signings and readings for Ballantine
  mystery authors
- Profiles of mystery authors
- Mystery quizzes and contest

To subscribe to MURDER ON THE INTERNET,
please send an e-mail to
join-mystery@list.randomhouse.com
with "subscribe" as the body of the message. (Don't
use the quotes.) You will receive the next issue as
soon as it's available.

Find out more about whodunit! For sample
chapters from current and upcoming Ballantine
mysteries, visit us at
www.randomhouse.com/BB/mystery